DASH

BLACKWINGS MC BOOK ONE

BY

TEAGAN BROOKS

Cathy

♡ Teagan Brooks

Adult Content Warning: This book contains sexual scenes, explicit language, and violence.

Cover Design by Dar Albert at Wicked Smart Designs

Dedication

To Mom, Dad, Spouse, and Spawn.

Contents

CHAPTER ONE

Ember

It was time. Time to leave. Time to start a new life, a real life.

Taking a deep breath, I quietly slipped out of bed. I arranged the pillows and blankets to make it look like I was still in the bed in case anyone decided to check on me. I knew they wouldn't. No one ever had.

I grabbed my backpack and slid it over my arms. The thing was almost too heavy for my small frame. I had crammed it as full as I possibly could. Once I left, I was not coming back. Ever. I didn't have many things, but it was a lot harder than I thought it would be to fit everything I wanted to take with me in one bag. After tightening the straps, I grabbed the gun I had hidden under my bed and tucked it into the back of my jeans. There was also one in the bottom of my backpack, but that wouldn't do me any good if I needed it during my escape attempt. After I strapped a knife to each ankle, I took one last look around my room.

I felt...nothing really. No happy memories threatened to bring tears to my eyes. I just felt empty when I looked at the room. My eyes fell on the window and a sense of excitement rushed through me. It was time to go.

I carefully raised the window in my bedroom just enough to climb through. When my feet hit the ground, I reached up and gently pulled the window back into place. Scanning the area, twice, I saw nothing but darkness ahead of me. Steeling myself, I walked as quickly and as quietly as I could toward the tree line. The farm I grew up on was located in the middle of nowhere and was completely surrounded by forest. It really was its own little hidden hell.

Once I made it to the tree line, I got my compass from my bag and started walking the route I had mapped out weeks ago. The cover of the trees allowed me to move faster, shielding me from sight while the sounds of the animals in the forest hid the noise of my movements. Even though I was blindly moving through the forest with nothing but a cheap compass and a sliver of moonlight, I made it to my destination in less than an hour.

I looked up at the large tree in front of me. Taking a deep breath, I started to climb. The farm property was surrounded by a 10-foot concrete wall topped with several feet of electric wire fencing. In order to get out, I had to climb up and over using the trees. I knew there were motion sensors and cameras scattered along the fence, so I had chosen to start with a tree that was several yards away from the fence. I moved from tree to tree without issue, refusing to look down. If I saw the fence below me, I would pause and start overthinking things, which would likely lead to me misstepping. I wasn't going to let that happen.

I kept moving and kept count of the trees. When I made it to the 10th tree, I finally looked down. I was on the other side of the fence! I had done it. I took a quick moment to catch my breath and tried to steady my nerves before I started climbing down. Once my feet hit the ground, I started running as fast as I could toward the tree line.

As soon as I emerged from the trees, I saw the car pulled over on the side of the road. It matched the description, but I remained exactly where I was, just outside of the line of trees. With only the tiniest bit of light from the moon, I could only be seen if someone was specifically looking for a person. I knew I had been spotted when the headlights on the car flashed twice. Breathing a sigh of relief, I jogged across the road and opened the passenger side door.

Reese turned to me and smiled, “You made it!”

I dropped into the seat, “Yes, I did. Let’s get out of here.”

“Okay. Duck your head below the window until we get closer to civilization.”

I laughed at Reese, but did as she said. I crouched in the front floorboard and looked up at her, “Thank you so much for doing this for me. I—”

She cut me off, “You don’t have to thank me, Ember. I know something weird goes on at the farm. I was happy to help you get out.”

“Still, I couldn’t have done it without you.”

We drove in a comfortable silence and my

mind wandered to when I first met Reese.

About a month into my senior year at Croftridge High, a new student named Reese joined our class. I was asked by our homeroom teacher to show Reese around the school, help her find her locker, and make sure she knew where all of her classes were located. It was all I could do to contain my excitement. See, as a "farm kid" I was only allowed to associate with other farm kids and even with them, it was very limited. We arrived at school together, we ate lunch together, and we left school together. We even sat together at every event that took place during school hours. If any one of the farm kids tried to make friends with "the locals," one or more of the obedient farm kids would tattle and the kid who broke the rules would be punished. I had heard that the punishment was a whipping given by one of the council members, but I had never broken any of the rules or seen any evidence that any of the other farm kids had been whipped.

Needless to say, it was near impossible to befriend someone outside of our circle of lunacy. I had been working on a plan to escape and get as far away from the farm as possible, but I couldn't do it by myself. I needed help and that help had to come from someone outside of the farm. For me, that help came in the form of Reese Walker.

As soon as we stepped out into the hallway, I introduced myself and started quickly giving her a brief explanation of my situation. She didn't laugh at me or look at me with repulsion like I had expected. She just stared at me with a sort of vacant look in her eyes and asked, "Why are you telling me all of this? You want me to help you or something?"

I could have cried right then and there, but I managed to hold it together. "Yes! That's exactly what I want, what I need. Would you be willing to help me?" She started to nod, so I continued spewing forth as much as I could before we ran out of time. "I'm not allowed to talk to anyone who isn't from the farm. If I do and get caught, I will be punished. So, when we go back to class, I won't be able to speak to you anymore, but it isn't because I don't want to. I have to obey their rules, but I do want to be friends with you. I hate having to follow their rules and do what they say. I know it is just going to get worse the older I get. I want out, but I can't do it without help. We are almost out of time. I'll drop a note in your locker explaining more. If you want to help me, write back and drop it in my locker, just don't let anyone see you do it. I'll show you where it is.

But if you don't want to help, I will understand, just please, please don't tell anyone else about this. Please."

The expression on her face never changed. She seemed sad or maybe lost, but I was too wrapped up in my own misery to ask. She responded almost robotically, "I won't tell anyone. I'll try to help you. Drop your note in my locker and tell me what you need from me."

I wanted to hug her and break out into a happy dance at the same time. Instead, I reached out and squeezed her hand, "Thank you so much. You don't know how much this means to me."

She nodded and we walked back into the classroom.

Reese's voice brought me back to the present, "Ember?" I looked up at her, still crouched in the floor. "We're here."

I blinked up at her, "Wow, that was fast. Um, is your brother home?"

"No, he's out for the night. It's just me and you."

This news eased a little bit of my anxiety. I was so worked up I was practically vibrating with nervous tension.

We entered the condominium she shared with her older brother and it was like entering a completely different world for me. I had never been in a home that wasn't on the farm. The houses on the farm looked exactly alike, inside and out, with the exception of one house. White siding, no shutters, small front porch. The inside walls were all white, all hardwood floors, all furniture was made of wood, any bedding or linens were white, almost no color of any kind anywhere. The buildings on the farm were very much the same.

I stood just inside the doorway in absolute awe. The living room was painted gray and had black leather furniture. Hanging on one wall was the largest television I had ever seen. Posters of motorcycles and street signs covered the walls.

Just beyond the living room was the kitchen, walls painted blood red with everything else, including the cabinets, countertops, and appliances in black. Even the sink was black. I had never seen such a thing. I couldn't stop turning in circles trying to take it all in.

I heard Reese giggle behind me, "I'm guessing your house was nothing like this."

I turned to face her, my eyes wide as saucers, "Nothing at all. Everything in my house is white or wood. And black, well that's just absolutely forbidden." I turned a full circle once more, "This place is amazing."

Reese smiled, "Let's go upstairs and see what you think of my room."

She opened the door to her bedroom and my eyes were filled with bright pink, black, and zebra patterns. She had a large bed with a wrought iron frame and several pieces of furniture placed around her bedroom, which was far bigger than the one I had just left. But the thing that seemed strange to me was that her room had two doors, in addition to the one we had just walked through. I turned my curious eyes to her, "Why are there more doors in here?"

She furrowed her brow and looked confused for a brief moment, before the blank expression she always wore on her face returned. She cleared her throat and explained, "The door on the left goes to my private bathroom and the door on the other side of the room leads to my closet. Go ahead and have a look."

I walked to the door she indicated led to her closet and pulled it open. I looked at her over my shoulder and remarked, "This is your closet? This is the size of my bedroom."

She tried to hide it but she didn't do a very good job of it. Pity. She was looking at me with pity. That's okay. I would have pitied me, too, but not anymore. I had managed to get out of there and I would rather die than go back. After the things I had learned or figured out over the last few months, Octavius and his men would just have to kill me if they found me because there was no way I was going to live the rest of my life on that farm or with the man who had "selected me."

Changing the subject, I plastered a smile on my face and said, "Let's see the bathroom." She led me across the room and opened the door to another room that was bigger than my old bedroom. It had a large mirror with two sinks in front of it, a toilet that was almost in a room by itself, a shower stall, and a deep bathtub that had holes in the side of it. "Why does your tub have holes in it?"

Reese smiled and said, "That's a whirlpool tub. I'll show you how it works later. Let's get something to eat and then get started on your hair."

I readily agreed. I had been so nervous all day, I hadn't been able to eat much of anything. Now that my actual escape from the farm was over, the mention of food made me realize I was starving. She pulled out her phone and used it to order a pizza. I knew a lot of kids had cell phones and they could do a lot of things with them, but I still thought it was cool that she could order food and pay for it from the little phone in her hand. Hopefully, one day soon, I would be able to do that, too.

After we ate and cleaned up, we went back to her room to start my transformation. Part of my plan to get away included changing my appearance. This was actually Reese's suggestion and a good one at that. I hadn't thought of changing how I looked to make it harder to find me. She had told me not to worry about any of that because she would take care of everything. Now it was time to see what she had come up with.

I sat on a stool in her bathroom facing the mirror. She stood behind me brushing my hair and explaining her plan, "First, I think we need to cut this hair. At school, you were the only girl who had hair this long. It's a dead giveaway. How much would you be comfortable taking off?"

I had never had anything done to my hair besides a trim, but that wasn't my choice. I thought about it for a few minutes and said, "Maybe a few inches below my shoulders. What do you think?"

She smiled at me and nodded her head, "I

think that would look great. We also need to color your hair. I picked up a few different shades I thought would look good. I'll go get them and you can pick which one you want to try."

She left the room and I began rubbing my palms together, a nervous habit I had been trying, unsuccessfully, to break since I was a preteen. It was an obvious tell, and everyone on the farm knew when I was nervous or frightened by something the second I started rubbing my palms together. I immediately slipped my hands under my thighs on the stool to prevent any further rubbing.

Reese returned to the room with six or seven boxes of hair color. She showed each one to me, but she wouldn't tell me which one she liked best or what she thought of any of them. "I'll tell you what I think after you pick. I don't want to influence the first big decision you get to make for yourself."

This was part of why I loved Reese. She appeared emotionless and distant most of the time, but she was a very thoughtful person and every once in a while, she showed it.

"Okay, um, I'll try this one." I held up a box of something called highlights.

"Good choice. That is the one I would have

picked. Ready?"

The next several hours were spent cutting and highlighting my hair. I still wasn't sure what exactly that meant, but Reese seemed to know what she was doing so I went along with it. I didn't really care what I looked like when she was done as long as I looked different. I was going for unrecognizable, no more, no less.

After washing the smelly stuff out of my hair, she forbade me from looking in the mirror while she finished cutting my hair and adding what she called layers. I sat quietly going over the things I had done the last few months, the things I had learned, and the things I still had to accomplish to finally be free and clear of the farm. She must have noticed that I was losing myself to my thoughts because she started talking to me and asking questions again.

I couldn't help but think how superficial we both were at times. She didn't want to talk about clothes and makeup and neither did I, but we did, because both of us wanted to talk about our real issues even less. I had told her very little about the farm and she didn't ask many questions. I wasn't sure, but I guessed it was because she didn't want to talk about whatever put the blank look on her face and kept it there.

I heard my name and blinked up at Reese. Judging by the expression on her face and her posture, she must have said my name more than once. “Sorry. Guess I spaced out for a minute.”

She pursed her lips and gave me a scrutinizing once over before continuing, “I said I wanted to get your makeup done and have you put on a new outfit before you look in the mirror. Is that okay with you?”

“Yeah, that’s fine, but, um, I’ve never been allowed to wear makeup before, so can you kind of teach me as you go along?” I don’t know why asking her to teach me to put on makeup bothered me, especially considering all of the other things I had asked of her, but it did. I felt unsure about it for some reason.

Reese placed her hand on my shoulder, “Relax, Ember. I planned on teaching you. I didn’t expect you to know anything about makeup. Sit right there on the floor by my bed and don’t look in any mirrors. I’ll be right back.” She returned carrying a plastic bag which she immediately upended and dumped the contents on the floor. “I bought you a makeup case and all the essentials you will need to get started. I had to guess on your foundation color, but our skin color seemed pretty close, hopefully, I got it right."

Emotion clogged my throat, making it hard to swallow. Finally, I managed to rasp out, "Thank you, Reese." I cleared my throat, "No one has ever done anything like this for me."

"No one has ever helped you escape from a crazy farm? I'm shocked," she held her hand to her chest, feigning surprise. Without missing a beat, she launched right into my makeup lesson. Thirty minutes later she had me trying on skinny jeans with a long, flowing top. She finished the outfit with ankle boots, a necklace, and then she handed a pair of earrings to me. I looked from the earrings to her and back to the earrings. I quietly said, "My ears aren't pierced."

That didn't faze Reese at all. She continued digging in her closet, "Yeah, I know. Flip the pack over. They're clip-ons. Give me a sec and I can show you how they work." Really, she thought of everything. I was beginning to wonder how I was going to continue on my journey without her.

After adjusting my clothing, checking my makeup, and brushing my hair again, Reese declared it time for the big reveal. She pulled me into the bathroom and instructed me to close my eyes. She turned me toward the mirror by my shoulders and said, "Open!"

I opened my eyes and my hand immediately went to my chest. I took a staggering step back and whispered, "That can't be me."

I saw Reese's face fall in the mirror, "You don't like it?"

"No, that's not it. It's amazing. I just can't believe that girl in the mirror is me. I'm, I'm..."

"You're beautiful." She softly smiled. I think that was the first time I had ever seen her genuinely smile. It was a sight to behold.

I half laughed and half sobbed, "I was going to say pretty."

She laughed, too, and then we sort of fell into an awkward silence. I couldn't find the right words to express my feelings. She had made me feel normal for the first time in my life and saying thank you just wasn't enough.

She patted my shoulder, "One thing about makeup, you should always remove it before going to bed. Leaving it on does nasty things to your pores, your pillows, and your sheets. Come on, I'll show you how the whirlpool tub works."

An hour later I was leaving her bathroom in my pajamas with a new promise to myself that I would one day have my very own whirlpool tub.

"I should probably get everything packed up and ready to go since we are leaving here first thing in the morning."

"Okay. All the stuff I kept for you is in my closet." She walked into her closet and came out with a duffel bag. She opened it and laid everything out on her bed. Since I had enlisted her help, she had stashed quite a bit of money for me. I had asked her to use some of the cash to buy me some clothes and a few other necessary items. I reorganized my things, making sure the most important items were in my backpack and things that could be replaced went into the duffel bag, in case I needed to drop it and run. With everything squared away, we lay down for what I was sure would be a night with little to no sleep. The success of my escape relied heavily on the events of tomorrow, which were uncertain at best.

Once I decided that I really was going to try and escape, I began sneaking around the farm, snooping and eavesdropping every chance I got. I had managed to learn the combinations to a few safes and the codes to enter some of the locked doors. I rotated the safes I stole money from and only took a few hundred dollar bills each time. I would then place the money in an envelope and slip it into Reese's locker at school.

My biggest problem was that I didn't have

any kind of identification. Through all of my snooping and sneaking around, I never came across birth records for myself or anyone else who lived on the farm. They had to have some kind of official documentation for us otherwise we wouldn't be able to attend public school. I didn't spend a lot of time trying to find the documents because I suspected they were likely fake anyway. Statements made during conversations I was secretly listening to led me to this theory.

When I explained my situation to Reese, in one of our many notes, I asked her if she could use the internet to find someone who could make some identification records for me. I explained that I needed more than just a license making me older than my true age; I was going to need a whole setup, birth certificate, social security card, a state-issued ID, and possibly a passport.

A few days later, she told me she asked her brother. Before my panic attack could even get off the ground, she continued on to tell me she said that one of her friends and her mother were trying to get away from the girl's abusive step-father. Her brother accepted that explanation and said they should go to the Blackwings Motorcycle Club and talk to Phoenix.

CHAPTER TWO

Ember

The next morning, Reese dropped me off at the end of the road that led to the Blackwings MC Clubhouse. Apparently, even though her brother was a member, he had insisted that she never come anywhere near the clubhouse. After a tearful goodbye and a promise to contact her soon if I could do so safely, I began walking down the street toward my new future.

When I got to the end of the road, I could see the clubhouse, but I couldn't get to it because it was surrounded by a large fence and the gate at the front was locked. I wasn't sure what to do next. I didn't see anybody around to ask or to open the gate for me.

Hoping to see someone, I started walking along the fence line. I was about halfway around the back when I finally spotted two men. Before I could say anything, one of them yelled, "What the fuck are you doing back here, bitch?"

I froze. He sounded like the men from the farm. That was how they talked to the women, always calling them something demeaning or derogatory, never using their names.

"Answer me, bitch. Now!" he yelled even louder.

I just stared at him. I couldn't speak. I could barely breathe. My heart felt like it was going to beat out of my chest. I thought the people at this place would be helpful, not openly hostile.

"Calm down, man. You're scaring the shit out of her." I couldn't see them very well, but one of them took a few steps closer and asked, "What are you doing back here, darlin'?"

I swallowed thickly and tried to still my shaking hands. "I'm looking for Phoenix."

They both looked at me strangely and the nicer one asked, "What do you want with Phoenix?"

The other one added, “Yeah, sweetheart, you’re a little young for his liking.”

I wasn’t sure what he meant by that, but I was beginning to get a little frustrated with these two. Reese’s brother said to come here and talk to Phoenix. I didn’t realize it would be this difficult to get to him. I huffed, “I would rather discuss that with him.”

“And you thought you would find him back here?” the big mean man asked.

“I went to the gate first. No one was there and I didn’t see a buzzer or anything, so I walked along the fence hoping I would see someone to ask.”

The big mean man again, “He expecting you?”

“No, sir, he isn’t.”

Both men chuckled, but I wasn’t sure why. The younger one said, “Walk back around to the front and we’ll let you in.”

“Okay, but is Phoenix here? I don’t need to come in if he’s not here.”

“Yeah, darlin’, he’s inside. I’ll take you to him.”

Oh, thank goodness. I wasn’t sure what I was going to do if he wasn’t there.

I was nervous. I hadn’t anticipated being led

into a building surrounded by an iron fence with a bunch of large men around. How would I get out if I needed to? What kind of danger awaited me inside the clubhouse? I could be trapped in there for years with these men, just like I was at the farm. I didn't want that. Not again.

We reached the front gate and I turned to the younger man. He was starting to punch in a code on a keypad I had not seen. "You know, it's really not that important. I'll just catch him later. Thanks anyway," I said quickly and turned to walk away. Before I could break out into a full sprint, a hand wrapped around my upper arm and yanked me back. I yelped and another hand came around to cover my mouth.

The younger man leaned down to my ear and asked in a low tone, "Now why are you trying to run off like that? Makes me think you're up to something." I shook my head from side to side vigorously, but he continued, "We don't like it when people who got no business being out here come sniffing around our territory, sticking their nose where it doesn't belong. So, we're gonna go inside and have a little chat."

As he slowly made his way into the warehouse, dragging me along with him, I began to shake and tears ran down my face. I was so stupid. Why did I think I could do this? I had never been off of the farm, except for school and the occasional—extremely supervised—trip into town for clothes or other supplies. I had no idea how to survive in the real world. I had only been able to survive in a world that was an illusion manipulated into my reality.

I was terrified. I couldn't even begin to take in my surroundings due to the tears blurring my vision, which meant I had no idea where they were taking me and no idea how to get out of this place. The man kept his hand over my mouth and his other arm wrapped around my waist as he pulled me deeper inside the clubhouse.

Finally, the man let me go, and I was pushed down into a chair. I wiped the tears from my eyes and face and looked around. I was in an office, facing a beast of a man sitting across from me behind a large desk. He did not look happy. I glanced behind me and saw two men standing guard at the door. The two men from outside were standing on either side of me.

The man at the desk spoke first, "What the fuck is this?"

"We found her snooping around outside the fence at the back of the warehouse, Prez," explained the big mean man.

I mumbled, “I wasn’t snooping, sir.”

“What the fuck were you doing then?” asked the beast behind the desk.

“Like I told them, sir, I’m here to see Phoenix. I went to the front gate, but no one was out there. I didn’t see a buzzer or anything, so I walked along the fence hoping I would see somebody to ask.”

“I see,” he growled. “Who’s supposed to be on gate duty?” I jolted at his tone. One of the other men answered his question.

“Get his ass in here now!” the beast roared.

When the man they called Pete came into the office, the beast stood. “When this lovely little thing came to the gate today looking for Phoenix, she couldn’t find anyone to ask.” Pete looked down as the beast rounded the desk. “So, she took a stroll along the fence to see if she could find anyone around to ask.” The beast was now toe-to-toe with Pete, who was still looking at the floor. “And do you know what happened next, Prospect?”

“No, Prez,” Pete mumbled.

“She was drug in here by Dash and Shaker, trembling from head to toe with tears streaming down her face!” he roared. “All because she was looking for me! Now get the fuck out of my office and plant your ass at that gate. I don't care if you shit your damn pants, you fucking stay there until I say otherwise." The beast looked to the men standing around the room. "The rest of you clear out, too. I'd like to talk to this sweet little thing without you mongrels looming around scaring her more than you already have."

The men quickly exited and the beast, apparently Phoenix, returned to his desk. He took in a deep breath, paused for a moment to study my face, and then settled back into his chair. "My apologies for the way my men treated you. Now, I'm Phoenix. What is it you want with me?"

Hesitantly, but with as much confidence as I could muster, I stated, "I need a new ID and the documents that would go along with that. I was told you could help me."

Phoenix pushed back from his desk and crossed his muscular arms over his impressively large chest. His face was a mask of indifference when he crushed my world. "I can't help you with that."

What? No. This wasn't happening. What was I going to do now? I didn't plan on this happening. I didn't come up with a backup plan. I had nowhere to go. They would find me and

I would have to go back. No. No. No. I couldn't breathe. What was happening? My chest hurt. Everything was blurry. Why couldn't I get air into my lungs? I needed to breathe.

A light tapping on my cheek startled me, causing me to suck in a huge breath of air. "That's it. Do it again. A little slower this time. Good. Good. A few more times." I did as I was instructed. After a few slow, deep breaths, I wiped my eyes with my hands. Phoenix was squatting in front of my chair, his hand gently resting on my knee, coaxing me to breathe.

He patted my knee and stood. "That's much better. Now, who told you I could help you with getting a new identity?"

Assuming honesty was the best policy at this point, I softly said, "Carbon."

Phoenix nodded, walked into the hallway, and yelled, "Carbon! Get your ass in here now!" Crap. Carbon was going to find out Reese lied to him, not to mention that she was the one that brought me here against his direct orders. He was going to be very upset with her. And it sounded like Phoenix was already upset with Carbon. This was not going to bode well for me.

A man with the same eyes and the same hair color as Reese walked into the office. If I thought

Phoenix was a beast, this guy was the beast's dad. What were they being fed around here? "What's up, Prez?"

Phoenix gestured toward me, "You know her?"

Carbon shook his head, "Never seen her before."

Phoenix looked back and forth between the two of us. "She says you told her I could help her get a new ID. So, which one of you is lying to me?"

Carbon looked down at the floor and pinched the bridge of his nose. He slowly shook his head before raising it to meet my eyes. "You're Reese's friend, aren't you?"

I almost choked when I tried to speak. "Yes." I turned to face Phoenix, "I've never met him, sir. I'm friends with his sister. She asked him for me. I'm not trying to cause trouble or anything. I just need someone to help me."

Phoenix didn't acknowledge me, but turned back to Carbon, "That true? Your sister asked you about this?"

Carbon shook his head. "Not exactly. She told me it was for her friend's mom. That she was being beaten by the step-dad, things were bad at home, and she needed help getting out. She never said anything about needing an ID. I told Reese to tell the mom to come by the clubhouse and talk to you. No more, no less."

Phoenix remained silent for several long minutes. Finally, he walked back to his desk and took his seat. He focused on Carbon. "That's all I needed from you. You can go." He turned back to me with narrowed eyes. "Start talking."

I think I may have yelped like a scared puppy. "I-I-I don't know what to say. Um, what do you want to know?"

Phoenix pinned me with a stern glare, "You know exactly what I want to know, but to humor you, I'll play your game. I want to know who or what you're running from. I want to know what kind of help you think you need and how you are planning to pay for that. I want to know what kind of trouble you might be bringing into my club, but first and foremost, I want to know what your name is and how old you are?"

I took in a shaky breath. Okay, I would start with the easy stuff first. "My name is Ember, and I'm 18 years old."

He raised a brow, "Can you prove that?"

I wanted to scream, "That's why I'm here," but I didn't think that would benefit anyone given the current tension in the room. Instead, I said, "I don't have any kind of identification, real or fake. The only thing I have is my high school diploma with my name on it."

"You're 18 and you don't have a driver's license?"

"No, sir, I wasn't allowed to get one."

"Birth certificate? Social security card?"

I shook my head. "I'm sure those things exist, or did at one time, but I don't know where they are or who has them?"

He looked at me incredulously, "Where are you from?"

Solemnly, I told him, "I grew up at the orphanage on the other side of town."

"What happened to your parents?"

I mechanically repeated the only answer I had ever been given when I'd asked the same question. "My mom died when I was born and my dad was never in the picture."

"Do you know their names?"

It was always hard for me to think about my parents, let alone talk about them. I swallowed thickly and cleared my throat, "I don't know my father's name, but I was told my mother's name was Annabelle."

Phoenix's spine went ramrod straight, his hands balled into fists. He asked through gritted teeth, “Her last name?”

I was taken aback by his reaction. He was obviously angry and he was starting to scare me. “Um, I never asked that. I assumed it was the same as mine.”

Phoenix scoffed. I noticed his fists clenched even tighter. He looked like he barely had his temper under control. “And what is that? Tell me your full name,” he barked.

His tone caused me to flinch, and I quickly eked out, “Ember Rose Blackburn.”

Phoenix jumped to his feet and roared, “Get the fuck out! Now!” The next second, he flipped his desk over, sending everything crashing to the floor.

No need to tell me twice. I jumped out of the chair, grabbed my bag, and bolted from the room.

I rounded a corner and slammed into a wall of muscle. Strong arms wrapped around me and held me in place, “Whoa. Where do you think you’re going?”

It was Dash, the nicer guy from outside. Shaking like a leaf with tears running down my face, I blinked up at him, “He-he-he told me to get out.” I immediately started squirming in his arms, trying to get away from him.

"Stop that," he ordered. "You're not going anywhere until I find out what's going on."

I hadn't made it far. I could still hear Phoenix yelling and destroying things in his office. "I need to go. He told me to leave. I want to leave. Let me go." He didn't. Instead, he tightened his hold on me. My only explanation for what happened next is that years of training and conditioning kicked in and instinct took over.

Since I was facing him, and he clearly did not perceive me as a threat, I swiftly brought my knee up between his legs. He released his hold on me and bent forward to cradle his manhood. I shoved the heel of my hand into his nose, sending him up and back. Using his momentum to my advantage, I swept his feet out from under him, sending him crashing to the ground and giving me the opportunity to run for my life.

I could hear voices in the hall behind me, but I didn't dare look back. I ran with everything I had. Once I made it through the front door, I thought I had a pretty good chance of getting away. I was halfway to the front gates when I suddenly hit the ground. "Gotcha!" an unfamiliar voice sounded by my ear.

"Get off of her, man. I got this," Dash angrily spat at the man currently crushing me.

“Sure about that?” the man crushing me snickered.

I didn’t have time for this. I had to go. I snapped my head back, successfully making contact with Crusher’s head. I rammed my elbow into his side and quickly pushed up and out. I leaped to my feet and took off.

I made it to the front gate, ready to climb up and over. Pete apparently had decided to do as Phoenix said and was standing by the gate. He stepped in front of me, his gun aimed steadily at my head. I probably could have taken him, even with the gun, but he wasn’t standing close enough. Every time I took a step toward him, he took a step back and ordered me to stay put.

I didn’t stay put. I had already decided that I would rather die than be sent back to the farm. Pete didn’t know it, but he had two options, let me through that gate or shoot me. I was fine with either. Pete had about three steps left before I had him backed against the gate. It was obvious to me by this point that he wasn’t going to shoot me, so I continued moving forward. If I could get close enough, I could disarm him and run for the hills.

Hands grabbed my arms from behind and lifted. Crap. It was Dash and Crusher, each man had one of my arms held tightly between both hands. "Pete, get her feet."

"No way, man. Phoenix told me not to leave the gate for any reason," Pete protested.

"Get her fucking feet or lose that Prospect patch, what's it going to be?" Crusher barked.

Pete reluctantly stepped forward and wrapped a hand around each of my ankles. Part of me wanted to kick him, but that would just be mean, it wasn't like I was going to be able to get away from the other two.

The three of them carried me back inside the clubhouse. I screamed, cried, fought, but nothing helped. As a last-ditch effort, I started begging. "Please don't hurt me. Please! I just came to ask for help. You don't know what my life has been like. I won't go back! I won't!"

My eyes found Carbon standing in the hallway. "How could you tell your sister to send someone here for help? No wonder you won't let her come around here. You're all just like them! All of you!" I screamed at the lot of them standing in the hall staring at the tiny girl being manhandled, not a one trying to intervene.

Phoenix appeared in my line of site and started barking out orders. "Carbon, get your fucking sister here right now. I want to know what she knows. Dash, lock that bitch in one of the cells. Byte, I got some shit for you to start digging into. The rest of you, do a perimeter check and I want a brother at each corner of the property, two at the gate, and two on the roof. No prospects. We aren't on lockdown, but we damn well might be depending on what we find out in the next few hours."

The men scattered, I assumed to carry out their assigned tasks. It amazed me that grown men would run off to do the bidding of another grown man just because he said so. It made no sense to me. If I ever got out of this mess, I wouldn't be taking orders from anyone ever again.

The three men carried me down a long hallway and through a door. When they started walking down a flight of stairs, I started to panic. "Where are you going? Where are you taking me?" I shrieked.

Dash made a sound low in his throat that sounded very similar to a growl. A chill ran down my spine when he spoke, his voice low and dark, "What did you think was going to happen when you walked into an MC and started causing trouble? Did you really think you could pull one over on us?" He scoffed, "We may look like big, dumb, bikers, but we're a lot smarter than people think."

I continued to thrash around, trying to break their hold on me. "I didn't do anything. I just came here and asked for help and that psycho in there started yelling at me and throwing things."

Dash squeezed the arm he was holding, "It would be wise for you to not disrespect our club's president, especially given the position you're in right now."

They carried me down another hallway, this one much darker than the first. We went through another door, into what I assumed was a room of some sort, but it was so dark down there I couldn't see much. I was suddenly dropped onto something that felt like a hard mattress or cushion. Then, I heard it, the click of a lock being closed sounded loud and clear through the blackness.

Another click and the room was illuminated with bright, artificial light. I gasped. We did enter a room. A room divided by bars. I was locked in a jail cell. The three brutes were on the other side of the bars smirking at me. I took in my surroundings, noticing that I was indeed perched on a disgusting looking mattress. My only other accommodation was a bucket in the corner. “No!” I screamed. “No, no, no! Let me out of here. Please! Please don’t do this!”

Pete and Crusher left without a word. Dash just stood there looking at me. All thoughts of him being the nice one were long gone. He was just like the rest of them. He sneered, “If you stop screaming, I’ll leave the light on for you.”

I shut my mouth immediately. I didn’t want to be left in the dark. Big tears poured down my face as the severity of my situation hit me. I wrapped my arms around myself and slid to the floor. Bringing my knees up, I buried my head in my arms and rocked back and forth, trying to keep my sobs as quiet as possible.

I looked up when I heard the door close. Dash was gone. He left me there all alone. My sobs grew louder. Was my life destined to be controlled by a man in a self-appointed position of power? What had I ever done to deserve my life turning out this way?

I continued to ponder the events of my life, trying desperately to figure out why mine was so messed up. Eventually, my thoughts had provided enough of a distraction for me to physically calm down some. My breathing had returned to an almost normal pattern and my tears had slowed considerably until I realized I had no idea how long I would be locked in the cell or when anybody would come back.

CHAPTER THREE

Dash

I secured the door and went back up to Phoenix's office. Finding no one in there, I headed to the room where we have Church. In there, I found Phoenix, Byte, Badger, Duke, Shaker, and Carbon. Carbon looked unsettled, very uncommon for our club's enforcer. Byte was furiously typing away on his computer. Badger and Duke were sitting on either side of Phoenix who was clearly barely holding his shit together.

I took my designated seat and addressed the group, "She's locked in the last cell on the right." Despite how I acted toward the girl, I hated every second of having to drag her back inside and lock her up. I would never admit it to anyone, but I was damn impressed with the way she knocked me on my ass and then fought off Duke. I wondered where she learned to fight like that. It was obvious that she had been through some kind of training; her skills were far more advanced than mine.

Phoenix nodded and cruelly smiled, "Good."

That pissed me off. He didn't have to drag her down there kicking and screaming, then lock her away in a nasty cell while she sobbed on the floor.

I did.

I saw the fear in her eyes, not him.

I felt her shaking in my arms, not him.

Before I could think better of it, I stood from my chair, "You want to tell me why the fuck I had to lock that girl in a cell and leave her on the floor sobbing so hard she could barely breathe?"

Phoenix jumped to his feet, fists balled, "Who the fuck do you think you're talking to like that, boy?"

Oh, he wanted to play the always-respect-the-president card? I stepped closer to Phoenix. "I think I'm talking to a man who isn't acting like the president I know, *brother*. You have never treated a woman like that. So, tell me, *Prez*, what did she do to deserve this?"

Phoenix growled and started to move toward me. I stood my ground, didn't even flinch. Badger and Duke jumped up quickly and got between us.

Badger, our club's VP, took the lead, "Dash, sit the fuck down and show some respect." He turned to Phoenix, "Phoenix, get your shit under control." Quietly, he said, "I'm not sure what this is all about, but this ain't like you. Take a step back and breathe, yeah?" Phoenix glared at him, but finally relented with a nod, and fell back into his chair.

A knock at the door helped break up some of the tension in the room. One of the prospects poked his head around the corner. "Carbon, your sister is here."

Carbon lifted his chin, "Send her in."

A beautiful woman with an expressionless face slowly entered the room. She found Carbon immediately and took quick steps toward him. She opened her mouth to speak, but Carbon cut her off, "Sit down, Reese. We need to ask you some questions."

She paused and quickly glanced around the

room. "Okay..."

Phoenix started before she ever made it to a chair, "How do you know Ember Blackburn?"

Something passed over Reese's face, like something just dawned on her. She promptly answered, "I know her from school. We graduated together last week."

Phoenix continued, "Did you ask your brother about help for her, not your friend's mom?"

Reese held his gaze, "Yes, sir."

"Why did you lie to him about that?"

I noticed a small tremble in Reese's hand, but there was a fire in her eyes while she maintained eye contact, "I'm sorry, sir, but I won't answer that question."

Carbon slammed his fist onto the table and yelled, "Damn it, Reese! She is in a lot of shit, and you will be, too, if you don't tell us what the fuck is going on right the fuck now! I'm talking shit I can't get you out of; shit I can't save you from. Talk!!"

Reese flinched. A look of fear briefly washed over her face. The next second, as if it never happened, all traces of emotion were wiped away, her eyes suddenly looking vacant. Her voice was almost monotone when she spoke, "I don't care what shit I'm in, Carbon. I won't betray her trust. I won't be the one who causes harm to come to her."

Carbon got in her face, continuing to yell at her, "What the fuck do you think is coming to her now? It looks like she's here to cause problems. She's locked in a cell right now. If you care so much about her, start fucking talking."

Reese sat silently and stared at Carbon while he laid into her. Shockingly, it was Duke who rose from his chair and stalked toward them. He grabbed Carbon by the shoulder and yanked him back. "Enough, Carbon!"

Carbon shrugged his hand off and returned, "This is between me and my sister."

The muscle in Duke's jaw flexed, his tell that he was about to erupt. No one wanted to see our enforcer and our SAA go at it. That would be one hell of a fight to break up. Sensing the mounting tension, Badger quickly stepped between the two raging bulls. "Carbon, out. That's an order." Carbon huffed and glared at Badger before he obeyed and reluctantly left the room.

Duke took the opportunity to squat down in front of a seemingly unflappable Reese. Softly, he said, "We can't help her if we don't know what is going on. What can you tell us?"

Reese remained silent for several beats.

Finally, she nodded and strongly stated, "She needed help to get away from where she grew up. She said she needed help getting an ID. I told her to come here. I don't know much more than that."

Duke reached out and squeezed her hand. "Thank you."

She looked up at Duke, her usually blank face full of trepidation. "Can I see her? Please."

He shook his head. "Not just yet, sweetheart—" He was cut off by the sound of Reese's chair scraping across the floor as she pushed back from him. It must have startled Duke, because he reached out to grab for her, his hand landing hard on her thigh.

Carbon suddenly burst through the door, "Get your fucking hands off my sister."

Phoenix stood and bellowed, "Everybody out!" He heaved in a breath, "Byte, stay. One of you take her to see the girl, but don't leave them alone."

Phoenix dropped back down into his chair, Byte continued his relentless typing, and the rest of us scurried out of the room.

Carbon, Duke, and myself took Reese down to see Ember.

Ember was still curled into a ball on the floor

crying. I don't think she heard us come in. She didn't move in the slightest when I pushed the door open.

I stepped forward and unlocked the cell. Reese immediately rushed in, pushing me out of her way as she went. She dropped to the floor and wrapped her arms around Ember. "Oh, honey. What did they do to you?"

Ember's head shot up. "Reese? What are you doing here?"

"Carbon told me to come," she hedged. "Are you okay? What happened?"

Ember sniffed and seemed to calm some just from Reese's presence. "I'm not sure. I was talking to that man named Phoenix, and all of a sudden, he started yelling and flipped his desk over. He told me to get out, so I did. I ran out the door, and he grabbed me." She pointed an accusatory finger at me. "I managed to get away from him and ran outside. Another man tackled me to the ground." She looked around the room again and pointed out Duke. "That one, but I got away from him, too. I ran as fast as I could to the gate. When I got there, another one of them put a gun in my face! Then, the three of them locked me in here." Ember started crying in earnest again.

"Shhh, it's okay. It's going to be okay." Reese rose to her feet and turned to face the three of us. She was furious. If I was a lesser man, the look she fixed us with would have sent me running. She settled her eyes on Carbon and screamed, "What the fuck, Carbon? You said he helped women! Is this how he helps?!?"

I had been leaning against the wall, carefully observing the scene before me. I stepped forward before things could escalate between Reese and Carbon. "Hold up a sec. I think we are all missing something here." I pulled my phone out of my pocket, scrolled to the name I wanted, and brought it to my ear. "Brother, can you come down to the cells?"

A few moments later, Badger came through the door.

I spoke to the room, "As I was saying, I think we are all missing something here. I'm hoping Badger can help us put it together since he has known Phoenix longer than any of us. Ember, can you tell us what you and Phoenix were talking about when he flipped his shit?"

She visibly swallowed, her fear palpable to everyone in the room, "He was asking me why I was here. He wanted to know my name and age. He asked where I grew up, which led to him asking about my parents. He started to get upset when I told him my mother's first name. He threw the desk when I told him her last name."

All eyes went to Badger. "Well," he drawled, "I might be able to help you if you can tell me how you answered all of those questions." I got the feeling Badger already knew how she answered those questions. Was he testing her?

Ember sighed, "My name is Ember, and I'm 18. I'm here because I wanted help getting away from the place where I grew up, which is the orphanage across town. My mother died during childbirth, and my father was never around. I don't even know his name. My mother's name was Annabelle. I never asked her last name, but I assumed it was the same as mine. My full name is Ember Rose Blackburn."

Badger's face paled and he took an unsteady step back, "Oh shit!" Okay, maybe he didn't know how she answered those questions before. He shook his head in disbelief. "You said you are 18. Uh, when is your birthday?"

Ember looked just as confused as the rest of us, but readily answered, "It's actually today."

You could see the wheels turning in Badger's head. He was trying to calculate something, holding out fingers as he silently counted. His eyes widened and he opened his mouth to speak. Before he could utter a word, a frantic Phoenix burst through the door. “Let her out!”

Ember and Reese looked at each other. Ember seemed to cling even tighter to Reese. They both slowly stood together but neither took a step forward.

Phoenix was still very tense, but this seemed to be a nervous tension rather than the previous rage that consumed him. What in the hell was going on with everyone around here?

Phoenix looked directly at Ember. His eyes softened and he lowered his voice, “I’m sorry if I scared you earlier. Please know that no matter how angry I am, I never have and never will lay my hands on a woman in anger.” Ember didn’t say a word, she just watched him curiously. He continued, “I do need to speak with you privately…” Ember was already shaking her head no, but he continued, “I understand if you’re not comfortable being in a room with just me, so how about I let you lock me in that cell and you can stand out here while we talk.” What was he doing? I glanced at Badger who just shrugged.

Ember hesitantly asked, “Can Reese stay with me?”

Before he could answer, Reese stated,

"Carbon and I will wait right outside the door, Ember. I promise."

Ember's eyes darted between Reese and Phoenix. Her gaze landed on me for a brief moment, surprising the hell out of me, before it settled on Reese. She visibly braced herself and nodded, "Okay."

I unlocked the cell. Ember and Reese made their way out keeping as far away from Phoenix as possible.

Phoenix hung his head. Was that shame? That wasn't like Prez. He had no problem admitting when he was wrong, but he stood by his actions, never apologizing. He once told me he would always make the best decision he could with what he knew at the time. If he turned out to be wrong, so be it.

Once the girls were out, Phoenix walked into the cell and sat on the rusty bed. I placed the key in the lock and asked, "You sure about this, Prez?"

He nodded. His voice was gruff and almost pained when he spoke, "Yeah, I need to talk to her, without an audience. If this will make her feel safe, I have no problem with it." I don't think he intended for anyone to hear his next words, but I did. "I deserve it anyway."

CHAPTER FOUR

Ember

Everyone left the room. I clung to Reese's hand until she pulled it from my grasp. "You'll be just fine. Carbon and I will be right on the other side of this door." I skeptically looked up at Carbon. "Contrary to his previous actions, my brother will step in and make sure nothing else like this happens to you. Right, brother dearest?"

"Watch it, Reesie," he scolded. "But yeah, after all is said and done, if I need to get you out of here, I will." I'm not sure if I believed him or not, but I had more pressing things to face.

Reese gently closed the door. I turned around and looked everywhere but at Phoenix. I had no idea what to do with myself. I couldn't recall ever feeling so uncomfortable. I started rubbing my palms together and had no desire to try and stop myself.

Phoenix took a step closer to the bars. I instinctively took a step back, or tried to. Apparently, I was already plastered to the wall. "I knew your mother."

I gasped. "You what?"

He continued, his voice thick with emotion, "I was in love with your mother. Wanted to marry her. Was going to marry her." He swallowed hard. "We had been dating for almost a year when she finally gave herself to me, which happened to be the night before I was deployed. I joined the Marines right after high school, just like my dad. It had always been my plan. Annabelle said she understood that. Said she would be there when I came back," he paused for a moment and cleared his throat. "Damn, this is harder than I thought. I came back for her, to marry her, and, and she was gone. No trace of her. I went to her parents' house and they were gone, too. No one knew where they went or how to find them. I looked for her. Searched everywhere for her. Never found her. I kept looking for her until I was deployed again. After that, without Annabelle, I just didn't want to come back here. And I didn't until about eight years ago."

I was fascinated to meet someone who knew my mother. I knew nothing about her except for her name and how she died. As much as I wanted to hear more about her, I didn't understand what this had to do with the situation at hand. "Why are you telling me this?"

"Let me ask you something first. Do you know what a Phoenix is?"

"Yes, I do." I was beginning to wonder if this man was mentally stable. He kicked everyone out to speak to me about a private matter, yet he's asking me about my knowledge of mythical birds.

"Good. Okay, so, your mother's name is Annabelle Rose Burnett. My name is Phoenix Black. Do you see where I'm going with this?"

I thought my knees were going to buckle. I placed both of my hands on the wall to stabilize myself. The dots were starting to connect, but I needed him to say it. "What are you saying?"

"I'm saying that with your mother's name and your date of birth, there's a very good chance that you are my daughter. Your name only adds to the likelihood."

The room spun and I felt myself falling. I heard Phoenix yelling something just before everything went black.

CHAPTER FIVE

Dash

I was waiting with Carbon and Reese in the hallway. I honestly don't know why I was there. I could claim it was because I had the key to the cell, but I could have given it to Carbon. I could say it was because I wanted to make sure Ember was okay, but I wasn't ready to admit that to myself.

The silence in the hallway was broken when yelling and some sort of clanging noise sounded on the other side of the door. I rushed in, Carbon and Reese right behind me. Phoenix was yelling and shaking the bars of the cell with every bit of strength he had. “Help her!” he screamed, pointing to the floor.

I followed his finger to see Ember crumpled on the floor in the far corner of the room. I tossed the cell keys to Carbon and went straight to Ember. I scooped her up and ran upstairs with her held tightly to my chest. I wasn’t thinking about anything other than making sure she was okay as fast as possible. “Patch! Somebody, get Patch!” I yelled as I ran toward my room.

I gently laid her down on my bed and smoothed her hair out of her face. She was breathing, but her eyes were closed and she wasn’t making any attempts to move. Damn, she looked white as a ghost.

Phoenix plowed through my door, breathing heavily, eyes wildly scanning the room. “What the fuck happened?” I demanded.

“I’m not sure. I think she fainted,” he panted.

“Why do you think that?” I asked. He wasn’t making any sense to me. Healthy young girls didn’t just drop to the floor without something being seriously wrong, did they?

Phoenix looked uneasy, “Uh, well, because I told her I think she might be my daughter.”

“What?!!” shrieked Reese. Fuck, it wouldn’t

be long before the whole damn club was in my room.

Phoenix turned and looked behind Reese, “Carbon, get Patch.”

Reese sat down on the bed beside Ember. She gently picked up her hand and started murmuring to her.

Patch entered the room moments later. “What happened?”

“I think she fainted. She might have hit her head. Be easy with her, she’s skittish, Patch,” Phoenix blurted. He really needed to get a handle on himself.

Patch focused on Reese, “You her friend?”

“Yeah.”

“You stay. Everybody else, leave,” Patch ordered.

I growled, “No fucking way, brother.” We were in my room and I’d be damned if someone else was going to come in here and tell me to leave. It had absolutely nothing to do with the gorgeous little creature in my bed.

Patch shrugged, “Fine. Just stay out of the way.”

He proceeded to examine Ember. It didn’t seem like he was doing a whole lot of anything except running his hands all over her body. I decidedly did not like that. I was on the precipice of planting my fist in his face when he determined she would be fine and backed off.

“Really? Then, why hasn’t she come to yet?” Reese quirked her head and narrowed her eyes, “Do you know what you’re doing? Have you even had any training?” she asked snarkily.

Patch snickered, “She has come to. She’s just playing possum.” He winked and leaned closer to Reese, “I’m trained in a lot of things, pretty girl. Medicine happens to be one of them.”

Ember’s eyes shot open and made a sweep around the room. She shrunk back toward Reese when her eyes landed on Patch, “Who are you?”

“Name’s Patch. I take care of the medical stuff around here when I can, seeing as how I’m medically trained and all. You had anything to eat today?”

Ember slowly shook her head. Patch looked to me, “Feed the girl. She’ll be fine.” Then he was gone.

“Prospect!” I yelled, inadvertently startling the girls. Jamie appeared in the doorway. “Bring her something to eat. Actually, bring something for both of them.”

Ember looked around the room, “Where am I? Where is everybody?”

"You're in my room. Brought you up here when you fainted. The others stepped out when Patch came in to take a look at you."

"Your room?" She started to sit up. "I'm, um, just going to go. I'm sure there's somewhere else I can—"

"No," I stated firmly. "Stay put. You need to eat and rest."

She glared at me. "I don't want to be in your room, okay?"

Ouch. That kind of hurt. I guess I couldn't blame her for feeling that way. "Look, I'm sorry about earlier. I was just following orders. You were perceived as a potential threat." I paused for a moment, trying to find the right words to convince her to stay in my bed, I meant in my room. "Nothing is going to happen to you. You were perceived as a threat and all I did was detain you. None of us hurt you. We would never do anything like that to a woman, even if she was a legitimate threat."

She rolled her eyes, "I seriously hope you don't think I believe that load of crap that just came out of your mouth."

She was frustrating the hell out of me, in more ways than one. "Will you just stay there and rest for a bit? At least until you have something to eat?"

"If I stay, will you leave?" she asked, one perfect eyebrow arched.

I smirked, "It's my room."

She blew me away when she grinned at me. I felt that grin deep in my chest. What was this girl doing to me?

Our moment was interrupted by a knock at the door. Phoenix was there, holding plates of food and drinks for her and Reese.

He hesitantly placed it on the bedside table for them and turned to leave.

She pushed herself up, "You don't have to leave, uh, sir."

He turned to face her, "Just wanted to make sure you were okay and see that you got something to eat." Phoenix glanced to the floor and back to her, "Uh, you can call me Phoenix."

Ember smiled like the cat that ate the canary, "Oh, good because I thought calling you 'maybe daddy' would be weird."

Phoenix chuckled and shook his head. "Right. I'll stop by a little later, give you some time to eat and rest."

CHAPTER SIX

Dash

When the girls finished eating, I turned on the television for them. Settling into a chair in the corner of my room, I started messing with my phone. I had no interest in the girly shit they were watching, but I had an inexplicable need to watch over Ember.

As my fingers tapped away at some mindless game, my thoughts were of nothing but Ember. The girl had my undivided attention. I had never met anyone like her. She was beautiful, in a different way than most of the girls that came around the club. She wasn't overly made up, she wasn't dressed like a whore, and it appeared that all of her body parts were the ones God gave her. In short, she wasn't trying to be attractive, she just was.

My eyes drifted to her form stretched out on my bed. It was probably wrong of me to shamelessly stare at her body while she was sleeping, but I never claimed to be perfect. She was a tiny little thing, maybe 5'1 or 5'2 and no more than 110 lbs. Even with her small frame, she had nice full tits, I would guess a D cup, and an ass that was begging for my handprint. Her long blonde hair framed her gorgeous face, perfectly complimenting her big blue eyes and pouty pink lips. I wondered if her nipples were the same color as her lips. I bet I could—

Duke walked in and halted my thoughts in their tracks. Damn it. I wanted to keep imagining her naked, writhing beneath me as I—

Duke cleared his throat, "You busy?"

"Nah, man. Have a seat." I gestured to the other chair I kept in my room.

"How's she doing, brother?"

"Not sure. She fainted. She ate. Then they fell asleep."

"Did Reese get something to eat?"

"Yeah, Phoenix brought both of them more than enough."

"You think she's Phoenix's kid?" he blatantly asked.

"Don't know. Didn't hear much of what happened. I've been in here with Ember and Reese since Ember fainted."

Duke nodded, "Ah, well, Phoenix was talking about it out in the common room. He said Ember claims to be the daughter of a woman named Annabelle Burnett who died during childbirth." He looked at me pointedly. Every member of the club had heard of Phoenix's Annabelle. "Ember turned 18 today. According to Phoenix, if his Annabelle got pregnant the one and only night they had sex, the baby would have been born around this time of year 18 years ago. He's convinced she's his kid because of the dates, her mother's name, and her name."

I leaned back in my chair and crossed my arms over my chest. "Could be. Annabelle isn't a common name, especially around here. As long as I've been around Croftridge, I've never heard of another Annabelle. It still doesn't explain why he couldn't find Annabelle when he came back. He was only gone for seven months. If Ember's story is true, Phoenix and Annabelle were both in Croftridge when Ember was born."

Duke nodded thoughtfully. "I hadn't put that together. It will be interesting to see what Byte comes up with." He paused, glanced at the girls, then, lowered his voice, "You know anything about this orphanage she grew up in?"

I shook my head. "Never heard of it. Only thing I know of across town is that creepy as fuck dairy farm."

"Same here. I didn't know there was an orphanage in Croftridge. I heard Phoenix telling Byte to dig into that, too."

"We shouldn't have to wait too long. Byte is fucking quick when it comes to that shit. How's Phoenix? Any better than he was earlier?"

"He's all fucked up over the way he treated her at first, thinking she was here to fuck with him or cause problems as soon as she mentioned Annabelle. Thing is, only a few people outside of the club know about Annabelle, and he knows that. I think he just didn't want to believe it. Annabelle's disappearance tore him apart, and it took him a long time to put himself back together. Now finding out that she had his kid and she died…" he trailed off and just shook his head. "That fucks with a man. I'm not sure how I would handle it."

A throat cleared behind me. We both turned to see Phoenix standing there, arms braced on the door frame. “I’m fine, brothers.”

“No disrespect, Prez.” I didn’t want him to think we were back here talking about the shitstorm that just blew his way for shits and giggles. I was truly concerned about the man. Phoenix had always been strong and steady, nothing like what we’d seen from him today.

“I get it, but I’m okay. I grieved for Annabelle a long time ago, accepted that she would never be mine. I loved that woman and a part of me always will, but the past is the past and can’t be changed.” He paused, glancing at the bed, “That girl in there is likely mine, and she’s here because she needs help. If it turns out she isn’t mine, I’m still going to offer her the club’s protection and help her in any way I can. Seems like she’s had a shit life so far. It’s the least I can do.” He poked his head a little further into the room. “How long have they been out?”

“About an hour or so. Soon as they ate,” I replied.

“Let me know when she wakes up. After all the shit today, I never did find out exactly why she came to me for help, other than wanting a new ID. She’s 18 now, she should be leaving the orphanage anyway, whether she wants to or not. She shouldn't need a new ID or help to 'get away from the place she grew up' as she put it. Something doesn't add up."

He was right about that. "You know anything about this orphanage? Duke and I have never heard of it."

Phoenix's eyes grew dark, "Byte located it. It's located on the same property as the dairy farm."

Duke and I both started to speak at the same time, but Phoenix cut us off. "We'll talk more about it at Church. When she wakes up, get a prospect to show her to her room and get them something to eat. Her friend can stay in there with her for now. Then, we'll all sit down and go over what we know."

***

The girls slept for several hours. Duke stayed in there with me the whole time they slept. I thought it was odd, but didn't comment on it. He seemed to be watching over Reese the same way I was watching over Ember. Since I was actively ignoring my feelings, I decided to actively ignore his, too.

When they finally woke up, Prospect Jamie led them down to the room Phoenix had arranged for them. Duke and I followed them for some reason unbeknownst to me. What was known to me was how good her ass looked in those tight as hell jeans she had on.

Ember suddenly whirled around. “Have you seen my bag? I’m not sure when I lost it, but I really need it. Can Reese and I go look around for it?”

“Duke and I will go find it. You and Reese check out your new room and get settled.” Did she catch me staring at her ass? Did I really care if she did?

I figured she dropped the bag during one of the scuffles earlier. If she dropped it when she was fighting with Duke outside, most likely someone would have already found it and brought it inside, so I went to look outside of Phoenix’s office first. I turned the corner and spotted it immediately, on the floor right outside of his office. Well, that was too easy. I reached to pick it up and noticed the zipper had come undone, her crap sticking out the top about to spill everywhere. I shuffled it around some, trying to get her stuff to settle so I could close it for her when a distinct green caught my eye. I pushed the clothes she had on top to the side and dropped my jaw at the site before me. “Holy shit.” I breathed. “Duke, go get Phoenix, but do it discreetly.”

I stepped into Phoenix’s office and started carefully placing the contents of her bag on his desk.

Phoenix walked in, followed by Duke. “Holy shit! Where did that come from?”

“Ember’s bag,” I replied, dumbfounded.

“How much is that?” he asked.

“Don’t know. You want me to count it?”

“Duke, you start counting. Dash, see what else is in there.”

I pulled out all of the stacks of cash, but the bag still felt heavy. No longer caring about her privacy, I tossed the clothes into a chair. I reached into her bag and pulled out a handgun from the bottom. I placed it on the desk and stuck my hand back into her bag, pulling out an even larger handgun.

“What the fuck is she doing with those?” Phoenix asked.

I couldn’t help it, I busted out laughing. Phoenix glared at me. “I’m sorry, Prez, but she is definitely your kid if she’s walking around with a Glock 19 and a Desert Eagle 1911 in her backpack.”

Duke chimed in, "And a little over a hundred grand in cash."

Phoenix chuckled, but quickly sobered. "Something must have really scared her."

My laughter died as well. "Yeah, and we're going to find out what that was." I paused for a moment. "You want me to take this back to her?"

Phoenix ran his hand over his jaw, "Take her the bag with the money and her clothes. Tell her we found the guns and put them in the safe. Carefully ask her if she has anything else on her."

I took the bag down to her room. "Uh, Phoenix put your guns in the safe, but um, your cash is still in there."

"You went through my stuff?" she accused.

"Yeah, we did, after I saw the money falling out of it," I answered, trying to sound indifferent.

Her eyes widened. "Don't worry, doll, it's all still in there." Relief washed over her face. "Now, I gotta ask, you got anything else on you we should know about?" She looked down and hesitated. "Not saying we're going to take it. Not saying we won't. But Phoenix wants to know."

She sighed and pulled up her pants leg to show me the knife she had strapped to her leg. Then she did the same with the other leg.

Damn, this girl just kept getting better and better. I whistled, “Nice.” She grinned impishly. “I suppose you can keep those for the time being. You want to keep the money with you or you want me to put it in the safe?”

Her cute little nose scrunched while she considered my offer. She stood and removed a large portion of the cash from her bag. “Can you put this in the safe for me, please?” Smart girl, keeping some of it handy if she needed it.

“No problem. You two stay here and stay out of trouble.” I winked. “We’ve got Church and then someone will be back for you.”

“Church?” Ember asked.

Reese answered, “It’s what they call their club meetings.”

Ember nodded, “Oh, like Council.”

“What?” Reese and I asked at the same time.

Ember turned toward Reese. “You know, like those student council meetings they had at school?”

Reese nodded and let it go, but I didn’t believe a student council was the council she referred to. Unfortunately, I didn’t have time to press her for more.

We had Church once a week, twice if you were an officer. The officers met around lunchtime to go over anything from finances and business issues to potential threats to the club. Meeting earlier in the day gave us time to tie up any loose ends or gather more intel, if needed, before Church with all of the members at 7:00 pm. That was our usual anyway. If we were waist deep in shit, Phoenix would call Church anytime he deemed it necessary.

Phoenix wasted no time informing those who didn't already know about Ember's presence in the clubhouse. He went over the events of the day, leading up to him suspecting her to be his daughter. The room erupted in shouts of disbelief as well as cheers and congratulations. Phoenix gave everyone a minute to quiet down. When they didn't, he slammed the gavel down hard and barked, "Shut the fuck up! I'm not finished."

The room fell silent immediately. "Ember said she grew up in an orphanage across town. I thought the only thing out that way was the dairy farm, so I asked Byte to find it." Phoenix held up what looked like an aerial view of some land. He pointed to a building on the picture, "This right here is what we believe to be the orphanage." He used his finger to circle most of the picture, "And this is the dairy farm. As you can clearly see, the orphanage is on the dairy farm's land. I would also like to know what these other buildings are, but that's neither here nor there at the moment. Do any of you know anything about the orphanage?"

Heads shook, no one had anything to offer except Badger. "One of the prospects, Jamie, I think, grew up in Croftridge. We could see if he knows anything about the orphanage or the dairy farm."

Phoenix shot Badger a look, "We grew up in Croftridge, too."

"Yeah, but there wasn't an orphanage, it really was just a dairy farm back then, far as we knew anyway. Plus, we were gone for over 10 years."

"Fine. Bring in Prospect Jamie."

Jamie walked in, eyes wide, his nerves on full display. That boy was going to have to toughen up if he was going to survive around here. Phoenix got right to the point, "You know anything about an orphanage on the other side of town?"

"Not much, sir," Jamie shakily answered.

"Tell us what you do know."

"Uh, the kids from there, they don't talk to the other kids at school. They always stayed together, ate lunch together, came to school together, and left together. They only spoke in class if the teacher asked them something. Other than that, I've only heard things about the place," he explained.

"What'd you hear?" Badger asked.

"Uh, well, the other kids at school said it wasn't really an orphanage. They said it is part of that dairy farm, that's why everyone at school called them the farm kids. People have said all kinds of things about the place—human trafficking, drugs, child labor camp, a religious cult. The list goes on and on, but that's all just what people say."

Phoenix asked, "You know Ember?"

He shook his head, "No, sir. I mean, I've seen her before, but I didn't recognize her until I heard her name. She didn't look like that at school and like I said, they didn't talk to anyone outside their group."

"What do you mean she didn't look like that?" I growled. She just graduated. So did he. How much different could she look?

"She had really long hair. Like down to her butt long hair, and it was a different color. She didn't wear any makeup and always had on those weird clothes the farm kids wore, sort of like school uniforms."

Phoenix shot me a warning look, then returned his eyes to Jamie. “Thank you. That will be all.”

When Jamie left the room, Phoenix continued, “Let’s table this for now. I’ll see what other information Ember can give us. Byte, have you found anything useful?”

Byte stood and cleared his throat, “No death records found for Annabelle Burnett. Can’t find anything indicating she is alive either. As for Ember, I was able to get into her birth records. She was indeed born to an Annabelle Burnett on today’s date, 18 years ago, here in Croftridge.” He paused and faced Phoenix, “There’s no name listed for the father.” He turned back to the room. “I have more recent satellite imagery of the farm property. The newer images show a large number of buildings on the property. It looks more like a compound than a dairy farm. I tapped into some financial records for the dairy farm, and it is barely turning a profit. The rumors around town have suggested the farm was being used as a front for something else, this pretty much confirms it.”

“Who owns the farm and the property?” Badger asked.

Byte looked down at his notes, “Octavius

Jones."

Phoenix and Badger cursed at the same time, "Motherfucker!" "Son of a bitch!"

Duke asked, "You two know him?"

"Not really. We went to high school with him. He was a little punk that was always causing trouble and starting fights. I beat the piss out of him one day for shoving a girl to the ground. Didn't see him around much after that," Phoenix explained.

"I'll see what else I can find on him," Byte added.

"Anybody got anything else?" Phoenix asked.

No one did. "You'll see Ember around the clubhouse until we get shit sorted. Until I say different, you treat her like she is my child; hands off and you protect her like you would me. Her friend is here with her, she also happens to be Carbon's little sister. Same goes for her, hands off and keep her safe. Neither of the girls are to leave the clubhouse for any reason until further notice. There will be hell to pay if anything happens to either one of them," Phoenix ordered.

With that, Phoenix dismissed Church.

CHAPTER SEVEN

Ember

Reese and I were watching television and talking when we heard a knock on the door. "Come in," we said at the same time, then broke out into a fit of laughter.

Phoenix opened the door, scowling at us. "You should ask who it is before you just allow anyone to enter your room."

I blinked up at him, "Are we not safe here?"

"Yes, you are, but you can never be too careful."

"Okay."

"I wanted to see if you two wanted to come

out to the common room and meet some of the brothers? They know you're here and everything that happened today. They've been told to be respectful to both of you and maintain your safety."

I looked to Reese for help. I was still very nervous around Phoenix and his brothers even though they seemed to be making a significant effort to make Reese and I feel comfortable around the clubhouse.

Reese softly smiled and took my hand, "I think that sounds like a great idea. Let's go."

Phoenix led us out into the common room and introduced us to every biker present. There were at least 20, maybe 30 bikers in that room. I would never remember everyone's name. I swear, sometimes I wondered if Reese had the ability to read minds. She whispered in my ear, "If you forget someone's name, it's right there on their cut." She pointed to the leather vest worn by the man currently standing in front of us. Right there on his chest was his name, Ranger.

"Thank you," I whispered back.

Ranger was an older man, but he seemed very kind. "If any of these jokers give you any trouble, you come see me and I'll set them straight."

I felt my cheeks heat as I stood there

awkwardly, unsure of what to say. Reese stepped forward, "That goes for me, too, right, Ranger?" she winked.

He chuckled, "Of course. I'll see you two at breakfast tomorrow morning."

After Phoenix paraded us around the common room, he showed us around the rest of the clubhouse. Then he dropped a bombshell on us. "Until we have this situation sorted, I don't want either of you leaving the clubhouse." I opened my mouth to protest, but he held up his hand and continued, "Just until we get some more information. Things aren't exactly adding up just yet. Inside these walls, I know that you're safe and that's what's most important right now."

"Okay," I reluctantly agreed. Part of me felt like I had gone from being trapped at the orphanage to being trapped in a motorcycle club, but another part of me was ecstatic that this man, who might be my father, cared so much about my safety.

"I do have more questions for you, but I think we've both been through enough today. You two are welcome to hang out here if you want, but I have to get back to my office and catch up on some work. I'll find you in the morning after breakfast so we can talk more."

"Okay, um, thanks for letting us stay and giving us a room."

He smiled a genuine smile, "No problem. You know where my office is if you need me." He turned and disappeared down the hall.

I wanted to go back to our room, but Reese convinced me to stay in the common room a little while longer. We sat down at a table near the bar and started talking about everything that had happened since she dropped me off that morning.

A young guy came over to the table and asked if we would like something to drink. "Could I have a water please?" I asked.

Reese rolled her eyes, "Bring two beers with her water."

The young guy nodded and went back to the bar.

"Reese! Have you lost your mind? We aren't old enough to drink alcohol," I whisper-yelled at her.

"We're at the Blackwings MC clubhouse, not some snooty bar in the city. Besides, it's just one freaking beer."

"You ordered two!"

"One for you and one for me."

I leaned closer to her, "I've never had any kind of alcohol. I'm not sure now is the best time to try something like that."

"One beer isn't going to get you drunk. Just give it a try. If you don't like it, don't drink it."

The young guy returned with a bottled water and two bottles of beer. I looked at him curiously when he uncapped our beer bottles at the table. "So you know it hasn't been tampered with," he explained. Tampered with?

Reese waited until he left and explained further, "People can put drugs into drinks that will make you really sleepy and have a hard time remembering what happened. They're usually called date-rape drugs or roofies. Rule number one in a bar or club, never, ever take your eyes off your drink or leave it unattended. By the time you realize what's happened, it's already too late. Now, give that a try." She gestured to the beer bottle in front of me.

I was just about to take my very first sip of beer when Dash and Duke sat down at our table. "Hello, ladies," Dash said.

"Hello," I awkwardly replied.

Duke cleared his throat, "I wanted to apologize for tackling you earlier today. I was just following orders and trying to contain you.

In all fairness, you gave as good as you got. No hard feelings?" He extended his hand toward me.

Deciding that I needed to have friends around the clubhouse and not enemies, I placed my hand in his and shook, "No hard feelings."

"Do you two want to shoot a game of pool with us?" Duke asked.

"Sure, as soon as Ember gives that beer a try. It's her first, ever," Reese told them.

I glared at her. They did not need to know that. She stuck her tongue out at me.

"No shit?" Dash commented. "What are you waiting for?"

"Uh, nothing I guess." Trying to ignore the fact that everyone was staring at me, I lifted the bottle to my lips and tipped it back like I had seen others doing. I took a large gulp and quickly swallowed.

I completely extended my arm, the bottle dangling from my fingertips, "Gross!! Somebody take it away!"

They all started laughing. Dash reached out and gently took the bottle from my outstretched hand. "It's an acquired taste."

"Not for me. I have no interest in ever tasting that crap again."

"All right, grab your water and let's get a

game started," Dash said.

I sidled up next to Reese, "I don't know how to play pool. Can you show me?"

I must not have said it as quietly as I intended because Dash was the one to answer. "I can. You can be on my team and Duke and Reese on the other team."

He explained the rules of the game to me, which seemed fairly simple. Next, he helped me pick out a cue stick and showed me how to hold it. I suggested he take the first turn so I could watch how he made a shot.

When it was my turn, I went for the easiest shot on the table. Leaning over the table, I held the cue stick like I had been shown and took aim. I tensed when I felt a firm body at my back and warm breath next to my ear. A shiver went through my body when I heard his raspy voice softly giving me instructions. After I made the shot and sent a ball into one of the pockets, I felt Dash's lips on the shell of my ear, "Well done, beautiful."

I felt myself blush and murmured, "Thanks," before quickly turning my face away from him. I didn't want him to see how he was affecting me.

We played a few more games of pool. Dash continued to stand close to me, whispering things in my ear and touching me every now and again. His proximity was making my stomach feel funny, but I kind of liked it. I kept playing for as long as I could, but when it got to the point that I was going to fall asleep standing there, I said, “This has been a lot of fun, but I’m going to head to bed. It was quite a day for me and I’m exhausted.”

Reese yawned and stretched her arms over her head, “Me, too. Catch ya later.” She looped her arm through mine and started toward our room. I think I was asleep before my head hit the pillow.

***

The next morning, I joined Ranger for breakfast in the common room. He asked me if I had any questions about the motorcycle club. I did, actually. I wanted to know about prospects, so I asked him.

After he explained the role of a prospect to me, he filled me in on all the things he had planned for the newest batch. “I think I’m going to have Pete shine all my shoes later today.” He leaned in closer to me, “You got any shoes you want shined?”

I was laughing so hard I almost choked on the bite of eggs I had just put in my mouth. That was how Phoenix found me, gasping for breath and sputtering eggs. “I was going to ask if I could join you, but I’m not sure if that’s such a good idea now.”

Ranger answered since I was still trying to compose myself, “I was just telling her how I like to break in the prospects. I’m going to have them shine her shoes when they do mine.” Ranger smiled brightly.

Phoenix shook his head at the older man’s antics, but sat down to have breakfast with us. “Is it okay if we talk out here or do you want to go somewhere more private, like my office?”

“Out here is fine.”

“You met Patch yesterday. He’s a club member, but he is also a doctor. He’s going to stop by later today to collect specimens from us for a paternity test. That okay with you?” he asked, hopefully.

“That’s fine with me.” I don’t know why he thought it wouldn’t be. If he really was my father, I wanted to know.

“I think we should know for sure, but regardless of the outcome, I will do everything I can to help you get out of whatever situation you're running from."

My eyes shot to his, but I was at a loss for words. Several beats of uncomfortable silence passed by as I stared at him. "Really? Thank you. You have no idea how much that means to me."

By this point, we were both finished with our meals. "Why don't we go into my office for the rest of our conversation?"

The man really didn't like to waste time. As soon as I got myself seated in the same chair as yesterday, he asked, "Why do you need help getting away from the orphanage? You're 18 years old now, you should be leaving there, whether you want to or not."

I began to fidget in my chair and started rubbing my palms together in my lap. "Well, uh, I always thought things were strange at the orphanage, but I didn't really know for sure because I didn't have anything to compare it to. Anyway, we weren't allowed to go anywhere other than school and very rarely we would get to go into town for shopping. It just felt like we were being kept away from the rest of the world and I didn't know why. I still don't know why. So, as the kids in the orphanage got older, we were assigned chores to be completed every day. Most of the time, my chores had something to do with cleaning one of the buildings on the property. A little over a year ago, I realized that I could hear conversations from other rooms in the building through the air vents, so I started listening. When I started hearing things that I didn't understand, I started paying more attention to the things going on around me and listening more carefully to certain conversations. I'm not sure, but I don't think the orphanage is really an orphanage and…" I paused and looked up at Phoenix. I wasn't sure if I should tell him this or not.

He had been listening intently to everything I said and encouraged me to go on, "You can trust me. No matter what you tell me, I won't make you go back there if you don't want to."

That was what I needed to hear. I exhaled in relief and continued, "Again, I'm not sure, but from what I overheard, I think they do something else out there besides dairy farming."

Phoenix asked, "Like what?"

I cleared my throat, "I'm not sure what, but I think it is illegal, and I think that the people who work there aren't working there by choice."

"You think they are being forced to work there?" he asked.

"Yes. I overheard them talking about how someone had been there for 10 years and would be there for 10 more to work off the debt they accrued," I explained. I hoped I wasn't making a big mistake by telling him all this information.

Phoenix had the strangest look on his face. I thought he was going to say something, but every time he opened his mouth, he just closed it again. Finally, he gently asked, "So, if it isn't really an orphanage, why were you there?"

"I honestly don't know," I said dejectedly.

"Okay, can you tell me why you need help leaving?" he asked softly.

I tried desperately to keep the tears at bay, "I overheard Octavius talking to his men in one of their council meetings. He said that it wouldn't be as profitable for me to work on the dairy farm once I turned 18, so he had 'put the word out.' Then, he said that I had been selected and would be picked up on my 18th birthday." Phoenix sucked in a sharp breath. "I think, I think he was trying to sell me." I managed to get that last part out before I burst into sobs.

Phoenix stood and rounded his desk. He knelt in front of me and put his hand on my shoulder. "Hey, hey, it's going to be okay. I won't let that happen to you."

I continued to sob, "I'm really scared. I don't want to be sold. I don't even know what that means!"

Phoenix wrapped me in his big arms and rocked me back and forth while holding me tightly to his chest. "No one is selling you. You're safe here. I won't let anything happen to you."

He held me until I calmed down. I don't believe I had ever felt so safe and secure. I pulled back and wiped my face. "I'm so sorry. Contrary to what you've seen of me thus far, I don't usually cry this much."

"It's okay. I can't imagine the past few days have been easy for you. You've held yourself together better than most would have." He walked back around to his desk and redirected the conversation, "I'm sure I'll need to ask you more questions about all this, but for now, I just have two more questions. Where did you get all that cash and why were you so heavily armed?"

I smiled sheepishly at him, "I knew that I would need money to get away, but we were never allowed to have our own money, so I stole it."

Phoenix blinked at me, "You stole over $100,000?"

I grinned, a little proud of myself, "Yes, but

not all at once. I found the combinations to several of the safes when I was cleaning one of the offices. I took a little money from different safes over the course of several months and gave it to Reese to keep for me. No one ever noticed."

Phoenix nodded, "And the guns?"

I shrugged, "All the kids at the orphanage were taught how to shoot at a young age. I've had a gun in the drawer beside my bed since I was 10 years old. There are guns and knives all over the place out there. They always stressed that it was important to know how to defend 'our place' if we ever needed to. We also spent a lot of time practicing hand-to-hand combat. Honestly, I thought all that was pretty cool so I didn't question it."

Phoenix rubbed his chin, "How many kids were there in the orphanage?"

"Usually, around 20 or so, I think. They kept us separated for the most part, different age groups on different floors, boys on one side and girls on the other, and we all had our own rooms."

Phoenix shook his head, "That sounds, lonely."

I agreed, "It was at times, but I was pretty good at finding ways to entertain myself. I wouldn't say it was terrible growing up there, but I wouldn't say it was great either. I mean, I was fed, clothed, sent to school, and I was never abused or anything."

Phoenix finished that sentence for me, "but you weren't loved either."

Sadly, he was correct. "No, I wasn't."

Phoenix stood, "I think that's probably enough for now. Patch will be by after lunch to get the samples for the paternity test. We should have the results in three to five days. He's going to run it under a false name, so you don't have to worry about anybody finding out that you're still around Croftridge. For now, don't go outside of the clubhouse without one of the brothers with you. Same goes for Reese. There's a little lake toward the back of the property and some walking trails through the woods. Get Dash to take you down there if you want to see it sometime."

I rose to my feet, "That sounds nice. I'll ask him. Thank you, for everything." As I walked back to my room, I wondered why he specifically suggested Dash.

***

Four days had passed since I arrived at the Blackwings MC clubhouse and I was in desperate need of clothes and toiletries. I knew Reese was in the same boat because she had been wearing my clothes since she didn't bring anything with her when Carbon told her to come to the clubhouse. I found Phoenix in his office and asked if someone could take us shopping.

"Yeah, that shouldn't be a problem. Are you ready to go now?"

I nodded.

"Okay, I'll send someone to your room to get you."

"Thanks!" I couldn't help but hope that it would be Dash who would take us shopping. To my surprise, Carbon and Dash showed up at our door half an hour later.

"Ember, Dash is going to take you to a few stores in town. Reese, I'll take you home to get some of your shit and bring you back," Carbon announced. Reese and her brother were two of the most mercurial people I had ever encountered.

I grabbed my bag and followed Dash out the door, trying to hide my smile.

CHAPTER EIGHT

Dash

I took her to the only shopping mall in Croftridge. It wasn't very big, but she should be able to get what she needed there. I stayed close by, but I tried to give her space to get what she wanted without making her feel uncomfortable. I'm sure she didn't want to pick out underwear with me standing beside her, though I wouldn't have minded providing my input.

She had just picked up a black lacy bra, making my cock twitch, when I was hit with an unmistakable feeling. We were being watched. I carefully scanned the area. I didn't want whoever was watching to know that I was on to them. Shit! I couldn't spot them, which made the hairs on the back of my neck stand up. If I couldn't spot them, they were watching from a distance, like with a high-powered scope. The feeling of being in the crosshairs was not a welcome feeling. I had to get us out of here and lose whoever was watching us.

"Are you about done here? I need to get back to the clubhouse to finish up a few things before dark, and we still need to stop by and get your shampoo and shit," I asked, harsher than I intended.

"Oh, sorry, I didn't realize you had to get back. I'll just pay for this stuff, and we can go." I wanted to sag in relief when she agreed to leave without putting up an argument, but I couldn't just yet. Not until I knew we weren't being watched anymore.

As soon as she paid for her things, I rushed her to the car. If I could have gotten away with it, I would have tossed her over my shoulder and sprinted the whole way. "If you're in that big of a hurry, I can get Carbon to take me to get my toiletries later," she suggested.

Fuck. I just wanted to get her out of here, not alert her to something being wrong, and I damn sure wasn't letting anyone else leave the clubhouse with her. "Oh, no, it's fine. We still have time to stop." I tried to slow down, but I was too anxious to get back to the car.

I threw Ember's bags in the back seat unceremoniously and sped out of the parking lot. "Slow down, Dash! Really, I can get the other stuff later."

I flashed a fake grin at her, "It's all good." I drove all over the place, taking shortcuts, back roads, and any other route I could think of to make sure we weren't being followed. I was utterly grateful that Ember wasn't familiar with the layout of Croftridge. She had no idea I was taking the most convoluted path to the drug store.

I pulled into a parking space close to the front door, and she immediately hopped out. "I won't be long. I promise." She rushed into the store before I could say anything.

I didn't want to let her go in by herself, but since there was only one way in and out and I was standing right beside it, I relented. She might need to buy tampons or something, and I'm sure she didn't want me looking over her shoulder while she did that. Girls were so funny about that stuff. Same thing with taking a shit. We know you have periods, and we know you shit. And yes, it does stink. Not a big deal.

It couldn't have been more than five minutes when she came jogging out of the store. "All done. Let's go." Was she serious? No woman could get in and out of a store that fast, though judging by the three bags she was carrying, I guess I was wrong.

When we got back to the clubhouse, I helped her carry her bags to her room. "Thanks for taking me shopping today. I hope I didn't keep you too long."

"You didn't. I've got plenty of time to finish up things."

She was fidgeting, shifting her weight from foot to foot. "Did you need something else?"

"Uh, yeah, Phoenix mentioned some walking trails out back and a lake. He said I could go check them out if I took someone with me. He suggested I ask you."

I smiled. Oh, he did, did he? "No problem. How about after dinner?"

"Sounds good. See you then."

After dinner, I showed Ember the walking trails and then accompanied her to the lake. I wouldn't call it a lake, but it certainly wasn't a pond either. It was big enough that you couldn't easily swim to the other side.

Phoenix's grandparents had a few benches placed around the lake so they could easily watch sunrises, sunsets, or just enjoy the lake with some shade in the middle of the day. I gestured to one of the benches, "Have a seat." I wanted to laugh, but managed to hold it in. Ember sat down as far away from me as she could possibly get. "I don't bite, sweetheart, unless you want me to." I winked.

She rolled her eyes, but remained silent. "So, do you know what you are going to do when you leave here?"

She shrugged. "I'm not sure now. Phoenix said he wanted to get the paternity test results back before helping me make any further plans."

"Do you think he is your father?"

"It sounds like it is possible. We kind of look alike, but I don't know what my mother looked like, so it's hard to say." The sadness in her voice was almost palpable.

"Talk to Phoenix. He probably has pictures of Annabelle around somewhere. Even if he isn't your dad, she is your mother. I'm sure he would let you see them."

Her eyes widened and she could barely contain her excitement. “Really? I’ve never seen a picture of her. All I’ve ever known about her was her first name and that she died giving birth to me.”

I smiled, “Come on. Let’s head back and see if Phoenix is around.”

When we got back to the clubhouse, Badger told me Phoenix had gone home for the night. He rarely stayed at his house, but I guess with everything going on, he needed some time to himself. I pulled out my phone and sent him a text.

Dash: Do you have any pictures of Annabelle you could show Ember? She has never seen her and has no idea what she looks like.

Phoenix: Yeah, I have some here at the house. I’ll bring them tomorrow.

Dash: Thanks, man.

I gently steered her toward her room. “Phoenix said he will bring some pictures tomorrow.”

“That’s great! Thanks for asking him.”

As we got closer to her room, I noticed that she seemed to be walking slower and slower. “Is everything okay?”

“Yes, it’s just that Reese was in a mood when her and Carbon got back earlier, and I was trying to give her some time to herself."

"Ah, well, we can watch a movie in my room if you want."

"That works. I get to pick the movie!"

CHAPTER NINE

Ember

I woke to the sound of wood splintering and men yelling. Wait, why were men in my room and why was it so hot?

"What the fuck is going on in here?" Phoenix roared.

I pushed myself up quickly to a sitting position. It was at this moment I realized two things; one, I wasn't in my room and two, my hand was on Dash's bare abdomen. Oh crap, did I drool on him while I was sleeping? I started moving my hand around to feel for wetness.

Dash caught my wrist in an iron grasp,

halting all movement. When he spoke, he didn't seem rattled in the slightest, "Nothing, Prez. We came in here to watch a movie last night and I guess we fell asleep. Look at us. We're both fully clothed with the exception of my shirt. Hell, I still have my boots on." He pointed toward the end of the bed where anyone could plainly see that we were both still wearing our shoes.

Phoenix just glared at Dash.

My cheeks flushed with embarrassment, "I'm so sorry. I didn't mean to cause any trouble. I'll just go on to my room now." I hopped out of the bed and quickly exited the room, making a beeline for mine. Of course, Reese was hot on my tail.

We entered the room, and Reese immediately started grilling me about what happened with Dash.

"Like he said. Nothing. We watched a movie, or started to, and I fell asleep before it was finished."

"Uh-huh, you two looked pretty cozy all curled up together."

I turned away from Reese to hide my face. It was cozy being curled up with him, and I wanted to do it again sometime. "Well, well, well, I think little Miss Ember just might have a thing for

Dash."

I whirled around quickly, "I most certainly do not have a 'thing' for him. I don't even know what a thing for him is, so I can't possibly have one."

"Oh, don't pull that innocent crap on me. You know exactly what I mean. You like him. I for one think it is great. Maybe they didn't completely screw you up at that crazy ass place you grew up. Besides, Dash is smoking hot. You could do worse."

"Are you insane? I don't like Dash. Yeah, he's attractive, but forming a relationship, of any kind, is not even remotely on my radar right now. My future is basically sitting on the end of a cotton swab in a lab somewhere. What's going to happen if Phoenix is my father? What's going to happen if he isn't? I thought I would be well on my way to starting my new life far away from this town by now, but I'm still here, just waiting."

Reese sat down on my bed, "Do you think you will want to stay in Croftridge if Phoenix is your father?" She sounded hopeful.

"I don't know. I've been trying not to think about it too much. I don't want to get my hopes up one way or the other, but it's so hard not to think about it. And even if he is my biological father, that doesn't mean he would want me to stay."

"Ember, you saw how he reacted when he figured out there was a possibility that you're his daughter. You know he would want you to stay, and I bet Dash would want you to stay, too." She waggled her eyebrows at me.

"I don't want to talk about this anymore right now. Let's go get breakfast and find something to do for the day."

"It's supposed to be pretty hot with clear skies today. Maybe we could go swimming," she suggested.

"I am not swimming in that nasty water! It's brown, and who knows what kind of creatures are living in it."

Reese laughed, "I meant the pool."

"They have a pool?" I asked, surprised.

"Yep. Go down the left hallway and through the door at the end. It takes you out to a large patio with an in-ground pool. They also have a hot tub out there, but I'm not sure how sanitary it would be to get in that."

"Um, I don't have a swimsuit," I confessed.

Reese smiled brightly, a little too brightly, "Good thing for you I have an extra."

"Of course, you do." I could tell just by the

grin on her face that she was up to something.

After breakfast, we returned to the room to change and I found out just what she was up to. "Reese!" I shrieked. "I'm not going out there in this!"

"Of course, you're not. You're going out there wearing this." She held up a sheer summer dress type thing. "But you're going swimming in what you have on." I was already shaking my head in refusal. "Ember, I know it is far different than anything you've ever worn before, but I promise you, you look fantastic. Just give it a go. If you hate it or are completely uncomfortable once we are out there, we'll come back to the room and find something else to do."

I reluctantly agreed and crossed my fingers that we wouldn't run into anyone on our trek to the pool. There was a fine line between bravery and stupidity. I wasn't quite sure which side this one fell on.

To my surprise, we made it out to the pool without running into anyone. Reese pulled off her cover-up without any hesitation and jumped into the pool. I stood there feeling awkward and uncomfortable. I had never shown this much skin outside of my bedroom. Ever. I started rubbing my hands together and glancing all around.

"Just take it off and get in. No one is out here." She dove under the water and popped back up, "If you want your life to change, you have to start changing things, doing things differently. Now, take a deep breath, tell yourself you're beautiful, take that thing off, and get in the damn pool." She placed her hands on her hips and glared at me.

She had a point. I was trying to start a new life, and to do that, I couldn't continue to do things the same way I always had. I just wished the swimsuit had a little more material and a little less shine to it. As it was, my breasts were barely contained in the two shiny gold triangles that made up the top, and it felt like half of my rear end was on display with the small amount of material that made up the bottoms. My underwear covered more than this! Great, now I'm talking myself out of doing this instead of talking myself into it.

Okay, deep breath. Check.

Ember, you're beautiful. Check.

Take the cover-up off.

Take the cover-up off.

"I'm about to get out of this pool, yank that off of you, and toss you in myself."

Take the cover-up off, quickly belly flop into

the pool, and come up choking on water. Check.

“That was graceful. Tell me, were you a swan in a previous life?”

“Shut it, Reese.”

“Oooh, some sass. Looks good on you, Ember.”

We stayed in the pool for a while before Reese decided we should layout and work on our tans. We climbed out of the pool and I found myself feeling much more comfortable with the bathing suit. I guess she was right.

I must have fallen asleep in the lounge chair because I woke to the feeling of large arms wrapped around me, immediately followed by the sensation of falling before I plunged into cool water. I vaguely heard Reese screeching in the background.

When I surfaced, Reese was already up and she was spitting mad. She was yelling a string of curse words that could make any biker blush at a smirking Duke and a grinning Dash.

My eyes met Dash’s and I couldn’t help but admire him. The man was very handsome and even more so when he smiled. He glanced down and his eyes seemed to fixate on my chest before he cleared his throat and averted his eyes.

“Ember!” Reese whisper-shouted. “Ember!

Your top…"

I looked down and right there for the world to see was my left boob, completely escaped from its triangle prison. Mortification the likes I have never experienced before coursed through me. I quickly turned away, tucked my boob back into the malfunctioning triangle, and fled.

Reese showed up in our shared room not long after my grand exit. "Are you okay?"

"Seriously? He saw my boob! Duke probably saw it, too!! I can never leave this room again. What if they tell Phoenix? My possible father will think I'm a hussy, especially after finding me in Dash's bed this morning." I fell back onto the bed with tears in my eyes.

"You do realize this is a biker compound, right? Your boob wasn't the first they've seen today, and probably won't be the last." I sat up staring at her with wide eyes. Surely, she was joking. "I know this is all new to you, but it was a boob. A nice one actually, but that's not the point. Stuff like that happens to girls all the time, especially in a bikini. You have to learn how to not let things like that bother you."

"How am I supposed to do that?"

"You acknowledge the situation, make a joke about it or apologize for it, something like that," she explained.

"What would you have done?"

"I probably would have tucked it back in while saying, 'You naughty little tit. I told you to stay put. No one wants a sunburned nipple, now stay in there and behave.'"

And just like that, Reese had me laughing and feeling better about everything.

She had just convinced me to go back to the pool with her when there was a knock on the door.

"Who is it?" Reese sang out.

"It's Dash. Is Ember in there?"

She looked at me and I nodded.

"Yes, she'll be out in a minute. She had to put her naughty tit in time out." I burst out laughing and smacked her lightly on her arm.

"Okay..." Dash sounded confused. "I'll just meet you at the pool. Do you two want anything to eat?"

"Yes, please. I think we slept through lunch," Reese answered.

"Okay. I'll have a prospect bring something out for you."

We spent the rest of the day with Duke and Dash at the pool. Dash even had a prospect bring dinner out for all of us. I had so much fun and just for a short time, I was able to forget about all of the things looming on the horizon.

CHAPTER TEN

Ember

It was three days later when Phoenix summoned me to his office. I was pretty sure I knew why he was calling me in there and I couldn't have been more nervous. Feeling like I was walking the proverbial plank, I ventured down the long hallway from my room to his office.

Entering his office, I found Phoenix sitting behind his desk, Patch occupying one of the chairs in front, and one empty chair clearly reserved for me.

"Come on in and have a seat," Phoenix said

and gestured toward the chair.

I glanced at it and started rubbing my hands together. “Um, if it’s okay, I would rather stand.”

“That’s fine, sweetheart. Just shut the door, would ya?”

“Of course.”

Patch cleared his throat, “I have the paternity test results.” He held up an envelope. “This was given to me sealed. I have no idea what the results are. So, who wants to do the honors?”

Phoenix and I stared at one another. I subtly shook my head. There was no way I could open that envelope and read the results. “Patch, I don’t think Ember wants to and I don’t know any of that medical jargon, so how about you open it and just tell us the results, yeah?”

“All right,” Patch nodded and tore open the envelope. He was silent for a few excruciatingly long seconds before he held up one of the papers and read, “Possibility of paternity is 99.99%.” Then, he changed the tone of his voice and said, “Phoenix you ARE the father.”

Neither Phoenix nor I said a word. “Oh, come on. Have neither of you watched those morning talk shows?” Patch looked back and forth between the both of us. “Guess not. Well, I’ll just leave these here with you,” he tossed the papers onto Phoenix's desk and left the room.

I didn't know what to say. I had tried so hard since all of this came to light to not think about it. I didn't want to hope one way or the other and set myself up for disappointment. I now realized, in doing that, I set myself up for lack of excitement as well.

Phoenix wasn't saying or doing anything. He was just sitting there staring at his desk. Hesitantly, I inched closer to him and put my hand on his shoulder. "Are you okay?" As soon as the words left my mouth, I saw it. The small drop of water on his desk, joined by another drop soon after. He was crying. This beast of a man was crying. Dare I hug him? Should I give him some privacy? No, Reese said to acknowledge the awkward situations.

"I need you to help me out here. See, I'm kind of socially awkward thanks to my upbringing, so I'm not sure what the appropriate response is to a beast man crying. Should I just pretend like you have something in your eye and go fetch you some eye drops?"

Phoenix looked up at me, his eyes red and full of unshed tears. Then, he threw his head back and laughed and laughed. He reached his big hand out and pulled me into his chest. It was at that moment, feeling his arms surrounding me, his laughter filling the air, and his tears wetting the top of my head, that I finally felt like someone loved me.

Phoenix's laughter died down, but he still held me to his chest, "Oh, sweet girl. I wish I had known about you. You would have been a welcome addition to my life, just like you are now. I know you're pretty much grown, but we just found each other. Will you stay here? At least for a little while, so we can get to know each other?"

"You want me to stay? Like here at the clubhouse or here in Croftridge?"

"Both. For now, I think it is best for you to stay at the clubhouse, at least until I find out more about this orphanage. Is that okay with you?"

"Can Reese stay, too?" I asked.

"Of course. Anything else?"

I pulled back from him and started rubbing my hands together. "What is it? You can ask me for anything. If it is within my power and my means, I'll give it to you."

"Do you have any pictures of my mother? I've never seen any and I've always wondered what my biological parents looked like."

He nodded and pulled open a desk drawer. “Dash mentioned something about that the other day and asked me to bring some.” He pulled out a photo album and placed it on his desk. He flipped to the first page and turned the album toward me. “This is Annabelle.”

I gasped and place my hand on my chest. I looked at him in horror. Jumping out of my chair, I pointed an accusing finger at the photo, “That is not my mother! Is this some kind of a sick joke or something? Let’s see how much we can mess with the poor little farm girl?!”

Phoenix was on his feet, too, “Of course not. Why the hell would you even think that? This is Annabelle! Why do you think it isn’t? How would you even know?”

Still pointing at the photo, my finger shaking like a leaf, “Because that woman’s name is Annelle. She worked at the orphanage when I was little. She was the nicest one there.”

“Is she still there?” he quickly asked.

“No, one day she was just gone. No one spoke of her ever again. When I asked about her, I was told to hush and never say anything else about her.”

“How old were you when she disappeared?”

I couldn’t remember exactly when it was. I

knew it was after I had started school because she was there when I left that morning and gone when I got back. "I'm not sure, maybe five or six."

"You're sure this is the same woman?" he questioned as he flipped to other pages filled with pictures of Annelle, or Annabelle.

"Positive. See that right there?" I pointed to the photo. "Do you know anyone else with a birthmark in the shape of a puzzle piece on their neck?"

He slammed the book closed and met my eyes, "You could have just said that from looking at the pictures. She had another identifying mark. What was it?" We had quickly gone from bonding as father and daughter to accusing one another of deceit.

I placed my hands on my hips and returned his stare, "She has a scar in the shape of the letter P on the inside of her right arm, just below her elbow. It was small and light, probably too light to show up in pictures." I felt an overwhelming urge to stick my tongue out at him.

He visibly paled and braced himself on his desk. "Did she tell you how she got it or what it meant?"

"She never said how she got it, but she told

me it was for her prince. She said she couldn't be with him at the time, but the P made her feel like he was still with her even though he wasn't. It made no sense whatsoever to me then, but I think I get it now. It's really for Phoenix, isn't it?"

He nodded and slowly rolled up his right shirt sleeve. He held his arm out to me and there, in the very same spot, was the letter A on his arm. He softly said, "The night before I left for the Marines, we used paperclips and a lighter to burn our first initial into one another." He looked up at me and more firmly stated, "Do not ever do anything like that."

Without thinking, I blurted, "Yes, Dad."

He smiled, "I like that."

I grinned in return, "I think I do, too.

CHAPTER ELEVEN

Dash

Phoenix had been in his office for most of the morning, and Ember was nowhere to be seen. I took the time to get caught up on some of my club responsibilities I had gotten behind on since Ember showed up.

I was in one of the storage buildings out back sorting through a shipment we had just received when I almost blew the head off of a prospect.

He screamed like a girl and threw his hands up in the air, “It’s just me! Don’t shoot!”

I grunted and put my gun back in its holster. “Fuck, man, let that be a lesson to you.

Don't fucking sneak up on people around here especially when we have weird shit going on. You make some noise, make yourself known. You're lucky it was me and not one of the brothers with a twitchy trigger finger."

He nodded, hands still in the air, eyes wide as saucers. "Put your damn hands down and tell me what the fuck you're doing out here."

"Uh, right, Phoenix said Church in 30."

"When did he say that?"

"Um, about 15 minutes ago. Sorry, I couldn't find you or Duke." He glanced around the storage shed, "Do you know where Duke is?"

"Haven't seen him. Did you call him?"

"Yeah, I called both of you and neither one of you answered."

"Shit. I must have left my phone in my room. I'll grab it and try to call him. Keep looking and I'll let Prez know what's up."

I was surprised and a little disappointed to find that I only had the one missed call from the prospect. I don't know what I was expecting. The one person I wanted to talk to was here in the clubhouse and, to my knowledge, didn't have a phone.

I hit Duke's name and got his voicemail after a few rings. I checked his room to see if he was passed out from partying too hard last night, but he wasn't there either. I tried calling him one more time and then said fuck it and headed to Church.

"Thanks for joining us," Phoenix griped at me. "Where's Duke?"

"Don't know. I was out back sorting through the shipment. Haven't seen him all day. I tried to call him a couple of times but he didn't answer." It made me feel a little uneasy. It wasn't like Duke to disappear without someone knowing where he was going, and it really wasn't like him to not answer his phone. Duke always answered his phone, didn't matter if he was fucking or taking a shit, he answered.

Phoenix ran his index finger and his thumb over his chin, "Have the prospects keep looking for him. Get one of 'em to ride into town and look around. If he hasn't turned up by the time we're finished in here, we'll all go out and hunt him down."

Phoenix rose from his chair and started right in, "You are all aware of Ember's presence in the clubhouse. Earlier today, Patch informed us that I am indeed Ember's biological father." Murmurs started to break out around the room, "Shut the fuck up until I'm finished." The room fell silent and he continued, “So, Ember is my daughter, and she has agreed to stay here in Croftridge for the foreseeable future so her and I can get to know one another.” I felt like a weight had been lifted off my shoulders upon hearing those words. “Since we don’t know what is really going on at that farm just yet, she will continue to stay here at the clubhouse. In addition, Reese will be staying with her. Now, about the farm and orphanage. Ember has confirmed that her mother, Annabelle, was actually living and working at the orphanage for several years. Ember doesn’t know when she got there, but she does remember that she disappeared suddenly one day when she was five or six years old. She was also going by the name Annelle at the time. Byte, see if you can dig up anything on Annelle. Try using Burnett, Black, and Blackburn as surnames.”

Phoenix sat down again and leaned back in his chair, “Now, about this farm, orphanage, or whatever. I want to know why my girls were there. I want to know what the fuck they are doing up there. We’ve all ignored that place for years. Yeah, the place has always been creepy as fuck, but it didn’t affect me and mine, until now. I want to know anything and everything about the place. And I want to know who in the fuck thought they could buy my baby girl. I want answers first, and then we are going to put a stop to whatever they are doing. Women and children will not be sold to fucking monsters in my territory. My club doesn't stand for that." Claps and words of agreement sounded throughout the room.

When everyone quieted down again, Badger asked, "How are we going to get those answers? It ain't like they're going to tell us anything if we ask."

"I've been thinking about this since Ember showed up. She said there are other kids there, and they rarely get to interact with each other. I'm guessing that's so they won't talk to each other and start figuring out that things aren't right with that place. I want to get the names of the farm kids they went to school with from Ember, Reese, and Prospect Jamie. They should be able to give us enough names to get started. I want Byte to get into the school's records for these kids and get parents' names and addresses. Then, we're going to start digging into the parents. We'll see what information that brings us and go from there. Anybody have any other business or issues to bring to the table?"

I cleared my throat and stood, "Anybody seen or heard from Duke today?"

Heads shook and several no's answered my question. Badger asked, "You think something's up?"

"I don't know, brother. It ain't like him to just disappear and he ain't answering his phone. I know everyone in this room has had the pleasure of Duke answering his damn phone when he really shouldn't have." Everyone chuckled at that. We had all heard Duke at some of his finest, or worst, depending on how you looked at it, moments.

"I've sent a prospect into town to ride around and look for him, and the others are scouring the buildings and land around here. Be at the gates and ready to ride out in 10. Dash and Carbon stay here with the girls and the prospects."

Phoenix banged the gavel on the table and dismissed Church.

I dropped my ass onto one of the couches in the common room. I couldn't shake the feeling that something was not right with Duke.

CHAPTER TWELVE

Ember

Reese and I walked into the common room to find something for dinner. I was shocked to find it completely empty. I looked to Reese, "Where is everybody?"

"How would I know? I've been with you all afternoon," she snapped.

Okay, so moody Reese had returned. Noted.

"I just think it's odd that no one is here. There are always at least three or four people in here," I explained, still looking around to see if I could spot anyone.

She looked around the room, that blank look on her face again, “Just enjoy not having to hear them fart or fuck.”

“What?!?” I screeched.

She rolled her eyes, “You should come out here after dark sometime. Take a look around.”

“It doesn’t sound like that is something I would actually want to do.”

“Probably not, but you should do it anyway. It would be an experience for you, that’s for sure,” she said flatly.

“Do you think we should go back to the room?”

“Why? Just because no one is out here doesn’t mean we can’t be out here. I’m freaking starving.”

“Fine. Let’s eat,” I grumbled.

We finished our dinner in silence. The entire time we were eating, not a soul came or went. It was eerily quiet, and I started to get a little freaked out. Where was everyone?

“I’m going to go knock on Phoenix’s door and see if he is in there.”

She nodded so I knew she heard me, but she continued to stare off into space. I should have asked her what was wrong and made her talk to me, but I had a strong feeling that something wasn't right, which meant Reese's issues would have to wait.

Phoenix didn't answer the door when I knocked and it didn't sound like anyone was in there. I was going to check, but the door was locked.

I walked down the hallway to see if anyone was around. All the brothers' doors were closed, and no sounds were coming from any of the rooms.

Once I got back to the common room, Reese was gone. What was with the disappearing act? I was really starting to feel creeped out at this point. I knew I was safe in the clubhouse, or at least I thought I was, but I didn't particularly like being left all alone, especially when it felt like something was going on.

On the way back to my room, I decided to knock on Dash's door. I figured he would be gone just like everyone else, so I jumped back when the door opened, "You scared me!"

"How did I scare you when you knocked on my door?" he asked, cocking his head to the side.

"I didn't expect you to answer. Where is everyone?"

He looked at me like I'd grown a second head, but then he answered, "Most of the brothers rode out a couple of hours ago. Me and Carbon stayed here with the prospects to watch over you and Reese."

I crossed my arms, "How are you watching over me and Reese when this is the first I have seen of you?"

He smirked at me, "One, I don't have to see you to hear you scream. Two, I've got this," he held his phone out to me.

I took it from him and saw four little squares on the screen. One was the common room, one was the front gates, and the other two were each hallway. "So, you've been watching these for the last few hours?"

"Something like that."

"Then where is Reese?" I challenged.

"In Carbon's room."

"Oh." He just took the wind right out of my sails. I don't know why, but I felt tense and nervous and I really wanted to argue with him. I huffed and turned toward my room. "See ya."

I felt his hand circle around my upper arm before I was pulled back to him. "Something the matter, darlin'?" he asked, his mouth far too close to my ear.

"No, I just wanted to know where everyone was," I answered shakily.

"I think you're looking for a fight." He placed his mouth right next to my ear, "You need to release some tension, baby?" Oh man, his warm breath felt good on my skin, and he smelled so good, and he... "You want me to help you with that?" Huh? Why was he talking? Oh...

"What do you mean? How would you do that?"

He laughed and stepped back from me. "I have many different ways, but this time I was referring to grappling or sparring in the ring. Didn't you say you had some hand-to-hand training?"

Oh, goody, goody gumdrops! I loved to get in the ring. I was practically vibrating with energy and my voice came out a lot louder than I intended, "Sounds great! Let's go!"

"Hold up, princess. Aren't you going to change?"

Was he stupid? "Why would I change clothes? If someone attacks me, they aren't going to let me change clothes first." I took a deep breath and hoped I wasn't making a social faux pas, "Do you need to change clothes, princess?"

The look on Dash's face was priceless! I must have gotten that one right. "I was going to go easy on you, but now you're in for it," he threatened.

I smiled to myself. Yeah, we'd see about that. "Bring it on, biker boy."

An hour later, Dash was laid out on his back, again, asking, "Where in the hell did you learn to fight like that? Seriously, I haven't had my ass handed to me in years, and you're a girl!"

"That's a bit sexist don't you think?"

"It's not sexist. It's basic logistics. Men are typically bigger than women. Men generally carry more muscle mass; therefore, are generally stronger than women. In this particular instance, I am most certainly bigger and stronger than you. Regardless of your training, logistically, you shouldn't be able to take me down, repeatedly."

"Yet I did, so ha!" Dash reached out, grabbed my ankle, and yanked. I landed on top of him so we were chest to chest. The next thing I knew, he had us rolled over with my arms pinned to the ground by his big hands.

He looked down at me and ordered, "I'm sure you know a variety of ways to get out of this, and any other time I would love for you to show me, but right now, don't you dare move." I was about to ask him why, when his lips crashed down onto mine. He was kissing me. He. Was. Kissing. Me. Crap, crap, crap. I didn't know what to do. His tongue was licking at my lips. I opened my mouth to speak, but his tongue slid into my mouth before words could escape. Oh, I liked that. I decided I would just do what he did. I slid my tongue into his mouth and he groaned. That must have been a good sound because he started kissing me with more intensity. Yes, I liked this, a lot.

He moved his hands to my hair while my arms circled around his neck of their own accord. He continued to kiss me, lightly biting my lower lip from time to time. He groaned again and pressed his body harder into mine. One of his hands slid down my body to my butt. He gave it a squeeze, then tilted my hips up toward him. He tugged on my hair, making my back arch and ground his hips into mine. I was completely lost in him and how amazing he felt like this.

Suddenly, Dash pushed back and jumped to his feet. He wiped his mouth with the back of his hand and had the other hand held out to me. "Ember, get your ass up. Now." Then, I heard it. The unmistakable rumble of multiple Harleys getting progressively louder.

I quickly got to my feet. "I'll, uh, just head back to my room."

He ran his hand through his dark hair and

looked down at his feet, “Yeah. That’s probably best.”

“Listen, Dash—”

He cut me off. “Just go, Ember.”

And so I did. I went back to my room, confused, a little hurt, and more unsure of myself than I’d ever been.

CHAPTER THIRTEEN

Dash

Fuck. Duke was missing, and there I was, making out with my president's daughter, when I was supposed to be watching over her and her friend. What the fuck was I thinking? Actually, I wasn't thinking. I had wanted to fuck her from the moment I first saw her. Spending time with her had only increased that desire. I had her under me, I saw an opportunity, and I took it.

I hated to do it, but I had to send her back to her room, or really, anywhere away from me so I could get my dick under control before Phoenix got here and strung me up by my balls for having my hands on his baby girl.

I couldn't help myself though. She was so damn beautiful. The way she was looking up at me with those big blue eyes, her mouth slightly parted in surprise from me pulling her down to the mat, but it was the way she took me down time and time again today that completely obliterated the last little bit of self-restraint that I had.

Fuck, thinking about her wasn't helping my dick behave.

Trying to focus on anything other than her, I made my way into the clubhouse. I met a fuming Phoenix and a group of disgruntled brothers in the common room. "You find him?"

"Fuck no! It's like he just vanished. Byte is going to try to ping his cell phone. If that doesn't give us anything, I'm going to have to call his sister."

Shit. Duke didn't like for his sister to be upset. He went out of his way to keep her from worrying about anything. I'm not sure what it was, but something happened in the past that resulted in her emotional stability being fragile at best and Duke becoming über protective of her.

"Everything okay here while we were out?" Phoenix asked.

"Yep. Reese is hanging out with Carbon, and Ember is in her room. Prospects didn't find anything when they were searching the grounds. I sent them to make some food. Figured you would be hungry when you got back."

"Thanks, brother. I'm going to my office for a bit. Byte, try to locate the cell phone and get back to me ASAP."

"Already on it, Prez."

***

It was early, really early, but most of the brothers were up. With Duke missing, I couldn't sleep; I'm guessing the same was true for the others as well. I had just swallowed the last of my breakfast when Phoenix rounded the corner, "Church, now!"

We all dutifully followed him into the room and took our seats. Phoenix didn't even bother to sit down. "After Byte was unable to get a location from Duke's cell phone, I called Duke's sister late last night. She hadn't heard from him, but said she would call if she did hear anything." He paused and looked to the floor. "She called just now. She got a call from Cedar Valley Regional Hospital a few minutes ago. Duke's there, and he's in bad shape. Before you ask, I don't know how bad or what happened. She's a mess of course. She asked that only Dash and I come to the hospital right now. We're going to take a cage, pick her up, and go now. Until I know more, travel in pairs and stay vigilant. Badger, watch over Ember and her friend."

Two hours later, the three of us were sitting in a private waiting room in the bowels of the hospital.

Harper was barely holding herself together. "They only take you in these private rooms if it's really bad. He's either dead, or they think he is going to be very soon."

She was right, but I didn't want to believe it. Denial was the name of my game. "You don't know that, Harper. There are a number of reasons they would bring us back here. Let's try to not jump to any conclusions before we talk to someone who knows what's going on."

Easier said than done. Three torturously long hours later, two people in blue scrubs walked into the waiting room. "Are you the family of John Wayne Jackson?" Any other time I would have laughed my ass off. The fucker better pull through because I couldn't wait to give him shit about his name. John fucking Wayne. The Duke. Ha!

Harper's pleading voice brought me back to the present, "...just tell me if my brother is alive. You can explain it all after. Just tell me if he is alive!"

Phoenix had his arm around her shoulder for comfort and I'm sure to help hold her up. The older doctor looked to Harper with kind eyes, "I'm sorry, ma'am. Yes, your brother is still alive. The next 24 hours will be very critical, but if he makes it through that, his chance of survival significantly increases."

She visibly sagged with relief, "What happened to him?"

"I'm sorry, I don't know the details of what happened or how his injuries came to be, but I can go over his injuries with you and what we did to treat them. May I speak freely in front of these two gentlemen?"

"Yes, of course, they're his family, too. Please tell us."

He cleared his throat, "Mr. Jackson was brought into the ED unconscious. He incurred significant trauma to his head which caused intracranial bleeding and swelling. To prevent irreparable damage to the brain tissues, we took him into emergency surgery to stop the bleeding, remove the blood, and relieve the pressure. He is currently in a medically induced coma which we will attempt to bring him out of sometime in the next few days, barring any unforeseen complications. He has a tube down his throat to help him breathe, and it will stay there until we wake him."

"When can I see him?"

"He'll be moved from the recovery room to the ICU within the next hour. As soon as he is in his new room, you can go see him. First, my colleague will go over the rest of his injuries."

Harper fell against Phoenix and wailed, "There's more?"

The other physician began to speak, "I'm Dr. Glassman, a trauma surgeon here at Cedar Valley. Mr. Jackson also had eight stab wounds, four on each side of his torso. Both of his lungs were punctured. We repaired a laceration to his liver and his colon, removed his spleen, and closed the other three stab wounds that miraculously managed to miss anything vital. I will be monitoring him closely for the next 24 hours to watch for any signs of further bleeding.

We have him on strong antibiotics and will be giving him some blood to help replenish what he lost."

Harper completely lost it. She was sobbing uncontrollably and clinging to Phoenix for dear life. I looked at the trauma surgeon and asked, "Have the police been notified?"

He nodded, "Yes. It's hospital policy to report these types of injuries to the authorities. Since no one was here for them to speak with, the detective left his card with one of the nurses. He also said he would be back later this morning to see if the family had been found."

"Where did they find Duke, I mean John?"

"I'm sorry, I don't know the answer to that. I was paged to the ED and we were taking him into surgery within minutes of getting the call. I'm sure the detective can answer that for you. I will say that the stab wounds appeared to be intentionally placed."

"What exactly does that mean?"

"Well, multiple stab wounds are usually all over the place, with some vertical, some horizontal, or some diagonal. Mr. Jackson had four vertical stab wounds evenly spaced down the left side of his torso, and the right side mirrored the left. I've never seen anything like it. I can't say for sure, but I would guess that he was already unconscious when they occurred because the wounds are very straight and clean, no tissue tearing or jagged edges, which are commonly seen when one is trying to fight off or escape their attacker."

"Thank you, doctor. Both of you," I said as I extended my hand to one then the other. Those words weren't enough. Duke was one of my closest friends, and these two men likely just saved his life.

They both nodded and turned to Harper, "Do any of you have any other questions?"

Harper was still somewhat hysterical so Phoenix answered, "I can't think of anything right now. Can she see him now?"

"I'll go check and see if he has been moved to his room. If not, it shouldn't be much longer." Phoenix shook their hands while I tried to comfort Harper.

As soon as we were alone, Phoenix asked, "What the fuck, brother? Eight damn stab wounds? Strategically placed? Who would have done this? Shit! We should have asked if he had his cut on." He was pacing back and forth, hands tugging on his hair.

"We can ask for his belongings if they aren't

in his room when he gets there. You know he was wearing it. You think somebody took it off of him?"

"They would have had to in order to stab him like they did. Fuck man, we gotta find that and his damn bike. But first, I want a brother in or outside his room at all times, and we're going to move Harper to the clubhouse."

Harper's head shot up. "No. I am not moving into the clubhouse," she vehemently stated.

"Sweetheart, we don't know what happened to your brother other than somebody attacked him and damn near killed him. He would want us to make sure you are safe," Phoenix explained softly.

"Then put a tail on me, post one of your boys at my house, but I am not moving into the clubhouse."

Phoenix sighed and ran his hand down his face. "Will you give me two weeks? You can stay in Duke's room, and you can come to the hospital as much as you want. If we haven't taken care of this within two weeks, you can go home and I'll put a man on you."

She huffed and gritted out, "Fine. Two weeks and no more."

"Agreed. Good to see you with a little

backbone, Harper," Phoenix told her.

She blushed and turned away from us. "Yeah, I've been working on it."

CHAPTER FOURTEEN

Ember

I woke to an empty room. I guess Reese stayed in Carbon's room last night. I was hoping she would have come back to the room before I fell asleep. I wanted to talk to her about what happened with Dash. I needed to talk to her about what happened with Dash.

When I went out to get breakfast, there were several bikers scattered around the room, but there seemed to be a quiet tension in the air. A quick glance around the room revealed no Reese, but Carbon was at a table in the very back corner. I made my way over to him. “Hey, have you seen Reese this morning?”

“Yeah, she’s in my room sleeping. You need something?” he answered without taking his eyes off of his food.

“No, I just wanted to check on her since she wasn’t there when I fell asleep last night or when I woke up this morning.”

“She’ll be all right,” he said casually.

“Why do you say that? Did something happen?”

Carbon looked shocked, “You don’t know?”

“Know what?” I almost yelled.

“About Duke,” he said, as if I should know what he meant.

“What about Duke?”

“He was missing.”

Was Carbon only capable of uttering one sentence at a time? I inhaled deeply and tried to keep my tone from showing my frustration, “Was missing. So, he’s not now?”

“No, he’s in the hospital right now, fighting for his life.”

“What?!?” I screeched.

“Yeah, Reese heard about him missing last night and was pretty upset, so she came to hang out in my room. She gets like that when things like this happen because of what happened to our family." I had no idea what happened to their family but it wasn't the time to ask. "Early this morning, Duke's sister called to tell Phoenix that Duke was at the hospital having emergency surgery. They said it was bad, but I don't know any more than that. When Reese found out, she cried herself to sleep in my room."

"Oh, wow, um, maybe I'll just go check on her," I hesitantly suggested. I wasn't sure if I was allowed to go into Carbon's room. These bikers had a lot of rules, and I hadn't learned them all yet.

"Nah, let her sleep. She'll come out and talk when she's ready. If you try to push her, she will shut down, and I've seen that shit last for months before."

"Okay, if you think that's best." I didn't really agree with him, but he knew her better than I did. "Is there anything I can do to help with stuff with Duke or things around here?"

Carbon looked at me and raised an eyebrow, "Can you cook?"

"Um, yeah, I can. I'm not a gourmet chef or anything, but I can make some decent meals. Why?"

"Because the prospects we have now can't

cook for shit. I swear people in prison eat better than this crap they're serving us. You start cooking for us and as long as it is better than this shit, I'll make sure you get paid."

"Oh no, I don't want any money. I've been staying here for free. I'll be happy to cook." Plus, it would give me something to do. If Reese was in one of her moods and Dash was busy, which happened more often than one might think, I was left to myself. I enjoyed reading and being able to watch whatever I wanted on television whenever I wanted, but I was used to being active and busy. I needed something to do that would either be physically challenging or productive in some way. Cooking for a large number of bikers would likely be both.

"Congrats, you're the new Blackwings MC Chef. Make whatever you want and if we don't have the stuff you need stocked, make a list and I'll have the prospects go get it."

"How many people do I need to cook for?"

"Usually around 20 for breakfast and 30-40 for lunch and dinner. If we are having a party or another club is visiting, the numbers will be a little different, but you'll know ahead of time," he explained.

"Okay, I'll be in the kitchen getting started."

"Better you than me, kid."

***

Hours later I had made lunch for 30 bikers, cleaned and organized the kitchen, made the longest grocery list in the history of grocery lists for the prospects, and was almost finished putting away the groceries when I heard footsteps coming up behind me.

I turned quickly to find a haggard-looking Dash striding toward me. "You okay?" I asked.

He shook his head and continued toward me. When I was within arm's reach, he slid his hand around the back of my neck and pulled me to him. His other hand went to the small of my back and his lips pressed against mine. He groaned and held me tightly to him while he kissed me with a ferocity I had not expected.

Finally, he pulled back, leaving me a bit dazed and unsure of my ability to stand independently. I placed my hand on his cheek and caressed it softly, "What happened?"

He pressed his forehead against mine and sighed. "Can't say much. Club business, but Duke is in the hospital and it's bad."

"I know."

He leaned back and furrowed his brows, "You know?"

"Carbon told me Duke was missing last night and was found this morning at the hospital having emergency surgery. How is he? Is he going to be okay?"

"Don't know, darlin'. He's in a medically induced coma right now. A machine is breathing for him. He was stabbed. It's fucking bad."

I gasped, "Someone did that to him? Why?"

"Don't know that either. Do me a favor, yeah? Keep to the clubhouse for a few days. You and Reese can go out to the pool, but don't leave the vicinity of the main building. Just until we know more."

I nodded several times. "Sure, I can do that."

"Church!" I heard bellowed from another room.

"I gotta go, darlin'." He gave me a quick kiss on the lips and then he was gone.

I still hadn't seen Reese. It was really hard for me to not go looking for her. I had to keep reminding myself what Carbon said. Still, I was worried about my friend, I was worried about Duke, and I was worried about my own situation.

Nothing better than a distraction in times like these. I set to work on making an outstanding dinner for everyone. It took me several hours, but it was worth it. By the time I finished cleaning the kitchen and putting everything back to rights, I was exhausted. I made it to my room, flopped face down on my bed, and promptly passed out.

***

The next few days passed by very much the same. Reese came back to our room, but she was like a zombie. She hardly said anything, barely ate, and she wandered around the clubhouse aimlessly. I was seriously worried about her and at a loss as to what to do. I approached Carbon about her again, but he assured me she would be fine and to just let her be.

There was also a new girl around the clubhouse, Duke's sister, Harper. She was rarely at the clubhouse, or rather, I rarely saw her at the clubhouse. I assumed she was spending most of her time at the hospital with Duke.

I was beginning to go a little stir crazy. The bikers were always busy, including Dash. Phoenix was either at the hospital or holed up in his office with strict orders not to disturb him. Reese was lost in her head. Cooking for the club turned out not to be as much of a time-filler as I had originally thought. So, there I was, bored, a little frightened, and very lonely.

It was getting late, dinner had been served, so I decided to go outside and read by the pool. Reese had brought some books she called trashy romance novels. I found the books not only entertaining, but for me, quite educational. I wasn't against having a sexual relationship with a man nor was I afraid of one, I just didn't know much about sex, other than insert part A into part B. Honestly, I hadn't given much thought to relations with the opposite sex until I met Dash. I was using Reese's books to learn as much as I could about sex, sometimes skipping ahead to just the intimate scenes. Even though I couldn't get enough of the books and I was learning a lot, I still didn't want anyone to know what I was reading or why I was reading it. So, when Dash crept up behind me and yanked the book out of my hands, I had a freak out of epic proportions.

"Give me that back, right now!" I screeched.

"What if I want to read it, too?" the sarcastic little turd asked.

"Then get your own copy." I continued to jump around like an idiot trying to grab it from him while he effortlessly held it out of my reach. Then, I promptly swept his legs out from under him, pinned him to the ground, and snatched the book from his thieving hands.

"Are we done here?" I glared at him.

"Nope. I wanted to take you out to the lake."

"I thought you said I needed to stay close to the clubhouse."

"You do unless you're with an officer of the club, and I just happen to be one of those."

"How convenient," I rolled my eyes.

"Shut it. Let me up so we can go."

"Fine." I was going for indifference, but on the inside, I was jumping up and down while rapidly clapping my hands. I truly enjoyed spending time with Dash, and I really, really wanted him to kiss me again.

When we got to the lake, there was a little canoe on the shore. "Where did that come from?"

He pointed to a shed just inside the tree line. "I think it belonged to Phoenix's grandparents. I've never seen anybody use it in the years that I have been here."

"Are you sure that it floats?"

He smiled proudly, "Yes, I am. I made the prospects row it across the lake and back earlier today."

I giggled, "That's just mean."

"Not really. Stuff like that teaches them

loyalty. If they want to be a part of this club, they have to be willing to risk their lives for any of the brothers. Testing out a canoe is nothing in comparison."

"Okay then." They were all about the brotherhood, and I just didn't get it. Maybe if I had grown up with a family and friends, I would understand, but I hadn't. This large group of men who would apparently die for one another because they belonged to the same organization just didn't make much sense to me.

He gestured toward the canoe, "Get in. I'll push it off and hop in." Moments later we were floating in the middle of the lake, watching a magnificent sunset.

Once it started to get dark, Dash pulled out a blanket I hadn't noticed before and spread it along the bottom of the boat. He lay down on top of it and held his hand out to me, "Come down here. It's easier to look at the stars lying down."

I carefully positioned myself beside him and took in the view. There were thousands of tiny twinkles scattered all over the dark blue sky. I had never had the opportunity to sit back and take in the night sky before. It was breathtaking.

"Beautiful, isn't it?" he quietly asked.

"Mmm-hmm," I agreed. I felt Dash's fingers

intertwine with mine, and he gave my hand a little squeeze. I turned my head toward his, and he slowly brought his lips to mine. This kiss was softer, gentler than the others had been.

He rolled onto his side and pulled me to do the same. My hands were in his hair, his were, oh my, his were on my butt again. Both this time, and they were squeezing it. And it felt great. Before I could stop myself, I moaned into his mouth. He must have liked that because his kissing and squeezing became more urgent. His hands started to roam all over my torso. I wasn't nervous, but a little unsure of things. I guess he sensed it because he pulled back and said, "If you want me to stop, just tell me."

"Okay," I quickly blurted and pulled his face back to mine. I did not want him to stop.

He pulled back again, "I mean it, Ember. At any time, if you want me to stop, just say so and I will."

"Got it. Stop and you'll stop. Now, stop stopping."

He grinned and dove back in. I had nothing to compare him to, but there was no way all guys kissed this good. I could do this with him for hours.

His hands were on the move again. I tensed

when I felt his hand against the skin of my stomach. He didn't move his hand for several moments, giving me the opportunity to tell him no. When I didn't say anything, he started moving his hand again. He slowly slid it up my stomach to right below my breast. He pulled back from me and met my eyes, "This okay, darlin'?"

"Um, yeah, yes," I stuttered out.

"I'm going to touch you. That okay?"

I nodded quickly. I wanted him to stop asking me questions, because I couldn't formulate answers.

"I need the words, darlin'."

Seriously? I couldn't say, whatever it was he wanted me to say. I had mustered up the courage to *do* things with him, speaking those things aloud had never crossed my mind. Thinking quickly, I said, "Continue, please."

He stared into my eyes the whole time his hand made its way over my breast to the top of my bra cup. Surprisingly, I found his unwavering eye contact comforting, encouraging even. He gently pulled the cup down and placed his whole hand on my bare breast. He groaned and lightly massaged it. Then, he moved his fingers to my nipple and I don't know what he did, but it felt like a bolt of lightning had hit me, tingling right down to the apex of my thighs. I shamelessly moaned and thrust my chest farther into his hand.

He brought his mouth down to my ear and rasped, "You like that, baby? Having my fingers teasing your pretty little nipples?"

"Mmm-hmm," I breathed, squirming as he continued to work his magic fingers on my nipples, now moving between the two.

"I'm going to pull your shirt up and pop those gorgeous tits out so I can see them before I put my mouth on them. I've been dying to know what color your nipples are and how red they'll turn after I suck them long and hard."

His words were causing the sensations at my core to intensify. I needed more and I had no problem asking for it. "Please, please, Dash."

"Love hearing you beg, baby."

The next thing I knew, both of my breasts were exposed, one being cupped by his big hand, the other being kissed and sucked by his mouth. I don't believe anything in my life had ever felt so good. I could feel the wetness between my legs, and I desperately wanted him to touch me there, too.

He switched breasts and by this time I was squirming all over the place, needing something,

I didn't know what, just more. Dash sat up and pulled me onto his lap so that I was straddling him. Our groins were pressed together and I could feel his hardness pressing into me. He continued to lavish my breasts with attention from his mouth and I began rocking my hips against him.

He let my breast pop free from his mouth and told me, "That's it, baby. Get yourself off. I want to see you come for me."

I must have looked confused because he asked, "Have you never come before?"

"Have I what?"

"Had an orgasm?"

Oh, I had read the word come in several books and knew what it meant, but I had never heard it spoken in this context, which confused my lust-addled brain. I blushed and looked away, "Um, no, I haven't."

He growled and placed his hands on my hips. He took my breast into his mouth and used his hands to move my hips against him. It felt incredible. Something was building down low, and the feeling kept getting more and more intense with each pass of my hips. This was the more I was seeking.

Dash jerked my hips even harder against

him and bit down on my nipple at the same time. Pain flashed for a split second before waves upon waves of the most exquisite pleasure pulsed through my core. I cried out Dash's name into the night air. He groaned along with me, thrusting his hips harder against me. I felt a stinging sensation on my rear end, and then I felt his hand rubbing and kneading the same spot. I was pretty sure he just smacked my bottom. Odd as it was, it felt rather good.

Dash let go of my breast and moved his mouth to mine. He thrust his tongue into my mouth, and then I felt another stinging sensation. This time on my arm. Why would he smack my arm?

Ouch! I felt another sting on my side. What was he doing? Before I could get a word out of my mouth, I was tossed into the water. Confused and disoriented, I tried to calm my panic and get myself to the surface. I relaxed my muscles and waited for my body to start floating. As soon as I knew which way was up, I kicked my feet and quickly brought myself to the surface.

I felt Dash's hand cover my mouth from behind seconds before I broke the surface. As soon as my head was above water, he whispered in my ear, "Shhh! Someone is shooting at us." I immediately tensed. "Stay calm. Stay quiet.

Phoenix and the boys should be here any second now. There's no way they didn't hear the shots. He knows you and I are out here. We just have to stay behind the canoe until they get here. Nod if you understand."

I nodded once and tried to suck in air as quietly as possible. He was right. Mere moments later, even though it seemed like an eternity, we heard Phoenix and numerous other brothers barreling toward the lake, firing shot after shot into the night.

Blessedly, there was no return fire from any direction. Shouts of "Clear" were called out around the lake, and then we heard Phoenix again, "Dash! Ember!"

"We're good, Prez," Dash shouted.

"Where the fuck are you?"

We drifted around the side of the boat and were blinded by the light Phoenix was shining in our faces. Thank goodness Dash thought to straighten my clothes while we were silently floating in the lake.

"You two okay?"

"Yeah, we're good."

"Thank God. Hurry up and get your asses over here. We need to get back inside," Phoenix ordered.

We swam over to the shore, which was a lot harder than it should have been. It'd been a long time since I swam any significant distance, but I was in fairly decent shape. This should have been easy. At one point, Dash grabbed one of my hands and was pulling me through the water.

As soon as we made it to where I could touch the ground, I put my feet down and walked the rest of the way. I took two steps onto the shore, and everything just stopped.

CHAPTER FIFTEEN

Dash

I had just stepped onto the shore and turned to see if Ember needed a hand when she dropped. I barely managed to get my arms underneath her before she hit the ground. I lifted her and had her cradled against my chest when I felt it. Her side was wet, warm, and sticky. I looked down to my hand and even though it was dark, I could tell that my hand was covered in blood.

"Fuck! Phoenix, she's hit!!" I yelled as adrenaline flooded my veins.

Phoenix started barking orders, "Get her inside now! Badger, find Patch and get him here yesterday! Byte, pull the feed from the security cameras and..."

His voice faded away as I got closer to the clubhouse. I crashed through the back door and damn near busted my ass tripping over my own feet in my mad dash to get Ember inside and get her some help.

"Bring her in here, brother." Patch's voice had never sounded so good. He was already in the small room he had set up to treat the club members when we were injured or sick. He had enough equipment and drugs in there that he could damn near perform surgery if need be.

I placed Ember's limp body on the table and Patch jumped right to it. "Take a step back, brother, so I can get a good look at her. You can stay as long as you stay out of the way." Any other time he would have had my fist in his face for speaking to me like that, but this was his turf, and Ember needed help. I silently nodded and took a step back.

Phoenix burst into the room, breathing hard, fear in his eyes. "How is she? She okay? How bad is it?"

"If you want to stay, calm down and stand

there by Dash. No disrespect, Prez, just need the room to work."

"Got it. Talk to me," Phoenix said.

"They got her twice. She took one to the arm, clean through and through, will just need some stitches. The other grazed her side. It's a deep graze. I'll clean it out and put a few stitches in it, too. She's going to need antibiotics to prevent infection, particularly because both wounds were submerged in lake water."

My momentary relief vanished with Phoenix's next question, "Why isn't she awake?"

Patch shrugged, "Probably just shock. This was likely more excitement than she's ever had, and once the adrenaline wore off, it was probably just too much for her. Happens all the time. She'll come to soon, usually happens as soon as I start numbing the area for the stitches."

He was right. He started with her arm. He asked Phoenix to hold down her other arm in case she woke up while he held the arm he was working on. He had just stuck her with the needle when her eyes flew open wide and she yelled, "Ow! Stop that! What are you doing?"

"Shhh! Calm down, darlin'. Patch is just numbing your arm for the stitches." Phoenix ran his hand over her hair trying to soothe her.

She looked confused, "Stitches? Why do I need stitches?"

"Darlin', you were shot," he explained.

She shrieked, "I was shot? SHOT?"

I stepped into her line of site. "Keep it together, Ember. Yes, you were shot. Twice, actually, but neither are severe wounds. You just need a few stitches. Try to calm down so Patch can get that done."

I felt it deep in my chest when she wordlessly nodded, laid her head back down, and let just one damn tear fall from her eye.

Phoenix continued to run his hand over her hair and spoke softly to her, "It'll be okay, baby. Everything will be okay. I promise."

Her breath hitched when she tried to talk. She was killing me. Never before had I felt someone else's pain and fear, but at that moment I felt hers. She was trying so hard to be strong. I was damn proud of her for that.

"I need you guys to talk to me. About anything. Just distract me. Please." She sounded desperate. It made me wonder if something else was going on with her. She was naive to the ways of the world and incredibly innocent, but even with the way she was raised, she was not weak. It wasn't the time or place, but I would be discussing this with her in the near future.

"What would you like to talk about?" Phoenix asked.

"I don't care. Anything. Just talk."

I saw Patch draw some fluid into a syringe from a small vial. "Ember, I'm going to give you a little something for the pain and a little something to help you calm down. Might make you a little sleepy, but won't knock you out completely."

"Okay, I think I would like that."

He patted her shoulder gently and gave her the medicine through the IV in her hand. When the hell did he do that?

Patch chuckled, "It was the first thing I did, brother. You were too busy checking her over for yourself to notice what I was doing." He shrugged and went back to working on her arm. Damn, I guess I said that out loud.

"Tell me about your family, our family. Do we have any other living relatives?" Ember looked to Phoenix, her face filled with hope.

He softly smiled at her, "My grandparents. They moved to a beachside retirement community in Florida about eight years ago."

Ember yawned, "What about your parents?"

Phoenix frowned slightly, "My mother and father died in a car accident when I was 15 years old. My father's parents were deceased when my parents were married, and both of my parents were only children. So, for our immediate family, it's just me and my grandparents, and now you."

"Are there any cousins?"

"Yeah, a few. Two of them live not too far from here. They are the President and Vice President of the Devil Springs chapter of Blackwings."

"So, it runs in the family?"

Phoenix chuckled. "My grandfather's brother started Blackwings MC. When he died, his son, Hawk, became the President. When Hawk died, his sons were too young to take over the gavel, so it was offered to me. Not long after that, Gram and Pop decided to move to the beach, so they gave me their house and this land. I took a vote, and we decided to move Blackwings here. When my cousins were old enough, they got a chapter of Blackwings up and running in their hometown where it originated."

She smiled as he spoke. Her eyes were closed, and it was obvious that whatever Patch gave her was working. Moments after Phoenix finished speaking, we heard a soft snore. Phoenix smiled warmly at Ember and reached down to hold her hand.

"All right, her arm is done. Her side shouldn't

take as long. Dash, hand me the bottle behind you," Patch instructed.

He set to work, and since Ember was clearly asleep, I figured it would be okay to speak freely. "How's Duke doing? Anything new?"

Patch looked up, "Yes and no. They weaned him off the medication used to keep him in the coma, but he hasn't woken up yet. He is breathing on his own, so that's good, but until he wakes up, we won't know how much, if any, damage was done to his brain."

"Is that normal? To not wake up once they stop the medicine," I asked.

"I wouldn't say it is normal, but it's not uncommon. At this point, nothing we can do but wait. Have the detectives found anything?"

Phoenix shook his head. "No, I talked to them this morning. They've got nothing. They believe someone was trying to send a message. What that message is and to whom it was directed, we don't know."

I completely agreed. "What kind of message do eight fucking stab wounds send? You'd have to know what that meant to know who sent it."

Ember mumbled something. Her face scrunched, and her brow furrowed. Even her little hands balled into fists.

"What did she say?" I asked.

"Couldn't make it out. What was that, Ember?" Phoenix asked.

It was still mumbled, but it was clearer this time, "Octavius. Eight."

Phoenix sucked in a sharp breath and whispered, "What the fuck?"

And then it clicked. "Hold up. Octavius? As in the guy that owns the dairy farm or whatever that fucking place is?"

Phoenix gritted out, "How many people do you know named Octavius? Especially around here?"

Patch stood. "Finished with her side. I want to give her a once over to make sure we didn't miss anything else. Phoenix, help me turn her on her side."

They repositioned her, and I watched Patch run his hands all over her. It took everything I had not to break his fucking hands. She was mine, and he was touching her, a-fucking-gain. I knew he was only doing it to make sure she was okay, but I still didn't like it.

Patch pushed her hair to the side and ran his hands over her neck. He froze, passed his hand over her neck two more times, straightened his spine, and cursed. "Fucking fuck! She's got a tracker in her neck!!"

I stepped forward, "You're shitting us, yeah?"

"Fuck no. It's right here!" he pointed to her neck. I couldn't see anything. Hell, I'd had my hands on her neck and never felt anything, but I wasn't about to share that little tidbit.

"Take it out," Phoenix growled.

"I can take it out, but I think Byte should be in here. He knows more about how these things work than I do," Patch said.

"We know how they work. Now get this damn thing out of my daughter."

I got what Patch was saying, or not saying. "Hang on a sec, Prez. I think Patch is saying he can take it out, but he might damage it in the process, yeah?" Patch nodded. "Think for a minute. If we remove it, but keep it in working order, whoever put it there won't know we found it."

Realization dawned on Phoenix's face. "Right. Get Byte in here."

Five minutes later, Byte held a still working GPS tracker in his hand, and Ember had one stitch in her neck.

Phoenix's eyes glowed. "I'm going to make them pay for this."

CHAPTER SIXTEEN

Ember

I groaned. My arm was throbbing, my side was throbbing, and I had an odd ache at the base of my neck. I groaned again, louder this time, and moved to get out of bed when a warm hand gripped mine, "Where you going, darlin'?"

I didn't know I wasn't alone, so I tensed upon feeling his touch and hearing his voice, immediately followed by a sharp wince. Through gritted teeth, I managed, "Dash, what are you doing in here?"

"Answer my question first," he smirked.

I turned away, “Uh, I need to use the restroom and brush my teeth.”

“Okay, sweetheart. Let me help you up.”

“I don’t need any help.”

“Yes, you do. If you rip those stitches in your side, I’m going to tan your ass.”

I huffed. “Try it, and I’ll drop you like a sack of bricks.”

He grinned mischievously at me, “Not while you’re hurt.”

I returned my own mischievous grin, “Fine. I’ll tell my dad.”

He narrowed his eyes, “Just let me help you get out of bed.”

I reached back to rub the back of my neck in frustration and discovered a bandage of sorts back there. “Hey, what’s this on my neck?”

He looked everywhere but directly at me, “Uh, you had a small cut there. Just needed one stitch.”

“You’re lying.”

He whirled around and looked directly into my eyes, “You had a small cut there that needed one stitch.”

I knew what he was doing. He was telling me the truth without telling me the truth. “Tell me, Dash, how did I get the cut?”

He glared at me, "Can't say. Club business."

Without thinking I jumped to my feet and yelled, "How is my neck club business?" Then, I promptly bent forward and clutched my side in pain.

"You know, you can be a real pain in the ass sometimes. Let me see how much damage you just did," he said, clearly annoyed with me.

I let him gently lift my shirt and look at the stitches in my side. "They're all still in there. You must have just pulled them really good. At least it isn't bleeding. You are going to have to take it slow for a few days while you heal."

"Okay, I get it. Now, can I pee, please?" I asked, my irritation as evident as his.

He gestured to the bathroom like a game show host, "Be my guest."

I did my business and brushed my teeth. My hair looked like I had stuck my finger in an electrical socket, so I quickly pulled it up into a messy bun. Once I was as refreshed as I could be, I returned to the room to find Dash lounging on the bed and Phoenix seated in a chair next to him.

"Have a seat, darlin'. Dash and I need to talk to you and ask you some questions."

That didn't sound good. I reluctantly took a

seat at the edge of the bed.

"First, how are you feeling this morning?" Phoenix asked.

I grinned and said, "I was doing okay until I pulled my stitches when I jumped out of bed because Dash said he was going to spank me."

Phoenix's eyes widened and he turned to Dash, "The fuck is she talking about?"

Dash was holding his hands up in a placating manner. "It wasn't like that, Prez. I was just trying to get her to let me help her get out of bed. I said if she ripped her stitches, I would tan her ass. I wasn't serious about it."

Phoenix just stared at him. Finally, he scoffed and said, "Yeah, we'll talk about that shit later." Phoenix then directed his attention to me, "Got a few things I need to tell you. Most of it you ain't gonna like. Then, I got a few things I need to ask you. You probably ain't going to like that either, but I need you to stay calm, listen to what I'm saying, and answer my questions as truthfully as you can."

Well, now I really didn't have a good feeling about this. "Sure. I'll try. Go ahead."

He audibly swallowed, "Last night, after Patch fixed up your wounds, he checked you over to make sure you didn't have any other injuries." He paused for a moment. He seemed nervous, like he was having trouble gathering his thoughts, and that did nothing to ease my anxiety. "There's no easy way to tell you this, so I'm just going to say it. He found a tracking device in your neck. Do you know what that is?"

My hand flew to my mouth, and I gasped. I couldn't speak, so I just nodded. I knew exactly what a tracking device was, and I could not believe that they found one in my neck. Well, I could believe it, I just didn't want to.

He continued, "Patch removed it, which is why you have a bandage on your neck. Did you know it was there or do you have any idea when it was put there?"

How could they? Those lying, evil people at that farm! Oh, something was going to be done about them. They couldn't be allowed to continue doing things like this. I tried to compose myself, but my anger was at an all-time high. "No, I didn't know it was there, but I do know when it was put there." Both Dash and Phoenix looked at me, confusion evident. "About a year ago, I had a physical with the physician that came to the orphanage. Everything was the same as always until he told me he found a suspicious mole on my neck that needed to be removed. He said it was so small that it would be easier to remove it instead of biopsying it. I didn't put it together at the time, but he had everything he needed to remove the mole with him that day, like he knew he would be doing it. I'm sure he was implanting the tracker and not removing a mole."

"Patch said you didn't have any scars back there. Removing a mole would leave at least some kind of mark, so you're probably right."

"So, they've known where I was this whole time? Do you think that's who shot me last night?"

"Assuming they were actively using the tracker, yes, they have known your location the entire time you've been gone. Is that who shot you? I can't say for sure, but I think it probably was."

"Why now? Why wait? I've been here for over two weeks now."

"That's true, but last night was the first time you've been in a place where they could get to you. They can't get close enough to thc clubhouse to target you, and they're not going to risk being caught taking a shot at you in broad daylight with a town full of witnesses."

"That answers my first question. They have been actively tracking me."

Phoenix nodded, "Seems that way."

"What am I going to do?" I cried. My breathing was starting to accelerate. They knew my location and they tried to shoot me. Correction, they did shoot me, twice. It was only a matter of time before they tried again.

Dash put his hand on my shoulder. "Hang in there, darlin'. There's more to discuss."

"Okay." I reached up and patted his hand on my shoulder. He grabbed my hand and gave it a little squeeze, but didn't let go. Just that simple touch from his hand provided me with a world of comfort.

Phoenix eyed our hands curiously, but continued on. "Now, this can't be repeated. Normally, I wouldn't even talk to you about this kind of thing, but I think you might be able to help us out. Can I trust you to keep this to yourself?"

"Of course. What is it?"

"Last night, we thought you were asleep from the meds Patch gave you. We were discussing Duke. We mentioned that the detectives thought someone was trying to send a message by what they did to Duke. Dash asked what kind of message eight evenly spaced stab wounds would send..."

I sucked in a sharp breath and whispered, "Octavius."

Dash scooted closer to me on the bed, and Phoenix leaned forward in his chair. "That's what you said last night. Actually, you said, 'Octavius. Eight.' Can you tell us why you said that?"

Fear was taking over, and tears pricked my eyes. I knew exactly why I said that. Dash squeezed my shoulders gently. "It's okay, Ember. You can trust us. Whatever it is, you can tell us."

I started rubbing my hands together, and my breathing picked up again. Dash ever so carefully lifted me into his lap and wrapped his arms around me. He spoke softly into my ear, "Just breathe with me. There is no reason to be afraid. No one is going to hurt you. No one can get to you. You're safe here. Just breathe when I breathe."

When I finally calmed down, Phoenix was staring at us with the strangest look on his face. I couldn't quite place it and didn't have the energy or focus to even try. I cleared my throat and began to speak. "As you know, Octavius owns the farm and the land the orphanage is on. I think he owns the orphanage, too. He's tied to it in some way. Anyway, he is obsessed with the number eight. He's the eighth one to inherit the farm or something like that."

"What does this have to do with Duke?" Phoenix asked.

"The stab wounds. If you draw a line across the top to connect the top two, a line across the bottom to connect the bottom two, connect the top two and the bottom two on each side, and draw an x between the ones in the middle, it makes an eight. It's his 'symbol' or something. He puts it everywhere. It's even worked into the product labels for the dairy farm. Take a look at the barn doors sometime."

Phoenix sat back in his chair and ran his hand down his face. "I'll be damned."

"Why would he do that to Duke? What message was he sending?" Dash asked.

"I don't know, brother, but he's a fucking fool if he thinks he can do this shit to one of my men and I'll let that stand."

Phoenix was angry. Like scary angry. I unknowingly scooted back a bit from him. He frowned, "Already told you, darlin'. You don't ever have to be afraid of me. I'll never raise a hand to you, and I'll never intentionally hurt you."

"I know that. I really do. I guess it is just a learned behavior from the farm. When the men were angry, the women shied away and disappeared. No one ever hurt me there, but I tried very hard to stay out of trouble. I watched the adult women and mimicked their behavior. I guess it will just take time for me to unlearn some of those things." I didn't like that my involuntary reaction had upset him.

He patted my knee. "You don't have to worry about anything like that here." He turned to Dash. "Let's go see if Byte has found anything on those names he got from Ember, Reese, and Jamie."

Dash got up and followed Phoenix out of the room. That reminded me. Where in the world was Reese? I really wanted to go find her, but my body wanted to rest. I climbed back into bed and was asleep in minutes.

CHAPTER SEVENTEEN

Ember

I don't know how long I slept, but I hadn't been awake very long when I heard someone knocking on my door. "Come in," I croaked.

Dash opened the door and strolled into the room. "I thought we told you to ask who it was." He raised his eyebrow and peered at me.

I rolled my eyes, "Give me a break. I was recently shot, twice I might add, and I just woke up about five minutes ago."

His features relaxed and he asked, "How are you feeling?"

"Better, I think. What time is it?" I asked as I

pushed myself up to a sitting position.

"Around 2:00 pm. You hungry?"

"I could eat."

"Be right back," he winked and walked out the door.

He returned with a plate full a food and a huge container of water. He put everything down and turned to face me, "We need to talk."

I threw my hands in the air. "Why does every conversation I have lately start with a variation of that statement?"

"A lot going on, baby. We're trying to get shit sorted as best we can."

I slumped back into the pillow. "I know, and I appreciate everything everyone is doing. I'm just frustrated and I feel like I'm missing a big piece of a messed-up puzzle."

"You're not alone in that. And you're right. You are missing a big piece. We all are. Unfortunately, there are only a few key people who can fill in the gaps, and we can't ask any of them right now."

"Why not?" I asked.

"Well, Duke isn't awake yet, no one knows where your mother is or what happened to her, and it ain't like we can go knock on Octavius's door. Even if we could get our hands on him, it's not like he would tell us anything," he explained.

"Did Byte find anything with those names we gave you?"

"You know I can't tell you that."

"Ugh! It might be club business, but it is also my business!" I shouted, though he didn't seem fazed by it.

"Sorry, darlin'. You'll have to take that up with your father."

"Whatever. What did you need to talk to me about?"

He sat down beside me on the bed, and I braced myself for whatever he was about to say.

"Phoenix thinks we need to move you to a safer location." I opened my mouth to protest, but he held his hands up and continued, "Hear me out. They know where you are and they obviously either want you back or want you dead. Since we found the tracker in your neck and removed it, we can move you to a new location without them knowing."

"They'll think I'm still at the clubhouse?"

"Exactly. Byte attached it to a battery pack or something to keep it running outside of a body and hooked it onto Chop's collar."

I gasped in horror, "No! You can't let them shoot the dog!"

"Calm down, darlin'. They're not going to shoot the dog. They're looking for you, not Chop. We only did that so it would still look like you were moving around the compound. If your little blinking dot sat still in one place all of a sudden, that would tip them off that we found it."

I still wasn't completely sold on the new plan. "If they think I'm still here, everyone that really is here will be in danger. I can't be the cause of someone here getting hurt."

He chuckled, "You don't get a say in that anymore, darlin'. This is how club life works. We're a brotherhood, a family. When those test results proved you were Phoenix's daughter, you were automatically under the protection of Blackwings, whether or not you wanted it or needed it. We protect what's ours."

"I'm not yours," I stated matter-of-factly.

He smirked. "I'll let you have that for right now, but you are Phoenix's. You only have to belong to one of us for it to matter."

"I'm not Phoenix's. I'm not yours. I'm not anybody's. I'm a freaking *person*!" I was on my feet, fists clenched, face red, and now my side was throbbing.

He grinned. The man had the gall to grin at me. "Calm down. You're getting hung up on the words and not the meaning. I'm not saying you're a piece of property to be owned. By saying you're somebody's, it means you're important to that person, that they care about you; therefore, the club cares about you. Now," his grin widened, "did you just almost curse?"

Did I miss something? "Huh?"

He teasingly pointed a finger at me. "You said freaking. Correction, you yelled freaking. I'm quite proud of you."

Was he serious? "Are you kidding me? You're in here telling me I am in more danger than we thought, and now I have to be moved somewhere else and you're focused on the fact that I said freaking. Freaking. Freaking. Freaking. There. Now tell me where I'm going."

He mumbled something that I didn't catch. "What was that?"

He cleared his throat and met my eyes. "I said, 'You'll be going over my knee if you don't watch that smart mouth.'"

I rolled my eyes. "We've already had this discussion once. Could we please get back to the main topic of conversation, and before you say anything irreverent, I'm referring to my future location."

He sighed and ran his hands through his

dark hair. “Right. Phoenix wants to move you out of the clubhouse to a remote location until he can get the situation with Octavius and the farm sorted. Badger mentioned that he has a cabin up in the mountains that would be safe for you. It’s not far from Devil Springs and only a couple of hours at most from here.”

I swallowed hard. “I’m going by myself?”

He looked at me incredulously. “Have you learned nothing while you’ve been here? Of course, you’re not going by yourself. I’m going with you, as well as two prospects.”

“What about Reese?”

“For now, it’s best if she stays here. We’re not sure if they have put together the connection between you two, but she has been around the clubhouse since they have been watching, so we need her to still be seen around here. We have to keep things looking as close to normal as possible.”

“Won’t they notice that you and two prospects are missing?”

“Nope. It will just look like me and the newbies have gone on a run.”

“How am I going to get to this cabin? If they’re watching, won’t they see me leave?”

He stood. “All you need to worry about right

now is getting yourself packed up. Let me know if you need help and I'll send a prospect in. We're leaving tonight, just after it gets dark."

"Fine. Can you find Reese for me? I have barely seen her since Duke was hurt, and I want to talk to her before we leave for the cabin."

"You haven't seen her because she has either been at the hospital with Harper or holed up in Carbon's room."

That seemed odd. Were Reese and Duke close? I thought she said her brother wouldn't let her hang around the clubhouse. "Were Duke and Reese close?"

He shrugged, "Don't think so. Never saw her around here before you showed up."

"Okay. Well, could you check Carbon's room and see if she's there? I want to see her before we go. I'm a little worried about her."

"Why?"

"I don't know. Just a feeling. She seems a little more distant than usual I guess." That wasn't a complete lie. She was more distant, but it was more than a feeling. I knew something was wrong with her, I just didn't know what.

He nodded. "I'll see if I can find her. Get started packing up. We're leaving even if you aren't ready to go, and we're not coming back if you forgot something."

"Got it." With that, he left me to my packing.

CHAPTER EIGHTEEN

Ember

"Are you sure this is safe?" I was sitting in an enclosed trailer with three motorcycles and Dash. The two prospects, Jamie and Pete, were pulling us using Badger's old Blazer.

"It's as safe as it can be. It's not like you are going to fall out or anything."

"I know that, but what if we have a wreck or they go off the side of the mountain. We don't even have seat belts!"

"Darlin', if they drive off the side of the

mountain, a seat belt ain't going to save you. Just try and relax. We'll be there soon."

I turned my head away from him. It's not like he could see me anyway, but still, I wanted that extra bit of distance. I was feeling far too many emotions at one time, and I wasn't sure how to handle them all. I was worried about Phoenix and the men back at the clubhouse. I was upset that I didn't get to see Reese or even talk to her before we left. Did she even know I had been shot? I was angry for being put in this messed up situation, but I didn't know where to direct that anger, so I couldn't process it very well. I was nervous about being alone with Dash and two prospects I barely knew in a secluded cabin on top of a mountain. If something happened, I could potentially be stuck up there by myself, or with two young men I didn't really know.

I was also scared. Really scared. What if Phoenix and the club didn't come out on top? What if Octavius found me again? Would he kill me or take me with him? Would he kill Dash and the prospects? This whole situation had the potential for me to lose everyone I'd come to care about recently. I wouldn't survive it if I lost everyone. I wouldn't want to.

I felt a warm hand on my shoulder, and then

I was being pulled into a solid chest. His other hand went to my face and his thumb slid fluidly across my cheek. I hadn't realized I was crying, but there I was, tears steadily running down my face. "Shhh, it's going to be okay, baby." He gently rocked me back and forth while soothingly rubbing my back.

I hiccupped, "You don't know that. What if everyone dies? He could kill Phoenix and everyone at the club, and then he could come to the cabin, kill you guys, and take me away." I wailed and buried my face in his neck.

He smoothed his hand over my hair. "This all you been thinking about?"

I nodded and sniffed. I hoped I wasn't getting snot all over his neck. How gross would that be?

"I'm going to tell you this one time, so listen and listen good. Phoenix is the President for a reason. This ain't his first rodeo. On top of that, he has years of military experience. He was highly decorated and highly ranked before he returned home. Badger is the VP because he is a close second to Phoenix. They can handle this. As for the four of us, we have a plan and a backup plan that we will go over when we get there. If anything goes wrong, we'll all know what to do. I'm not going to promise that something won't happen to me, but I will promise that Octavius will not get to you."

"Dash, don't say that," I pleaded.

"Do you know why Phoenix sent me up here with you?" I shook my head, I really had no idea why, but I was very happy that it was Dash he sent. "Because your father knows that I would lay down my life for you just as fast as he would. When there is a cause close to the heart, people fight a lot harder for it."

I pushed back from him just a little so I could look at his face. It was hard to see him, but the tiny touch light on the other side of the trailer allowed me to see the shimmer of his eyes. "Why would you do that?"

"Because I care about you, Ember. A lot. I know you just came from a shit situation and this is a whole new world for you, so I've been trying to give you time to get adjusted and settled, but know this, you are mine."

This time, it didn't make me angry when he said I belonged to someone, to him. Not at all. I couldn't help the smile that slowly spread across my face. My voice came out raspier than I intended when I asked, "What exactly does that mean?"

He leaned closer, so his lips were right against

the shell of my ear. For a few moments all I felt was his warm breath, and then he spoke, "It means you are mine. In every way. Body, heart, and soul."

"And you will be?"

"Silly girl. I'm already yours." He nipped at my earlobe, and then pressed a warm kiss on my neck, which made me shiver. He carefully pulled me to him and arranged me so that I was straddling him.

My arms went around his neck and I slid my fingers into his thick hair. I felt really awkward, but I had to know, "So, you're like my boyfriend?"

He scoffed. "Do I look like a fucking boy to you? And I damn sure don't want to be your friend. I'm your man, darlin'. You good with that?"

"Yeah, I think I'm good with that." I tried to hide it, but I knew he heard the tremble in my voice. I wanted to be with him. I enjoyed his company, I felt safe with him, and I really liked the things he had done to my body. Still, I was nervous. I'm sure he had plenty of experience with dating and sex, while I had none other than what I had done with him. How could he even want to be with someone like me? I wouldn't even know how to make him feel the way he made me feel the other night. I mean, the romance novels Reese had me reading explained a lot of stuff I had never even heard of, but reading about it and doing it were two very different things.

"Hey, what's going on in that head of yours?"

"Nothing," I answered quickly, too quickly.

He gave my hips a gentle, but firm squeeze. "Don't lie to me. If this is going to work between us, we have to be honest with each other. No matter what. You can talk to me about anything."

My mouth suddenly felt dry. I decided I would say it fast and get it over with. "I-don't-know-how-to-please-you-because-I-don't-have-any-experience-and-I'm-afraid-that-will-make-you-not-want-me." It all came out like one really long word. I sucked in a huge breath and waited to see how he would respond.

His voice was soft when he spoke, and I could hear his smile, "Baby, I know you don't have a lot of experience. I prefer it that way."

"Y-you do?"

"Yeah, I do. I get to be the one who helps you figure out what you like and don't like. I'll show you what I like and what I don't. I never expected you to just know those things."

I sighed in relief and laid my head against his chest. At least one of my current problems had been solved.

"We need to stop talking about this. It's making me hard and I'm not touching you like that while you're hurt."

I smiled against his chest, "Okay, Dash."

He lightly slapped my butt. "Get some rest. We'll be there before you know it."

***

I couldn't fall asleep. I had too many thoughts flooding my mind and too many emotions flooding my heart. Even with all of my inner turmoil, I felt safe in Dash's arms. Because of that, I didn't make a move to get up when I felt the Blazer come to a stop, followed by the engine shutting off.

"Come on, beautiful. We're here," Dash murmured against my ear.

I gingerly got to my feet. My body was sore from straddling Dash for hours and my wounds were starting to ache again.

"I'll get you something to eat and some pain medicine once we get everything inside."

"Thank you. What can I help with?"

"Not a damn thing. Stitches, remember? Go inside, and pick out a bedroom. Then plant your ass there until I come bearing food," he said, jovially.

So, that's what I did. The cabin was the definition of remote, but it was a lot bigger and nicer than I expected. I assumed we would be staying in something equivalent to a hunting shack, but that was not the case. This place was two stories with four bedrooms and four bathrooms. In addition to the living room, kitchen, and dining room, it had a large game room, an attached two car garage, a screened in porch with a hot tub, and a large, open deck.

I made my way upstairs and checked out the bedrooms. All the rooms were about the same size and decorated similarly, the only difference I noticed was the size of the bed in each room. I wondered if Dash and I would stay in the same room or if that was being presumptuous. We had slept in the same bed once before, but we didn't consciously go to bed together that night. I would just err on the side of caution and pick a room with a queen size bed, leaving the king size, another queen, and two twin beds free for the picking.

Prospect Jamie brought my bags to my room. I thought now would be a good time to shower. I felt sticky and grimy from being in the back of that trailer for a few hours.

When I stepped out of the bathroom, dressed in my pajamas with a towel wrapped around my hair, I found Dash sitting on my bed, a plate a food and a drink on the nightstand, and a scowl on his face.

"What's wrong?" I asked.

"Why did you pick this room?"

I shrugged. "Was I not supposed to pick this one? I can move to another one if it is a problem."

"It is a problem, and your things have already been moved to another room."

"Okay..." What was his problem? He told me to pick a room. I did.

"Did you hear me say that you are mine?" he snapped. I nodded.

"That means you sleep in my bed. Doesn't mean we have to do anything you aren't ready for, but it does mean you sleep beside me. Especially when my number one priority is keeping you safe. You are safest by my side."

"I'm sorry, Dash. I wasn't sure what to do, and I didn't want to assume that we were staying together."

He sighed, but his expression softened, "I get that, but what did I tell you? We have to talk to each other. Next time you aren't sure about something, just ask me, yeah?"

"Yeah, okay." He made it sound so easy, so simple, which brought my insecurities to the surface. I had been trying so hard to fit in with everyone and overcome my social awkwardness instilled by my sheltered upbringing, but one little incident made me realize I still had a long way to go.

He picked up the plate of food and the drink. "Come on. I'll take you to *our* room. I'll come back and get your stuff from the bathroom while you're eating."

"Did you eat?"

"I'll grab something after I get you settled. I'll bring it back up here so we can go over plan A and plan B if things go sideways."

I had just swallowed the last bite of food when Dash came through the door with his own plate of food. He sat down and began talking while eating. "If everything goes smoothly, we will just hang out up here until Phoenix gives the all clear. I have a couple different burner phones that I will use to check in with Phoenix at a set time every couple of days. I'll start checking in more often as he gets closer to taking down Octavius's operation. If I call in at the set check-in time and Phoenix doesn't answer, we will grab our stuff and go to the Blackwings clubhouse in Devil Springs. It's about 30 minutes from here. You with me so far?"

I nodded, listening intently. I wanted to make sure I didn't miss anything he said.

"If Phoenix doesn't answer at the set check-in time and we can't leave here, we will leave everything as is in the cabin and go to the underground bunker. I will show you where it is and how to get in it if I'm not able to go with you right away. In the bunker, you will find a satellite phone with a few numbers already programmed in it. One of those numbers belongs to Copper, President of the Devil Springs chapter. He's also Phoenix's cousin, yours, too. You call him and say, 'This is Phoenix's Spawn. Code Flame.' He will know what to do. You stay in the bunker until Copper calls you back on the phone and says, 'Flame extinguished. Phoenix shall rise.' This means the problem has been taken care of, and it is safe for you to come out. Now repeat that back to me."

I did as he asked, and I think I surprised him that I was able to recall everything he said after just one explanation. This wasn't my first time dealing with strategic planning. At least some of Octavius's crazy was coming to be of good use.

"Well done. We will go over it again tomorrow and every day until we can go back to Croftridge. Tomorrow, I will show you where the bunker is located and also where we have a stash of weapons. Do not, under any circumstances use anything that sends out a signal of any kind, no phones, no internet, basically no electronics whatsoever."

"Got it."

"That's it? No complaints, no comments, no questions?" he asked, surprised.

"I came from a life where this was a part of my daily routine. Octavius wanted us to always be prepared to defend ourselves. As I got older, I thought he was suffering from extreme paranoia and a bit mentally unstable. Now that I know he is involved in some more than questionable activities and dealings, it makes more sense. To answer your question, no complaints, no comments, no questions."

He pulled me to him and planted a kiss on my temple. He didn't say anything else, just held me for a long while. Finally, he softly murmured, "Let's get some rest. We never know what the next day will bring."

CHAPTER NINETEEN

Phoenix

They had been gone a week. A week and I didn't have much more than I had when they left. Byte hadn't been able to find much with the names we got from Ember, Reese, and Jamie. So far, the parents of those kids turned out to have records for multiple drug-related charges. It made sense that they would have lost custody of their kids, but the kids would have been taken through the county for temporary placement or placement with extended family, not sent to an orphanage. I thought maybe we needed to dig further into the past. The farm was up and running way before I was born. Was it just a dairy farm at one time or was it always a facade to hide other activities? I didn't know, but I knew just who to ask.

I picked up my phone and dialed a number I should have dialed much more often. He answered on the second ring, "Phoenix, my boy! How are you?"

"I'm good, Pop. Sorry it's been so long since I have called you and Gram. Things have been busy lately, and I've got a lot on my plate at the moment."

"You sound stressed. You need my help with something?" That was my Pop, always looking out for me and willing to lend a helping hand without knowing the need first.

"Maybe. I have a few questions I want to ask you, but first, I have some news to share with you and Gram. Is she around?"

"She is, but before I get her, I need to know, is this going to upset my love?" Another reason why I loved this man, the way he loved my Gram.

"I don't think it will upset her, but it will come as a shock to you both. Probably should be sitting down for it. I almost fell on my ass when I found out."

"Oh, hell, did you knock up one of those club whores? You're Gram has been waiting on babies from you for a long time, but she won't like that this is how they're coming to be."

"No, Pop, nothing like that. Just get Gram, put me on speakerphone, and both of you take a seat," I instructed.

Moments later I heard my Gram's sweet voice. "Phoenix, my sweet boy, how are you?"

"I'm good, Gram. Got a lot going on right now, but it ain't all bad. That's part of the reason I called," I paused and cleared my throat, "I have some news to share with you and Pop."

She squealed with delight. "Oh, please tell me I have a great-grandbaby on the way!"

It was harder than I thought it would be to tell them about Ember. I'm a grown ass man. It's not like I was going to get in trouble for having an 18-year-old kid I knew nothing about, but I was worried they would be disappointed in me. I've always wanted to make them proud, and I wasn't sure this would.

"Phoenix?" Pop sounded worried, "You still there?"

"Yeah, Pop, sorry, this is just hard for me to say," I rasped out. My mouth was suddenly dry. Grabbing the bottle of whiskey sitting on my desk, I took a huge pull and relished the burn as it went down.

"You can tell us anything boy. You ought to know that by now. Man up and spit it out," Pop ordered.

"I recently found out I have an 18-year-old daughter. DNA tests confirmed she's mine." Silence. Nothing but silence from the other end of the phone.

Finally, I heard a sniffle. Damn it, Gram was crying. Pop softly asked, as if he already knew the answer, "Who's her mother?"

Pain stabbed at my chest. It always did when I thought about her. It had been 18 years, and it was just as sharp as it was the first time I realized she was gone. I choked out, "Annabelle."

I heard gasps and more sniffling from the phone. I knew Gram was gearing up to fire off 50 questions before I could even answer one, so I quickly spoke again. "Let me tell you what happened and how I found out about her. I think that will answer most of your questions."

"Sure, son. Go ahead."

I spent the next 30 minutes filling them in on how I found out about Ember. Gram interrupted here and there with random questions about her physical appearance, her personality, etc... It was

Pop's silence that had my nerves on edge. I'd left out the parts about the suspicious activity at the dairy farm, the tracking device in Ember's neck, her getting shot, and how she was hidden away in the hills with three of my men for protection. Gram didn't need to know about all that right then, if ever.

Gram sounded like she was about to explode with glee. "When can we meet her? We can come there. I can book us a flight for tomorrow or the next day. Do you have a picture of her? Send it to your Pop's phone for me. Oh, and what—"

"Gram," I interrupted, "now's not a good time for you and Pop to visit. Like I said, she came here with her friend looking for a job; she wasn't looking for her biological father. She needs time to accept that her whole life was a lie, and we need time to build a father/daughter relationship before I go throwing more unknown family members at her. I'm sorry, Gram."

"No, no, sweetie. You're absolutely right. I'm just so damn excited about this. I can't wait to meet her. Please tell her that, and even though we haven't met her, we love her already."

"I will, Gram."

"Send that picture to your Pop. I've got to go. I have to call all of my friends and tell them I'm finally a great-gram! Love you, sweetie!"

"Love you, too, Gram."

I heard rustling, and then Pop's voice filled my ear, "It's just you and me now so cut the bullshit and tell me the truth." And that's why my Pop was one of the best lawyers in the United States. He could smell bullshit from a mile away, and he got straight down to business.

"That orphanage where she grew up, it's owned by the man that owns the dairy farm on the far side of town. It's located on the same land as the farm, just on the other side and surrounded by other buildings. She didn't come here looking for a job. She came here looking for help escaping from that place because she found out she was being sold on her 18th birthday."

Pop pulled in a large breath and slowly blew it out. "You gotta be shittin' me."

"There's more, Pop. It's the reason why I haven't called before now to tell you about her."

"Go on," he urged.

So, I told him everything I knew at that point. Everything except where she was. We were talking on a secured line, but I still wasn't risking her location being discovered. "This leads to the other reason I called. What do you know about that dairy farm? Anything that might help me find out what is going on there and put a stop to it?"

Pop sighed, "Phoenix, you better take a big swallow of whiskey and sit down. Now it's my turn to tell you a story." Oh shit.

I did as he said and braced myself for whatever he was about to tell me.

CHAPTER TWENTY

Ember

We had been at the cabin for a week and, surprisingly, it had been a very busy week. Each day we went over the various plans in place, practiced target shooting with various guns, and walked the grounds. That was my favorite time of the day, walking hand in hand with Dash through the mountain forest surrounding the cabin. Sometimes we would silently enjoy each other's company, but most of the time we shared stories from our pasts and things about ourselves.

After just one week, I felt like I knew so much more about Dash, like his real name. Reed Lawson was 27 years old. He grew up in Devil Springs. Like most of the other Blackwings members, he joined the military after high school. He didn't stay in as long as some of the others did, but he was deployed twice before coming back to Devil Springs. Once home, he planned to prospect for Blackwings, but Phoenix had moved the club to Croftridge. He happily moved, too, leaving his mother and younger sister behind in Devil Springs. He didn't say as much, but I got the feeling that he didn't have a good relationship with either one of them.

After our walks and talks, I would make dinner for all of us while Dash, Jamie, and Pete checked weapons and secured the cabin for the night. After dinner, we would climb into bed together and fall asleep wrapped in each other's arms. This was usually preceded by a lot of kissing and roaming hands. Well, Dash's hands roamed. He would hardly let me touch him. We hadn't done much more than what we did in the canoe. He had touched me down there, but not on the inside. He would just rub my clit in circles until he made me have an orgasm. Then, he would get up and take a shower. I knew what he was doing in the shower, because I watched him one night. It made me want him to play with my clit all over again. I didn't know if he was waiting for my stitches to come out before he went any further or if he thought I wasn't ready yet. Either way, it didn't matter. I got Jamie to help me take my stitches out on our sixth night at the cabin while Dash was in the shower. I had no stitches, and I was ready for the next step. Really ready. I just didn't know how to tell him.

I stretched and looked over to Dash. He was softly snoring beside me. I took a minute to just look at him. He really was a handsome man, but looking at him in that moment, seeing how peaceful he looked while sleeping, made me realize how much tension he had been carrying around with him every day. I gently ran my hand down the side of his face and gave him a quick kiss on the forehead.

I got out of bed and made my way downstairs to make breakfast for everyone. I was doing it at the clubhouse, so I continued to make meals for the guys that were here. I had discovered wireless headphones and an amazing stereo the first day we were at the cabin. I used them every morning while cooking breakfast. Sometimes for the other meals, too, if the guys were outside, but I left them off if they were inside so we could easily talk.

I had gotten to know the prospects better, too, or one of them anyway. Jamie was the same age as me and very friendly. He liked to joke around and keep things upbeat. He had also attended Croftridge High and, surprisingly, went to prom with none other than Reese Walker.

Pete was probably a little older than me, but I wouldn't know because he didn't talk much. He kept to himself most of the time and never smiled. I got the feeling he didn't like being at the cabin very much. I also got the feeling that he didn't like me, but I couldn't really say why. He hadn't said or done anything to me; it was just the way he looked at me sometimes. I figured I was probably just being paranoid. If he was really acting strange, Dash or Jamie would have noticed it. It was hard to maintain your sanity when you didn't know what was going on back home other than someone was out to get you while you were hidden away in the mountains.

I grabbed my trusty headphones, cranked up the volume, hit play, and got to work. I was dancing around the kitchen while cooking, like I did every morning. Every other morning,

I finished making the food and had time to go back upstairs and change clothes before anyone else woke up. That morning was different. I was standing at the stove, shaking my butt and finishing the last of the eggs when I was grabbed from behind. My muscles moved from memory, no input from my brain required. I threw my left elbow back until it made contact, leaned right, and swung my right fist until I hit what felt like a cheek. My attacker hit the ground with a thud. I quickly grabbed the large knife I was using to chop vegetables.

In the fray, the headphones must have been knocked off my ears because I heard Jamie yelling, “Ember? What the fuck? Dash?”

Dash? Huh? I looked down. Oh, crappity crap. Dash was on the ground looking every bit like a pit viper ready to strike.

I dropped the knife on the counter and took a step back. “Dash, I’m so sorry. I didn’t hear you come up behind me, and it scared me.” I looked up to see Jamie holding a gun pointed at Dash, but looking back and forth between the two of us. Prospect Pete also had his gun drawn, but it was pointed at me, yet again!

Jamie looked unsure of what to do. “Dash?”

“Put the guns down. Both of you and turn

the fuck around," Dash barked.

Both prospects turned and put their guns away. Dash quickly jumped to his feet. He was spitting mad. "Ember," he growled, "upstairs, now."

"L-let me just take the eggs off the—" I started.

He cut me off repeating the same order, "Now! The prospects can take care of the eggs. Upstairs! Go!"

I had never seen him so mad. I really wasn't sure what I had done, so to prevent matters from getting worse, I did as he said and scurried upstairs to our bedroom. My hopes for a brief reprieve to gather my thoughts were dashed when he came through the bedroom door right behind me.

I turned to face him. "Why are you so mad at me? I'm sorry I hit you. I really didn't know it was you."

Through gritted teeth, he said, "I'm not mad about that." Before I could ask what he was mad about, he grabbed my wrist and pulled me into the bathroom. He flipped the bathroom light on and pointed toward the mirror. That was when I saw it.

I gasped and covered my face with both of

my hands. "I had no idea. I'm so embarrassed."

"You may not have known about the shirt, but you should have had some 'idea' about the shorts." He made little quotation marks with his hands.

I shook my head. "I really didn't. See." I proceeded to unroll the waistband of my shorts, which lengthened them several inches. "I've never worn these before, and they were too big. They kept sliding down my hips, so I rolled the waistband to make them stay up until I finished cooking. I was going to come back up and change as soon as I was done."

He was still breathing a little heavy, and his face was still red. "Stay here." Then he turned and left. I heard him descend the stairs. There I was, standing in the bathroom because he told me to, just like the obedient women from the farm. Just do as you're told, and don't worry about the reasoning behind it. Only, this time, it felt different. I didn't mean to upset him with my see-through top and my indecently short shorts, but I had. I didn't want to upset him any further. Not because I was afraid of him—I wasn't—but because I wanted to please him by doing what he asked. Was that normal? At that very moment, I realized that I didn't care if it was considered normal or not. It felt right to me, and that's what I was going to do.

And that's how Dash found me when he returned. Standing in the bathroom grinning from ear to ear at my latest realization. "You want to tell me why you think you have a reason to be smiling like that when you just showed your tits and ass to two prospects?" He placed his hand on my shoulder and gently turned me to face him.

"I'm smiling because I realized that I stayed right here where you told me to because I wanted to make you happy and not because I was scared of you. Then, I wondered if it was normal to think that way and decided that I didn't care if it was normal because it felt right to me, and that was all that mattered."

He was on me in a flash. His body crashed into mine at the same time our lips met. One of his hands went to my hair and the other went to my butt and lifted. I wrapped my legs around his waist while both of my hands went to his hair.

He started walking. I went to pull back so he could see where he was walking, but he growled and tightened his hold on my hair to keep me in place. Well okay then, just as long as he wasn't going to try to walk down the stairs.

He took a few more steps and then we were falling. I wanted to scream, but I couldn't with his glorious tongue filling my mouth. Suddenly, my back hit the mattress, Dash coming down on top of me, never breaking the kiss. He took us to the bed.

The.

Bed.

He groaned and started kissing along my jaw toward my ear. "I need to make you mine, baby. Please let me make you mine."

It was hard for me to focus on anything but him, let alone form coherent sentences. Panting aside, I managed to get out, "I thought I already was yours."

Apparently, he liked that response because his movements became more intense and less controlled. He bit down on my earlobe and rasped out, "You are, baby, but I need to claim your body. I need to be inside you, baby."

I loved hearing him say he needed to, not that he wanted to. He felt so good on top of me, pressing my body to the bed with his, ravishing me with his mouth. Before my nerves could get the better of me, I whispered, "Okay, Dash."

"You sure?"

I most certainly was. I had been thinking

about the physical aspect of my relationship with Dash since our night at the lake. I didn't know what was going to happen in regards to Octavius. After Reese explained to me what being sold probably meant, I soon decided that I wanted my first time to be with Dash, not with someone who had purchased me. It was probably wrong of me to think like that, but my entire life was a glowing example of things not turning out like I thought they would. I didn't hesitate to answer him, "Absolutely."

He sat back on his heels and had me stripped completely naked in what had to be record-breaking time. I was grateful for that; it didn't give me time to become self-conscious. He tossed my clothes across the room, stood, and stripped himself of everything but his black boxer briefs. That didn't quite seem fair. "I know I'm new to this and all, but aren't those supposed to go, too?" I pointed to his boxer briefs.

He smirked. "Greedy girl. Love that you want me to take my cock out, but I need to get you ready for it first."

Get me ready first? I didn't have time to figure out what that meant. Dash grabbed my thighs and pulled me toward him. He leaned his big body over me and brought his lips to mine. His mouth moved to my neck, across my collarbone, and down to my breasts. He latched onto my nipple and began to suck while he rolled my other nipple between his fingers. My fingers dove into his hair, and I groaned loudly.

"You like that, baby?" He murmured against my breast.

I arched my back, pressing my breasts into his face, tugging lightly on his hair. "Uh-huh," I breathed. I felt him grin against my skin.

He slowly kissed his way down my stomach. Before I realized what he was doing, he made it to his destination. I felt his warm, wet tongue between my legs. It was by far the most glorious sensation ever. Waves of pleasure washed over me. He licked and sucked while I wriggled and squirmed. It felt so good, but I needed, something else.

I tightened my legs around his head and thrust my hips up toward his face. The throbbing between my legs was maddening. I was right there on the edge, but couldn't quite make it to the other side. Dash chuckled. The infuriating man knew what he was doing.

I opened my mouth to tell him what I thought about that when I felt his finger slide inside me. First one, then he added another. He moved them in and out a few times causing me to moan shamelessly. Suddenly, he curled his fingers at the same time he sucked hard on my clit. He kept his fingers curled and pumped them a few times while lightly biting down on my clit. I exploded into an orgasm so powerful it left me seeing stars.

When I came back to reality, Dash was hovering over me, his hands braced on either side of my face. I felt him at my entrance. He leaned down to gently kiss my lips, then, looked at me with a question in his eyes. I gave him a little nod and reached up to capture his lips again. He pulled back and shook his head slightly. "I want to see your eyes when I take you for the first time."

He kept his eyes locked on mine as he slowly entered me. I felt incredibly full, but it didn't hurt like I thought it would. I wouldn't say it felt great either, but I did like being that close to him. He continued to slowly push himself into me. He briefly kissed my lips before he ran his nose along my jaw. He sounded pained when he asked, "You okay, baby?"

I couldn't speak. I was overcome with the intensity of the moment, so I just nodded my head. He jerked his head up and met my eyes. I nodded again and softly smiled.

He leaned back down, placing his mouth next to my ear and breathed, “I’m going to move now, baby. If you need me to stop, tell me, and I’ll stop. It will kill me, but I’ll stop.”

It came out as a whisper, “Okay.” And then he started moving. Slowly at first, he pulled back and thrust forward. When I started meeting his thrusts, he picked up the pace. I couldn’t help the moans and sounds of pleasure that escaped me.

“Baby, you feel so fucking good,” he grunted. “So, fucking tight. Fucking perfect.”

How was he forming sentences? The only coherent things coming out of my mouth were “Yes” and “Dash.”

“I’m not stopping until you come again. I want to feel your sweet pussy squeezing my cock.” He pushed up, sitting back on his heels. He draped one of my legs over his arm and used his other hand to rub my clit as he moved in and out of me. Half a dozen more thrusts and I came, screaming his name and gasping for breath. He dropped forward and shoved into me once, twice, three more times before he groaned my name and stilled.

He kissed me sweetly and cradled my face in

his hands. “You okay, sweetheart?”

I smiled and nodded, “I’m good.”

He reached down between us. I didn’t know what he was doing. Then, I felt him slide out of my body. I looked down and noticed him holding the condom that was covering him. “I’m going to get rid of this, and I’ll be right back.”

Thank goodness he remembered the condom. It hadn’t even crossed my mind. How could I have been so thoughtless? I was berating myself when a warm sensation between my legs startled me.

“It’s okay, baby. Just cleaning you up,” Dash said as he gently ran a warm washcloth between my legs.

I blushed furiously, “I could have done that.”

“I know, but I wanted to,” he smirked and sauntered back to the bathroom before returning to the bed and wrapping his arms around me.

Tucked against Dash’s chest, I felt like that was where I was meant to be. I don’t think it had anything to do with sex. I felt a strong connection to him before that. Yes, he was the first guy I’d had any kind of physical or emotional relationship with, but I felt like he was my forever. Maybe I was being naive and setting myself up for major heartbreak. Who finds their forever love on their first try?

"I can practically hear you thinking. What's going through your head, pretty girl?"

"I was just thinking about you and me, and what's going to happen when all of this is over," I said, choosing my words carefully.

He gave me a little squeeze. "When all of this is over, I'm going to talk to your father, which I should have done before I took you to bed, but I can't do anything about that now. Then, you need to decide if you want to stay in your room at the club for a little longer, move in with Phoenix, or get a place with me. The timing is up to you, baby, but we will be moving in together, getting married, and eventually starting a family."

I looked up so I could see his face, "You're serious about all this?"

"Of course, I am. Aren't you?"

"I want to be. I mean, I am, I just thought that maybe I was making more out of this than it really is. All of this is new to me, having a relationship, having sex, having these feelings."

He sat up a little, "What feelings?"

I felt my cheeks redden and turned my head away from him. "I don't know how to describe them."

"You in love with me, darlin'?"

Now I really felt like a stupid little girl. "I don't know how that feels, so I can't answer that question."

"I ain't ever been in love, but I imagine it feels like you can't breathe without the other person. When you're apart, you can't wait to see them. Everything seems better when they're around. When they hurt, you hurt. When they cry, you cry. When they smile, you smile. You would give your life to save theirs, but if you lost them, you would lose yourself, too."

I cast my eyes away from him and chewed on my bottom lip, fighting the urge to rub my hands together. That was exactly how I felt about him, but what if he didn't feel that way about me? "In case I didn't make it clear, sweetheart, that's exactly how I feel about you."

My head shot up, eyes wide. "Really?!?" I all but shrieked.

He grinned slyly, "Yeah, darlin'. I love you."

I pushed back and launched myself at him. "I love you, too."

I pressed my mouth to his and slid my fingers into his hair. He pulled me over him so that I was straddling him. It was then I realized we were both still very much naked. I continued kissing him until he firmly gripped my hips and pushed me back.

“What’s wrong?” I asked.

He grinned, “Nothing, baby. I just needed to grab a condom. I couldn’t take you sliding that sweet pussy over my cock much longer.”

Oh, had I been doing that? “Sorry,” I mumbled.

“Nothing to be sorry for,” he said as he rolled the condom down his shaft. Good grief that thing was big. How in the world did it fit? He laughed, “Quit staring at my cock, and ride me.” He grabbed my hips and lifted, positioning me above his hard length.

He used one hand to hold his…cock up against me. “Slide down it, baby,” he rasped out.

I did as he said, and oh my stars this was a whole different kind of wonderful. I wasn’t sure what to do next, though. I looked to Dash for help, pleading with my eyes. He seemed to understand my dilemma without me having to say it. He took hold of my hips and started to guide my movements. He had me bouncing up and down and rocking back and forth.

“Baby,” he breathed. “You look so hot riding me, with your tits bouncing in my face.” He leaned forward and sucked a nipple into his mouth. He sucked hard and slapped my butt with his hand.

The little twinge of pain in my nipple and the sting on my backside pushed me right over the edge. I lifted myself up and slammed back down on him over and over while my orgasm pulsed through me. He groaned and then held my hips still as his entire body shuddered.

Sweaty and out of breath, I had a sudden realization, “Do you think Jamie and Pete know what we’ve been doing in here all morning?”

Dash smirked, “You think I would ever let anybody hear you come, especially the first time my cock’s buried inside you?” He raised an eyebrow and looked at me pointedly. “Fuck no I wouldn’t. I sent those two cockheads to the store to replenish our supplies for two more weeks. They shouldn’t be back for another hour.”

“You planned this?” I asked.

“Yeah, same as you did. Know you got Jamie to help you take those stitches out last night. I’ll spank your ass for that later tonight.”

My mouth dropped open, “For what exactly?”

“For letting another man see what’s mine and touch what’s mine. Don’t care that he was taking your stitches out. He was touching your bare skin. You don’t like it, don’t let another man touch you.”

I studied his face for a minute and realized

that he was serious. "I can't control other people, Dash. There's no way for me to keep another man from ever touching me again. What about Phoenix?"

"You can control it when you are the one lifting your shirt up so he can get to your skin. And Phoenix is different. He's your father. Hell, he's probably going to beat my ass when he finds out I've touched you without coming to him first."

I gasped, "You're kidding, right?"

"Nope. Club rules. I showed him disrespect with my actions and will have to accept whatever punishment he dishes out."

"You do realize how barbaric that is, right?"

"Don't care. It's how the club works. Better get used to it because you don't get a say in any part of that."

Wanna bet? There's no way I was going to let my newly discovered father beat up my new man all because of some caveman club rule. I knew just how to go about getting my way, too.

"Come on. You've got to be starving since you missed breakfast. Let's get something to eat and then practice our plans before we start on our other stuff today. I also want to take some more supplies out to the bunker just in case we need to use it."

I wanted to roll my eyes. We had practiced the same plans every single day. I had it. He had it. Jamie and Pete had it. I had to constantly remind myself that they were doing this for me, and it would seem terribly ungrateful of me to balk at his suggestions.

We spent the rest of the day doing exactly what he said. When we got back to the cabin after adding supplies to the bunker, the sun had set. I was exhausted, and my body was aching, one place a bit more than others. Just as I finished my snack, I heard Dash call my name from upstairs.

I walked up the stairs at a snail's pace. "In the bathroom," Dash called out. When I entered the bathroom, Dash was standing beside the huge garden tub. He had filled it with a bubble bath that was calling my name.

He gently smiled when he saw me. "Between this morning and our exercises, I thought this might help with sore muscles and other stuff." He almost looked embarrassed. Aww, big bad Dash was embarrassed about drawing a bubble bath for his recently deflowered girlfriend. There was nothing I could do to stop it. Laughter burst from my lips.

"What's so fucking funny, Ember?" he huffed.

Bent over at the waist, I was struggling for breath between laughs. I held my hand out in a placating manner. "It's. Just. Nothing gets. To you. But a bath. For me. Makes you blush."

He slapped me on the butt, hard. "Get in the damn tub, woman."

I yelped at the sting and quickly obliged. I undressed and carefully climbed into the tub. Sinking down into the warm water felt so good to my aching muscles. I closed my eyes and let out a contented sigh. Just as I was about to lay back and get comfortable, I felt the water displace behind me. "Slide up a little and make room for me."

"Biker boy is going to take a bubble bath?" I teased.

"I swear, Ember, if you don't shut your mouth, this will be the last time I do something like this for you," he growled.

I turned my head back to him, "I'm just teasing you."

"Yeah, yeah." He didn't seem as amused as I was.

"This was very nice and thoughtful. Thank you." I leaned back against him and laid my head on his chest. I could have easily gone to sleep like that. If only the water would stay warm, and there wasn't the possibility of drowning.

"Don't get too comfortable. I don't want you falling asleep in here."

I chuckled, "I was just thinking the same thing."

We stayed in the tub until the water started to get cold. He helped me out and helped me get dressed. Once in the bed, he gave me a chaste kiss on the lips, told me he loved me, and rolled me so my back was to his chest. Okay, not what I had expected to happen post-bath.

"Can't tonight, darlin'. You're already raw and sore from me fucking you twice this morning. Shouldn't have done it that second time, but I couldn't stop myself. You need a day or two to heal before I stick my cock in you again."

How did he...? "Are you a mind reader or something?"

He scoffed, "Ain't a mind reader, but my ears work just fine. You said that out loud."

Really? I must have been more tired than I thought.

"Yeah, you and me both. Now get some rest. Tomorrow is a check-in day."

CHAPTER TWENTY-ONE

Dash

I parked Badger's old Blazer in the lot of the little diner at the base of the mountain. It was a small town with nosy townsfolk. Badger knew most of the people around the area and let them know to not be alarmed when they saw his Blazer being driven around by two different young men—me or Jamie. So far, the people had minded their own business and left me to it when I had driven down to check in with Phoenix. I hated leaving Ember up there, even if she was with Jamie and Pete, but there was no way in hell I was bringing her down here with me.

I pulled out my latest burner phone, waited for the exact time we planned, and dialed Phoenix's number. The phone continued to ring, and a pit started forming in my stomach. He always answered by the third ring. Always. Fuck. Fuck. Fuckity fuck. Fuck!!!

Taking a deep breath, I reminded myself to stick to the plan. I waited the longest five minutes in the history of my life and called Phoenix again. My heart rate increased and more sweat beaded on my forehead with each unanswered ring.

I got out of the car, smashed the phone, destroyed the SIM card, and pulled out a new phone. My shaking hands were making it take a lot longer to get the phone activated than necessary, which only added fuel to my adrenaline fire. I finally got the damn thing activated and placed a call to Badger. No answer. Motherfucking son of a bitch!

Screw the rest of the details. Something had obviously gone down, and I had no idea when or what happened. Hell, Octavius could have people on their way to the cabin at that very moment. I needed to get back up there and get Ember to Copper's clubhouse.

My tires squealed when I peeled out of the parking lot. I dialed Copper and pressed the phone to my ear. Please answer. Please answer. I let out the breath I didn't realize I was holding when I heard someone pick up on the other end of the line. He didn't say a word, but I knew he was there.

"Birds in the nest aren't chirping."

I heard a low muttered curse and then, "Contain the flame. Crew coming to you." The line disconnected.

I tossed the phone out the window and hopefully over the side of the mountain. I hauled ass up the narrow, curvy road, praying I kept it between the ditches and got back to my girl in time to get her to safety. Originally, I was to bring Ember to Copper's clubhouse, but contain the flame was code for put her in the bunker. I wanted to know why the plan changed, but I didn't have the brainpower to think about it right then. Copper was about 30 minutes out, but given the situation, I had no doubt he would be there in about 15 minutes.

Finally, the cabin came into view. I relaxed a little when nothing looked out of place. I came to a screeching halt in the driveway and ran as fast as I could to the back door. Crashing through the door, I yelled for Ember to grab her things. I went straight to the safe to grab our guns and our go bag. I pulled the safe door open, and everything went black.

CHAPTER TWENTY-TWO

Ember

The sound of a fast approaching vehicle followed by screeching tires startled me. I jumped up and ran to the window. Relief filled me when I saw that it was Dash, but it quickly vanished when I noticed the look on his face as he ran toward the cabin. Crap. Something was wrong. Really wrong.

I heard him come through the door and yell, "Ember, grab your bag and get down here! We're going to the bunker!" I grabbed the bag I'd basically kept packed and ready since we arrived, grabbed the gun Dash kept in the nightstand, and headed for the stairs.

I stepped into the hall and froze. From upstairs, I had a clear view of the kitchen and living room downstairs. Jamie was sprawled on the floor of the kitchen, blood oozing from his head. My gaze quickly darted to the living room. To my absolute horror, Pete was standing behind Dash holding a gun. It seemed to happen in slow motion. There was nothing I could do to stop it. Pete lifted his arm and brought the butt of the gun crashing down into Dash's head. I watched helplessly, and thankfully soundlessly, as my love crumpled to the ground.

Resisting the strong urge to scream, I quickly backed into the bedroom. I dropped my bags on the bed and moved to the corner of the room by the bathroom. From there, I could see the bedroom door, but anyone entering the room wouldn't have a clear view of me right away. I could also barricade myself in the bathroom and escape through the window if need be.

I checked to make sure the gun was loaded, racked the slide, and aimed at the door. I inhaled slowly through my nose and exhaled through my mouth, over and over, trying to keep the panic at bay.

It wasn't long before I heard footsteps rapidly approaching. Then I heard his voice. It sent cold chills down my spine. "Ember! We need to go! Are you still in here?" Pete sang out.

One more slow inhale and slow exhale. I kept the gun trained on the door. Seconds later, Pete sauntered through the door, his gun loosely held in his hand. It took seconds, but I will forever remember each and every detail of those few seconds.

Pete's head turned in my direction. His eyes landed on me. He noticed the gun. Realization flickered in his eyes, then fear. He knew he didn't have time, but he tried to bring his gun up and aim it at me. Before he lifted his hand an inch, I squeezed the trigger. Once, twice, three times. My aim was true. Abdomen. Chest. Head. He fell backward, eyes wide open, arms limp by his side. He hit the floor with a sickening thump, his arms bouncing and flopping before settling awkwardly at his side. Blood was quickly pooling on the floor, from what I assumed were large exit wounds. I took one tiny step forward, then two more. His chest wasn't rising. He wasn't blinking. The silence in the room was deafening. And that's when I screamed as loud and for as long as I could.

I fell to my knees and screamed again. My screams turned into sobs. Suddenly, my brain came back online. Dash. Jamie. They were downstairs and they were hurt. And something else was wrong. Dash was running when he got here, and he went for the safe. Crap. Crap. Crap.

I would have to cry later. I got my butt up and flew down the stairs. I crashed into a body the second I rounded the corner to the living room. “Dash!” I shrieked. “Are you okay? We have to go. Like now. Oh my gosh. Jamie. Where is Jamie?”

“Ember!” Dash roared. I stopped my rambling and blinked up at him. “We’re okay. Where the fuck is Pete?”

I buried my face in his chest and wailed, “He’s upstairs in our bedroom.”

Dash pushed me back, “What happened? Did he hurt you?” Fury was rolling off of him in waves.

I shook my head, tears streaming down my face. “No. I think he was going to though. I saw him hit you with his gun, and I’m guessing he hit Jamie, too.”

“Go over there with Jamie. I’m going to kill that fucker,” he growled.

Quietly, I told him, “I already did. I shot him

when he came in there after me."

"Aww, baby." He wrapped his hand around the back of my neck and pulled me to him. "I hate that you had to do that, but you did good, baby. You sure you killed him?"

I nodded into his chest. "Hit him in the gut, the chest, and between the eyes. He was gone before he hit the floor." My breath hitched with the last few words, and the sobs started all over again.

Dash stepped back and placed both hands on my shoulders. He bent down so we were eye to eye. "Listen to me. I need you to pull it together. I don't know what is going on, and we can't afford to waste any time. Now, I need to go up there and check Pete's pockets. See if he had a phone or something that might tell us what he was up to. I'll grab your bags while I'm up there. I need you to grab the go bags and help Jamie. Copper and his crew are on their way, but we don't know if anybody might be ahead of him. Get me? As soon as I come back down, we're moving to the bunker."

"Got it. Go. Hurry." He took off up the stairs while I grabbed the bags and went to Jamie. He was still on the kitchen floor, but he was now sitting up, propped against the cabinets.

He smiled sheepishly when he saw me, "Knew you'd be okay."

I gave him a small grin, though it probably looked more like a grimace. "I'm glad you knew it. I sure didn't." I looked him over from head to toe. "Do you think you can stand?"

"I'm going to have to." He inhaled deeply and heaved himself up, using the counter as support. "Damn my head hurts like a motherfucker."

"I'm sure it does. You okay otherwise?"

"My vision is a little blurry, but I think that's to be expected. I'll be all right. We heading to the bunker?"

I nodded. "As soon as Dash comes back down. He's checking Pete's pockets for a cell phone or something that may tell us why he turned against us."

Right on cue, Dash entered the kitchen with my bags and a few other items in his hands. "Come on, let's get you to the bunker."

"I'll take the bags if you can help Jamie. His vision is still a little blurry, and I think his legs are a little weaker than he is letting on," I informed him.

I took the bags, Dash slid his arm under Jamie's shoulders, and we all quick stepped it to the bunker. Once we were sealed in tight, I sagged into one of the chairs, feeling the first inkling of relief.

Dash handed a drink and some pills over to Jamie before dropping down into a chair beside me.

“Did you find anything on Pete?” I asked.

“Yeah. A phone that isn’t one he’s supposed to have, his wallet, and this weird necklace.” He tossed all of the items onto the table.

The necklace slid to a stop right in front of me. I covered my mouth with both hands and rose to my feet. Dash was quickly on his feet, too. “What’s the matter?”

I stabbed my finger at the necklace. “That! It’s an Octavian Crest.”

“A fucking what?”

“An Octavian Crest!” I shrieked. “He was one of Octavius’s men!”

“Son of a bitch!” he cursed.

We both turned to Jamie when he spoke, “Son of a bitch is right.” He had Pete’s phone in his hand and was scrolling through it. “Looks like he sent a text out about the time you got back from the check-in.”

“Who was it to? What did it say?” Dash demanded.

“I’m guessing to Octavius. It’s saved as ‘8’.

It says, 'signal received. Will unload extras and secure main package for pickup. See you soon.'"

"Fuck!" Dash grunted, now pacing the room. "Anything else?"

"Yeah. A response from 8. 'You have two hours. Be ready.'"

Dash grinned and said in a menacing tone, "We'll be ready. That's for damn sure."

CHAPTER TWENTY-THREE

Dash

"How long do we have left?" Jamie asked.

"About an hour and a half, I'm guessing. Copper and his crew should be here soon. I want you two to stay here in the bunker while we handle Octavius and his men. You stay down here until me, Copper, or Copper's VP Bronze comes to get you. Same deal, one of us will call the phone, identify ourself, and give the passphrase."

"No disrespect Dash, but what do you want us to do if something happens to all three of you?"

I liked how this kid thought. He was definitely going to be a good brother to have when he got his patch.

"Good thinking, but that's not a possibility," I lowered my voice to prevent Ember from hearing the next part. "Since we don't know what went down at our clubhouse, Copper had his VP and a skeleton crew stay behind in case everything goes to shit. The club overall couldn't withstand losing the mother chapter's President and VP as well as the nearest chapter's President and VP. The other chapters are too new or the current leaders are too new."

Jamie nodded. "Makes sense. No one else knows about the bunker?"

"Nope. Copper didn't even know until the day we came up here, and Bronze should have been told before Copper and the crew rode out today."

The satellite phone started ringing. I accepted the call, but didn't speak. "We're here." Never had another man's voice sounded so sweet.

"Come to the bunker's entrance. I want Ember to meet you. She needs to know who you are," I told Copper.

"Be right there, brother."

Moments later, I opened the hatch, and Copper climbed down. His eyes went to Ember,

"I'll be damned. You look just like your mother. I'm Copper, President of the Devil Springs Blackwings and Phoenix's cousin, yours, too." He held his hand out to her.

She shook his hand and stared at him with wide eyes. "You knew my mother?"

His eyes softened. "Not well, sweetheart. Saw her with Phoenix a few times, but they didn't come up to Devil Springs much, and I wasn't in Croftridge that much at the time. If you'll excuse me, we ain't got time for pleasantries; I believe we have some business to handle." He turned to face me. "What do we know?"

"The prospect we brought up here with us belongs to Octavius. They've been texting the whole time we've been up here. Octavius knows she's at the cabin and is on his way here."

Copper pulled his gun and pointed it right at Jamie. "And you ain't killed him yet?"

Ember screamed and jumped in front of Jamie. "Not him! The other one. And I did kill him!"

Copper put his piece away and grinned, "You get that from our side of the family. I bet your daddy will be damn proud. All right, continue."

"According to the phone messages, their plan was for Octavius to send a signal for the prospect to get rid of me and Jamie and have Ember ready for pick up. Octavius thinks he is coming up here to pick up Ember and Pete. ETA 75 minutes or less."

"You know how many are coming?"

I shook my head at the same time Ember spoke, "He'll come with eight men."

"How do you know that?" Copper asked.

"He is obsessed with the number eight. He's also weird about the number nine and the number three. His son's name is Nivan, which means nine. Eight plus one is nine. He will come with eight men. I can guarantee they will arrive in three white Suburbans, three men in each vehicle."

"This fucker is certifiable, yeah?" Copper mused.

I nodded. "Sounds like it."

Copper smiled maniacally, "Nine's going to be easy. We keeping any alive?"

"I think we should keep Octavius alive and anyone who might be important to him, if we can determine who that might be," I offered.

Ember interjected, "His son is most important to him. He will be in the third vehicle, Octavius will be in the first, and Octavius's right-hand man, Hector, will be in the second vehicle. Each will be wearing white and will be sitting in the middle row. That's how they've always traveled to meetings or wherever they go."

Copper laughed, "What a fucking idiot. He's making this way too easy."

Ember quietly added, "They'll have guns. Probably two or three each."

Copper patted her shoulder, "Don't you worry, sweetheart. We've got guns, too. A lot of guns." He clapped his hands together loudly. "Let's get to it."

I grabbed Ember's hand and pulled her to me. Wrapping my arms around her, I buried my face in her neck and breathed her in. I didn't want to leave her there, but I had to do this. She was mine damn it, and no way in hell was Octavius getting away with the way he had treated her and what he was still trying to do to her. "Stay here with Jamie. No matter what, only open that hatch for me, Copper, or Bronze. Okay?"

She nodded her head and sniffled. Aw, shit. I couldn't handle tears right then. She looked up at me with fear in her eyes, but blessedly no tears. "Be careful."

"I will." Fuck it, I didn't care who was watching. If this was my last chance, I was taking it. I covered her mouth with mine and kissed her as if it was the last time I would ever kiss her, because it very well could be the last time. I pulled back and met her eyes, “I love you, baby. So damn much.”

She shyly smiled, “I love you, too, Dash.”

I needed to get out of there before I changed my mind and stayed there with her. “Let’s go.”

Copper climbed out first. I hopped out right behind him. He turned around and shot me an appraising look, “Phoenix know about that?”

“I think he has an idea, but I haven’t specifically said anything to him. Didn’t want to do it over the phone during one of our check-in calls. I plan to talk to him face to face as soon as we get back, assuming he’s still there to talk to.” My voice trailed off with the last part. I was trying valiantly to not let my worry for my brothers take over. I could worry about them once Octavius and his men were taken down.

Copper placed a supportive hand on my shoulder. “Don’t go there, brother. He’s alive. I feel it,” he tapped his chest with his fist, “in here.”

“I hope you’re right.”

“I am,” he replied, as if it was a given fact.

***

An hour later, we were all in position awaiting the arrival of Octavius and his minions. I was practically vibrating with anxiety and pent-up rage. "Calm your tits, man. You ain't going to do anyone any good if you can't get a shot off or hit your target because of twitchy fingers and sweaty hands. Find your zone and get your fucking head in it," Copper ordered.

I nodded. Fuck, he was right. I was letting my concern about my brothers and my fear for Ember's safety cloud my mind. I needed to focus. I had a job to do. A simple job. Wait for them to exit the vehicles. Shoot to kill the ones not wearing white.

Breathe in.

Breathe out.

Not wearing white. Shoot to kill.

Exits driver seat. Shoot to kill.

Exits front passenger seat. Shoot to kill.

Breathe in.

Breathe out.

My zone. I found it. The calm washed over me. My hands steadied. My vision sharpened. My ears homed in on the sound of tires crunching over gravel. They had arrived. It was go time.

Just like Ember said, three white Suburbans came to a stop in the cabin's driveway. The occupants remained inside for several long moments before we finally heard the first click of a door opening.

Copper whispered into his earpiece, "Let most or all of them get out before you start shooting. Going black." Copper turned off his earpiece. There would be no more changes or adjustments to the plan. No more communication between the contact men scattered around the property, each with a small group of brothers.

Breathe in.

Breathe out.

Doors started opening. Men exited the vehicles. Three were out of the second vehicle, two from the first and third. Come on, what were they waiting for?

A good 30 seconds passed before the last two doors opened simultaneously, and the last occupants stepped out. The doors shut immediately followed by a cacophony of gunfire and screams that filled the air. Bodies violently dropped to the ground until there were only three standing. Three dressed in all white, each standing beside a different vehicle.

The next thing I knew, I was in front of Octavius

with my gun to his head with no recollection of how I got there. “Gotcha motherfucker.”

He glared at me with hate-filled eyes. Then, the ballsy fucker spit in my face. Spit. In. My. Face. Oh, fuck no. I slammed my gun into the side of his head. The pussy dropped like a sack of bricks. I pressed his head into the ground with my boot, keeping my gun trained on him at all times. “Gonna need some rope and some duct tape!”

I tied Octavius’s arms behind his back and tied his ankles together. Then, because I’m an evil bastard, I slipped a loop of rope over his head and used the end to tie his wrists and ankles together. Next, I slapped a piece of duct tape over his mouth. I’d be damned if he spit on me again. I hated that shit, and he was going to pay dearly for it.

Copper and his SAA, Judge, secured the other two, while the rest of the crew checked the bodies on the ground. I had no doubt that each one on the ground was dead, but you could never be too careful.

“Hey, Judge, come check this shit out,” Copper called out while he was walking toward me.

Judge came over and whistled, “Interesting.

How does that work exactly?"

"It's pretty simple. I tied a running bowline knot, slipped the loop over his head, pulled the end taut, and wove it through the wrist and ankle ropes before tying it off. If he tries to undo his wrists or ankles, he'll choke himself," I proudly explained.

Copper and Judge shared a look, grinned, and walked back to the men they had restrained. They undid the ropes and retied the men just like I had tied Octavius. Copper dusted his hands off. "Thanks, Dash. I love learning new tricks."

"Listen up!" Copper shouted. "First off, well done, brothers!" Hoots and hollers filled the air. When the cheering died down, Copper continued. "We still have work to do. We don't know the situation that awaits us at the Croftridge clubhouse. Phoenix and Badger are currently MIA. I want four of you to stay behind and clean up the bodies. There's also one in the house, right, Dash?"

I nodded, "Yeah, in the master bedroom upstairs."

Copper turned back to the group. "One body in the master upstairs. So, four stay for cleanup and disposal. When you're finished, check in with me. I'll likely have you come to Croftridge.

The rest will come with me and Dash to the Croftridge clubhouse now. Toss these assholes in the trailer and lock it down. Better yet, Spazz, dose 'em up first. I need a few brothers to take these cages back to Croftridge. We'll load your bikes in the trailer. Any questions?"

Copper's enforcer, Batta, spoke up, "Where's the girl?"

Copper looked to me, "Go get her, brother. Let's take her home."

CHAPTER TWENTY-FOUR

Ember

My fingernails were completely chewed off and my hands had been rubbed raw. I was a ball of nerves and nothing was helping me get a handle on it. I jumped about two feet in the air when the satellite phone rang. I dove for it, but Jamie got to it before me. He accepted the call and said nothing.

The sweetest relief washed over me when I heard Dash's voice saying the passphrase. Tears wet my cheeks as I inhaled for what felt like the first time in days.

Jamie opened the hatch and stepped to the side so I could climb out first. About halfway up the ladder, Dash reached down and pulled me out. He squeezed me so hard it almost hurt, but I was probably doing the same to him.

"We got him, baby! We got him!" he exclaimed.

Sobs wracked my body. I was finally free from the hold that man had over me my entire life. I was almost afraid to believe it.

"It's over, baby. Come on, let me take you home," Dash murmured in my ear.

Home. I had a home. A place where I was loved and wanted. A family. I gasped. "Phoenix!"

"Shhh, we're going to find him now. You and Jamie are riding in one of the Suburbans with me, Copper, and Judge." He started to pull me along with him to the vehicles, but I dug my heels in.

"Wait! Where is Octavius?" I shrieked.

Dash smirked, "He's tied up at the moment."

"You mean that literally, don't you?"

"You know me so well, baby. Now move it. Oh, and try not to look down," he warned.

"Why?"

"Just in case Copper's guys haven't moved all of the bodies yet," he said as nonchalantly as one would say, "Just in case it rains."

That statement should have disturbed me or at the very least, bothered me on some level. It didn't. Not in the slightest. I simply nodded and followed him to the SUV without looking down.

Once we were on the highway, the guys started making plans. I guess I got to be a part of "club business" this time since they had no way to prevent me from hearing their discussion. Unfortunately, the unknown situation that lay ahead of us kept me from enjoying that little fact.

Copper turned around in the front seat to talk to Dash. "When was the last time you spoke to Phoenix?"

"I talked to him yesterday. I usually checked in every few days, but as of yesterday, he wanted me to start checking in every day. He didn't say why, and I didn't ask. We kept things to a bare minimum."

Copper rubbed his chin and stayed silent for a few moments. "I'm thinking he was onto something. Do you think he knew about Pete?"

"No way. He would have never sent him with us if he did."

Copper scoffed, "I know that. I meant, do you think Phoenix found out in the last day or two?"

Dash was shaking his head no before Copper even finished speaking. "Phoenix would have come up here himself if he had discovered the truth about Pete."

Copper nodded, continuing to rub his thumb and forefinger over his chin, the same way Phoenix did, "Yeah, yeah, suppose you're right about that. I'm just thinking out loud here, trying to piece it together. So, by the time we get there, it will have been 28 hours since there has been any contact with Phoenix. You try any of the other brothers?"

"Just Badger. My orders were to try Phoenix a second time five minutes later if he didn't answer my first call. If he didn't pick up on my second try, I was to call Badger. If Badger didn't answer, then I was to call you."

Copper pulled out his cell phone and dialed, "Bronze, see if you can get in touch with anyone from Croftridge." He paused for a moment. "Yeah, man, we got the sons of bitches. Heading to Croftridge now. Phoenix and Badger are MIA." He paused again. "Thanks, man. Talk in a few. Yep." He turned back to Dash. "Got Bronze trying to get somebody. Let's assume he can't get anyone on the phone. How do you want to play this? We can't go bursting in there guns blazing with her in tow."

"I say we leave Ember in the car with some of

your guys. The rest of us take Octavius and his goons in through the front door, guns to their heads. If anybody is in there waiting to ambush us, they won't unless they want us to kill their precious leader. If we do get attacked, we can use them as shields, and your boys can take Ember back to Bronze."

Copper nodded, "Phoenix will be proud of you, Dash. I know you're an officer, but you're a relatively new officer. Today, you've essentially been functioning as the club's president. You've handled your shit and thought things through as well as Phoenix or me."

I think I saw a little color appear on Dash's cheeks. "Appreciate that, Copper."

We rode in a tense silence until Copper's phone rang. "Whatcha got?" "Uh-huh." "What did he have to say?" "Who the fuck is that?" "Yeah, yeah, fuck me, man, really?" "All right, I will." "Thanks, brother."

Copper turned back to face us, "Bronze called every brother in the Croftridge chapter, and Duke's phone was the only one that was answered, except it wasn't Duke, it was some chick named Reese."

I sat up straight in my seat. "Reese? Is she okay?"

"Don't really know. Bronze said she didn't even give him a chance to tell her who he was. She just told him her name was Reese and Duke couldn't come to the phone. He said she then proceeded to cuss him for all he was worth and hung up. Who is she and why does she have Duke's phone?"

Dash leaned forward and pinched the bridge of his nose. He sighed, "You know Reese, she's Carbon's little sister."

Copper grinned, "Little Reesie Piecie?"

Dash chuckled, "That'd be the one."

"Excuse me," I cut in, "Can I call her? She'll talk to me."

Copper looked to Dash, who made the correct choice and indicated for Copper to hand me the phone.

"What's Duke's number?" I asked.

Dash dialed for me. I wanted to cry when Reese's voice filled my ear. I had missed her so much over the last two weeks. "Reese, it's Ember."

"Ember! Holy shit, girl! Are you okay?" she yelled into the phone.

"I'm fine. Listen, I don't have much time, but I need your help."

"I don't know how much help I can be.

Carbon told me not to leave Duke's room for any reason whatsoever until he himself said I could." Her next words were whispered, "He said it was a matter of life and death."

"What? When did you talk to Carbon?" Both Dash and Copper leaned closer upon hearing Carbon's name.

"I didn't exactly. He sent me a text about five hours ago, I think."

"Okay, and you're in Duke's room?"

"Yeah, at the hospital."

"Are you the only one there?"

"Yep. Harper went back to the clubhouse this morning."

"How is Duke?"

"He's awake, but won't speak and is a general pain in the ass most of the time. The only reason I'm here now is because he needed something and no one else was available to bring it to him. Before I could leave, Carbon texted me and told me to stay."

"I think right now it is the best place you can be. Listen, stay there like Carbon said. I have to go, but I should be home soon."

"Wait! What did you need help with?"

"I needed to ask you some questions, but you already answered them. I really have to go.

I'll talk to you soon. Stay safe, Reese." I quickly disconnected the call before she could say anything else and handed it back to Copper.

"She got a text from Carbon about five hours ago telling her not to leave Duke's hospital room until he came to get her. He told her it was a life or death situation."

"Fuck, man. That means something must have gone down at the clubhouse, and Carbon somehow managed to get a text out to her while he could," Dash surmised.

Copper told Judge to pull into the nearest gas station. Once there, he got out and quickly informed the other guys of the new information and the current plan. He was back in the SUV and we were on the road in no time. We would be there soon. I couldn't shake the feeling that what awaited us was going to be less than pleasant.

CHAPTER TWENTY-FIVE

Dash

The open and unmanned gates were the first sign that something was wrong. The second sign was the body of a prospect lying on the ground beside the gates, a knife protruding from his chest. The third sign, the clubhouse doors were wide open.

Judge stopped in the lot and turned to Copper. "I'll stay with Ember and the prospect. If you'll send me Batta and Tiny, we can keep her safe using less men."

"Good thinking, Judge. I'll send them your

way. Dash, you ready?"

"Yep, let's do this." I turned to Ember. "I'll be back as soon as I can. If Judge thinks he needs to get you out of here, you don't fight him on that. Just go with him, and I'll come when I can, okay, baby?"

She nodded and her eyes started to fill with tears. "Stay safe. Love you."

"Love you, too, baby." I gave her a quick kiss on the lips and got out of the SUV.

Tiny and Batta climbed in per Copper's orders, and I thanked each as I passed by them.

Rounding the back of the last vehicle in our little convoy, I found our three prisoners on the ground, awake, but still groggy from the drugs. Good, they'd be easier to handle.

We removed everything except the ropes around their wrists and the tape across their mouths. Jerking Octavius to his feet, I placed my gun to his head. Copper grabbed Nivan, and Spazz grabbed Hector. We silently approached the clubhouse, frog-marching our prized prisoners. Spazz shoved Hector through the front door. We hung back a few feet to see if there would be any activity. Nothing. Spazz stuck his head around the door. "Don't see anybody and don't hear anything."

Copper shouted to his guys behind us, "Split into groups of three or four and let's get this building cleared. Check every room."

Twenty minutes later, the building was cleared. We found nothing. Not a soul was there, and not a clue as to what happened to everyone was found. No blood, no evidence of a struggle, nothing.

Copper placed his hands on his hips, "I'm kind of at a loss as to what to do now. I figured we would at least find something to go on if we didn't find them here."

Octavius started to laugh and shake from his spot on the floor. Hector maintained his hate-filled stare. Nivan, surprisingly, looked terrified. Interesting. I ripped the tape off Octavius's mouth. "The fuck you laughing at?" I kicked him with my booted foot for good measure.

"You are all a bunch of leather-clad idiots," he cackled, sounding like a rabid hyena.

I kicked him again, harder this time. "You gotta point you want to make? I'm getting really fucking tired of you and your bullshit. I'm about *eight* seconds from putting a bullet between your eyes. *Nine* from putting one between your son's eyes."

His laughter immediately died, and his face

filled with rage. "How dare you disrespect what I stand for?" he bellowed.

I smirked, "You did that all by yourself, oh Eight the Great." The men around me burst out laughing.

I didn't think it was possible, but Octavius's face grew even redder. "You'll never find him. You need me to find him! He needs me to lead you to him! I'm the one with the power. I'm the one that is important. I'm the one that is needed. Not your precious fucking Phoenix!!"

I looked to Copper, my eyes wide, "You know what Ocho is going on about?"

Copper shook his head. Spazz narrowed his eyes and really looked at Octavius, studied him. "You're the Jones boy, aren't you? People called you Tav in high school, until Phoenix beat your ass in front of the whole school and you yelled, 'I'm Octavius Jones. You'll never get away with this.' Am I right?"

"He didn't beat my ass! I chose to walk away! Because I'm better than him!!" he screamed.

Copper leaned back on his heels and blew out a low whistle, "I'll be damned." He turned to me and lowered his voice, "There's more to this than what's on the surface. I'm guessing it runs a lot deeper than any of us ever would have imagined. Old Tav has apparently had a beef with Phoenix since high school."

"All this because he got his ass handed to him one time in fucking high school?" I asked.

"Like I said, I get the feeling it runs way deeper than that. Let's lock them up in the cells downstairs. We might have to get creative, but I think using his son to get to him is the way to go." An evil smile appeared on Copper's face. A lesser man would have backed away in fear. Don't get me wrong. It fucking scared me, but I wasn't about to let that show. "What do you want to do with Ember?"

"Let's put her in the panic room with Jamie," I suggested.

"Go get her and I'll get Octapussy and his boys settled into their new accommodations," Copper ordered.

He didn't need to tell me twice. I jogged out to the SUV waiting to whisk my love to safety. When I opened her door, she launched herself into my arms. "Is everything okay? Did you find my dad?"

I slowly shook my head, "We didn't find anything in there."

"What do you mean?"

"Just that. No one was in there. It didn't look

like there was any kind of struggle, no blood or broken glass, just an empty clubhouse."

She started to tremble in my arms. "What are we going to do now? We have to find them!"

"Club business, baby. Listen, I'm going to have you and Jamie hang out in the panic room while Copper and I work out our next move. Okay?"

She sighed, "Okay. Fine."

"Hey. What's that about?"

"I'm just frustrated. I never know what's going on. You won't let me help with anything. I just sit in a room and wait for you to come get me."

"Sitting in a room where I know you are safe and out of harm's way is helping me, more than you think. As for not telling you things, there's a reason for that, which I will explain when we have more time. Right now, I need to get you and Jamie down to the panic room," I explained.

"Fine. Lead the way to my newest hiding spot." I chose to let that one go. She'd had to deal with a lot of shit since she walked into the Blackwings clubhouse. It was completely understandable for her to be frustrated. Add to it that her dad was missing and we had the man responsible for it, as well as holding her prisoner for her entire life, in our custody, she was handling everything remarkably well.

I entered the code to the panic room, pulled the door open, and almost fell to my knees at the sight before me. Right in front of me were all of my brothers. Every single one except for Duke and Phoenix.

Badger wrapped both arms around me and squeezed to the point of pain. "I'm so damn glad to see you, brother! We've been trapped in here for hours and we have got to find Phoenix."

"How the hell were you trapped in there? There's an access panel right beside the door. You just enter the code and the door opens."

"That crazy fucker must have changed it. I'm not sure. They came through the front doors throwing concussion grenades. Next thing I know, we're packed in here like sardines in a can, and the passcode won't open the door," Badger explained.

"You talking about Octavius?"

"Yeah. He came in here spouting all kinds of crazy shit about him and Phoenix. I saw one of his men grab Phoenix and stick a needle in his neck before they started throwing those grenades everywhere. I don't know what they did with him. No one else saw anything."

“We’ll find out soon. Copper and his boys are here. We’ve got Octavius and two of his men locked in the cells. Killed six of his men at the cabin. Well, seven if you count Pete the piece of shit prospect,” I told him.

“You killed Pete?”

“Nah, Ember did. Found out he was one of Octavius’s men. That’s how we got the jump on Octavius. We can talk about it later. I need everybody out so I can put Jamie and Ember in here until we’ve found Phoenix and dealt with Octavius.”

“Everybody move out. No one leaves the clubhouse. Somebody check the gates. If they’re open, lock ‘em up. Officers, come with me to the cells,” Badger ordered.

Byte stepped forward, “I can reset the codes to the panic room from my laptop. I just need about 10 minutes to do it.”

All eyes went to Ember when she spoke, “I think I might know the passcode. May I try it?”

“How would you know that?” Badger asked.

“I lived under his rule for 18 years. You tend to pick up a lot of things over that amount of time. I was able to break into his safes and steal almost $100,000, wasn’t I?”

“Point made. Help yourself,” he gestured to

the access panel.

Ember waltzed into the panic room, punched some buttons, and lights started flashing. The girl never ceased to amaze me. “Nice job. What’s the code, baby?”

She rolled her eyes, “8-O-C-T-A-V-I-U-S-8.” The man really did have serious issues.

“You and Jamie go on in and get comfortable. I’ll be back as soon as I can.” I leaned down to give her a quick kiss and realized every brother from my club was staring at me. “Later, guys.” I looked back to Ember, “Love you.”

“Love you, too.”

CHAPTER TWENTY-SIX

Dash

Copper about fell on his ass when he saw me and the other Croftridge officers walking toward him. "Where in the fuck did they come from? Phoenix with you?"

"They were locked in the panic room. Phoenix wasn't with them though," I explained.

"How do you get locked in a panic room? I thought it was supposed to work the other way around?" Copper asked.

Badger grunted, "Octafuckhead had a tech guy change the passcode for the inside panel."

Copper still looked confused. "So, how did

you get the door open?"

"He's either really fucking stupid or way too cocky, or maybe both, because the dumbshit didn't bother to change the code to open the door from the outside. When Dash came down to put Ember and Jamie in the panic room, he found us."

Copper grinned, "Never thought the day would come that I would be happy to see your ugly mug." He pulled Badger in for a slap on the back. "You got any idea what happened to Phoenix?"

Badger looked to the floor and slowly shook his head. "I saw one of the Octacunts jab a needle in his neck right before they started throwing concussion grenades. When we all started coming around, we were locked in the panic room, and Phoenix wasn't with us."

"Ah, I was wondering how they managed to get all of you brutes in there without there being a few bodies scattered around." Copper clapped his hands together loudly, "Enough with the chit-chat, let's see if we can get our caged birds to sing. You want your guy or my guy to do the honors?"

"Eh, let 'em both have some fun. We've got three for them to play with." Badger chuckled and headed toward what we called our interrogation room.

It was time to get the party started. We had Octavius's son gagged, stripped down to his boxer briefs, and strapped to a metal table in the middle of the room. Octavius was tied to a chair and blindfolded. The other guy was tied to a chair on the other side of the room, gagged, but not blindfolded. Carbon was standing beside his tool box of torture, bouncing on the balls of his feet like a kid ready to rush the candy store. Copper's enforcer, Batta, was pacing the length of the room, casually swinging a baseball bat by his side, and whistling an eerily upbeat tune.

I considered both of these men my brothers, would do anything for them, but it straight up creeped my shit out when I saw them let their crazy out first hand. Kidnapping our president was the most severe offense either of them had dealt with in their years as a club enforcer. Add to that trying to kidnap and sell his daughter, killing a prospect, and nearly killing Duke, I wasn't sure I would be able to handle what they dished out. I'd seen both of them work someone over, for far less than what these three had done, and that was hard to stomach.

Copper and Badger exchanged a look,

communicating silently. They each turned to their respective enforcer and nodded. Let the games begin.

Carbon's voice was ice cold when he spoke, "Remove his blindfold." Copper ripped it off his head. Whatever reaction we were expecting, didn't come. The expression on Octavius's face remained the same. He actually looked bored.

Carbon covered his hands with vinyl gloves and picked up a pair of rusty bolt cutters. "Where shall I start?" he mused. The boy's eyes widened, and he started to thrash around on the table, sounds of fear and panic escaping around the gag. Still no change from Octavius. "Cover his eyes."

Copper looked curiously at Carbon, but did as he asked and replaced Octavius's blindfold. What was he doing?

As soon as it was in place, Carbon quickly turned and faster than anyone should be able to, he snipped off Hector's thumb with the bolt cutters. Hector grunted and groaned around his gag. Octavius's posture changed. It was slight, but I saw it, and from the looks of it, so did Carbon.

Carbon made eye contact with Batta and gestured to Hector. Batta silently crossed the room. With one swift motion, he swung the bat and hit Hector's left knee. Hector screamed loudly behind his gag. This time, Octavius sat up as straight as he could, listening intently. Interesting.

My skin broke out into goosebumps when I heard Carbon's chilly tone, "Ready to talk?" Octavius was visibly trembling, and beads of sweat had formed on his forehead, but he didn't respond. "Okie dokie," Carbon sang. He returned to Hector and removed a toe with the bolt cutters. He stepped out of the way so Batta could bring the bat down on Hector's right forearm.

Hector immediately started gagging and heaving. Carbon looked down at him and shook his head, "Pussy. Already puking." He sighed, "Remove his gag. Can't have him choking on his own vomit and dying just yet." The gag was removed, and Hector spewed forth the contents of his stomach. He screamed in pain, puked again, and sucked in huge lungfuls of air. "Octavius!" he screeched. "Help me!"

Octavius stiffened. His face turned red, and his breathing doubled. Then, he bellowed, "No!" He was trying with everything he had to get out of the chair. "What have you done to him? Let me see him! Get this off of me!"

Carbon chirped, “Don’t think so. Start talking or we keep going.”

Octavius had stilled, I assumed to contemplate his next move. Unfortunately for him, Carbon wasn’t a patient man. Apparently, Hector wasn’t either.

“Octavius! What the hell are you doing? Talk! Help me!! Make this stop!”

Carbon turned to Hector and arched a brow. “I don’t know what he did with him. I would tell you if I did. I swear it,” Hector rambled.

“That doesn’t help me with my problem at all. Sorry.” Carbon laughed, “Oh, wait, no I’m not.” Two seconds later, Hector was missing half of his ear.

Hector’s high-pitched screeching could outdo a banshee on any given day. “My ear!! Help me, please, Octavius, please make it stop!” Hector was sobbing for all he was worth, blood oozing from his hand and his foot, and was that, oh hell, had he pissed himself?

“I find it interesting that he seems to care more about what happens to Hector than to his own son.” Carbon said to the group. “Or, is that a ploy to spare the boy?” Carbon cackled like a crazed maniac. “Damn, I’m so fucking giddy I’ve started rhyming.” Carbon shook his head and just like an etch-a-sketch, his face was wiped clean. The ice-cold killer was back. "Remove the boy's gag. I want to hear his screams."

Carbon slowly approached the table, hands steepled in front of him, index fingers tapping together as he surveyed his tools. "Stop!" Hector bellowed, louder than I thought he could manage in his current state. "That's not his son!!"

"Shut your mouth, Hector!" Octavius yelled.

"Why? You're shutting yours enough for the both of us!"

"Not another word out of your mouth!" Octavius commanded.

"Why? What are you going to do about it? You may not know what it means to be a real man, but I do, and I'm not about to let that boy be tortured because of you and your stupid obsession with Phoenix!"

Octavius was shaking with rage. "You don't know anything!! It's not stupid. I have every right to hate him! He ruined my life, and then he did it again and again and again. No way am I telling these imbeciles anything about him when I finally have power over him!"

"It is stupid. No one knows what he did to you and if no one knows, it can't be that bad. You can't always win. You can't always be the best. You can't always have all the power." Hector paused for a moment, heaving in breaths before he changed tactics. His voice was less anger-filled and almost encouraging. "Don't you see, Octavius? You do hold all the power right now. Only you can decide if this stops or if they continue to torture me and that boy. At least get him out of this. You are the only one who can do that."

Octavius seemed to brighten at Hector's words. "You're right. I do have the power." He grinned evilly and looked toward Hector, "I don't give a shit what they do to you or to him."

"Enough!!!" Carbon bellowed. Even the boy, who had been thrashing around on the table and yelling into his gag the entire time Hector and Octavius were bickering, stilled. "Gag them!" He yelled, pointing at Octavius and Hector. Carbon walked to the table and sliced through the boy's gag with a wickedly huge knife. "You his son?"

The boy quickly shook his head, "N-n-no. And I know where Phoenix is!"

Carbon bent down to the boy's face and bared his teeth, "You ever see a clown pull a string of handkerchiefs out of his pocket?" The boy hesitantly nodded. "That's how it will look when I pull your intestines out through your mouth if I find out you're lying to me."

The boy squirmed but didn't break eye contact with Carbon. "I'm n-not lying. I saw him shove a man through the doors that led to his basement. The man was tied up and looked like he couldn't stand very well. I don't know if that's Phoenix, but he was dressed like those guys." The boy motioned with his head toward those of us on the sidelines. "He had that same leather vest on."

Carbon turned to face Copper and Badger with a raised brow, as if to say, what now?

Copper and Badger had some silent conversation through a series of grunts, nods, and hand gestures. It was truly amazing to watch. Copper stepped forward, "Take those two back to their cells." He looked to the boy and narrowed his eyes, "We're going to let you up, but you ain't leaving this room just yet. I'm going to ask you some questions, and you're going to answer all of them. If I think you're fucking with me, I'll let Carbon and Batta loose on you, got me?"

"Y-yes, sir."

Once the boy was released from his restraints, he sat up on the table and answered every question Copper asked. When Copper was finished, the boy continued to talk, telling us anything and everything he thought we might want to know.

Copper stood, “Let’s go get our president.” He clapped the boy, who we now knew was named Coal, on the shoulder, “You’re coming with us.”

CHAPTER TWENTY-SEVEN

Dash

I stopped by the panic room to let Ember know we were heading out to get Phoenix. She, of course, hit me with a barrage of questions that I couldn't answer. I promised her I would come get her as soon as we got back, and then I would answer as many of her questions as I could. She didn't seem to like that very much, but she kissed me and told me to go bring her dad back.

Ember didn't know it and would likely be pissed as hell at me when she found out, but I had her and Jamie remain in the panic room even though there was a skeleton crew of members staying behind at the clubhouse. I didn't know how things were going to go once we got to the farm. Anything could happen, but I knew she was safe as long as she stayed in that room.

From what Coal told us, we should be able to enter the property without issue as long as we were in the SUV's we drove back from the cabin. "They've got a chip or something on them that opens the gate. The gate can't be opened without one of the chips," Coal explained. "Once we're through the gates, we can drive one SUV to Octavius's house and the other two need to go to the building with his main office in it."

"Why can't we all go to his house?" Badger asked.

"Because they never do that. He goes home to change into fresh clothes, while the others go to the office and wait for him to arrive."

"How far is the office from his house?" Copper asked.

"Not far, maybe 50 yards or so."

"How many people will be at the office building?" I could see the wheels turning in his head; Copper was already mapping out a plan of attack.

"There shouldn't be many, if any, at this time. When he has been out for business, he calls the members of his council that weren't with him and tells them when to meet him at his office. It's really just the executive council members and a handful of their sons who are old enough to start trying to climb the ranks that you have to worry about. The workers aren't going to try to stop you, and I seriously doubt any of the kids would try anything either."

Copper rubbed his thumb and forefinger over his chin, "How many of these council members and kids are there?"

Coal started holding up fingers and mouthing numbers, trying to quickly tally up a number to give Copper. "Should be about six council members and four sons, I think. I don't know them all, and I'm not exactly sure who was in the other SUV's when they drove up to the cabin."

Copper started nodding his head, still rubbing his chin. "We can handle 10. I've got Octavius's phone," he held it up and wiggled his hand. "And looky here, an old text to a bunch of men telling them to be in the main office for a council meeting in 15 minutes."

We all laughed. This guy really was an idiot. He left trails and clues all over the place and did half ass jobs, like only changing the inside code for the panic room, but his biggest mistake, besides crossing us, was being a creature of habit. When someone always did the same thing, followed the same routine, never changed their ways, it made stuff like this too damn easy. Too. Damn. Easy.

I leaned back in my chair and crossed my arms over my chest, "So, we're going to ride in there, send one SUV to the house and the other two to the office, find Phoenix, then send a text to have them come to us, yeah?"

Badger grinned, "Sounds about right to me."

Copper slammed his palm down on the table and stood. "Me, too. Let's roll."

Suburbans or not, cramming eight big bikers into one did not make for a fun ride. Not a one of us would be considered small, and from the smells surrounding me, some wouldn't be considered clean either. Copper and Badger were up front while Coal was tucked in between me and Carbon. The kid looked terrified. I don't know if it was because of what we were about to do or if it had more to do with Carbon. Either way, the kid couldn't freak out on us. He was the only one who knew where Octavius's house and the office building were.

Trying to help him maintain his composure, I started talking to him. “You said your parents work at the dairy farm?”

He startled at the sound of my voice, but quickly recovered. “Yes, they do, but they work on the real side, not the other side.” He had said something like that earlier, but we weren’t after those details at the time.

“What’s the real side and the other side?”

He turned to me with eyes so full of hope, “You’re not going to let him come back, right? Octavius?”

“No, we’re not. Why?”

“I’ll tell you if he’s not coming back, but if he is, I can’t say. It could put my family in more danger. I’ve already put them at risk by what I’ve already told you,” he told me, his voice trembling as he spoke.

“He ain’t coming back. That I can assure you.”

“Okay, well, the real side is the actual dairy farm. The other side looks like it’s part of the dairy farm, but it’s where they package drugs and guns to be shipped out.”

“I see. Does everyone there know about the drugs and the guns?”

He shook his head. “No, I don’t think any of

the workers at the real farm know about it. He's managed to keep everything separate."

"So how do you know about it?"

"I was somewhere I shouldn't have been and overheard them talking. I was supposed to stay within a certain area of the farm, but there was a pond nearby, and I wanted to go swimming. I had to pass by part of the fake farm to get to it, and I overheard some of the workers talking. I wanted to know more, so a couple of days later, I went back over there and hid behind some crates. I watched them for a while and left. When I got outside, Octavius was standing there. He told me he wouldn't beat me bloody and fire my parents, if I agreed to owe him a favor. He didn't tell me what the favor was or when he would ask for it. That's the reason I was pretending to be his son. I didn't know why he wanted me to do it, and it seemed easy and harmless, so I agreed."

"Will the workers who handle the drugs and the guns be a problem for us?" I asked.

"No way. They aren't there because they want to be. They do that because they have to." Well, color me surprised.

"Why do they have to?"

"Because they owe Octavius money. He loans money to the people, I don't know why, and when they can't repay him, he brings them and their whole family, if they have one, to the farm. They have to stay there and work their debt off," he explained.

"Their whole family?"

"Yep. The men work on the farm and in the field, the women do the cooking and cleaning, and their kids are kept in a completely different part of the farm."

"The orphanage?" I guessed.

He looked confused. "There's no orphanage out there. Just a building where the slave workers' kids stay while their parents work off their debt."

I tried to keep my face neutral even though my blood was boiling. "Do you know any of the kids?"

"Not really. I was homeschooled my whole life, but those kids were taken to school. Most of the kids weren't there for too long, a few years at most. Ember, the girl at the cabin, she's been there for as long as I can remember. I've never talked to her, but I would see her around the farm every now and again. I knew she was one of the kids from the other side, because the kids on my side were allowed to play together and socialize. I always wanted to talk to her, she seemed so lonely and sad, but we weren't allowed to interact with the kids on the other side."

My jaw clenched. I could feel my molars grinding together. I didn't want to ask, but I had to know. "Do you know why Octavius went to the cabin to get her?"

"I only know what he told me. He said she had been kidnapped by a biker gang, and we needed to go save her."

"So, you didn't know he was planning to sell her, probably to be used as a sex slave by some creepy motherfucker?"

Coal gasped and a look of horror washed over his face. "He what?" I nodded. "No, I had no idea. I would have done something, or tried to do something to stop it. You have to believe me."

"Relax kid. I believe you." I did believe him. He would make a terrible poker player because his eyes gave him away.

"Chit-chat time is over. We're here," Copper announced.

We all fell silent. You could hear the gravel crunching beneath the tires as we flawlessly rolled through the gates to the land of lunacy. It was getting dark, so it was hard to get a good look at the place, but you could easily tell the place was huge.

Coal sat forward and gave Copper directions to Octavius's house. When the house came into view, Coal pointed out the office building. Badger relayed that information to the SUV behind us through his earpiece.

Copper pulled into the driveway with ease. Coal pointed to the doors that led to the basement. For some reason, I assumed we would be going inside the house to get to the basement. Worries of tripping alarms and hidden cameras had danced through the back of my mind the entire way there. An exterior entrance? Alarms and cameras or not, this would be a piece of cake.

"All right boys, check your weapons and be ready. We're going to file out on my count. Batta and Tiny will breach the door, Judge goes in first, followed by Batta and Tiny, then Dash, with Badger and me bringing up the rear. Byte you hop in the driver's seat and be ready to roll as soon as we're out with Phoenix. Coal, you stay put. Byte, shoot him if he tries to run. All right, on my count. One. Two. Three."

We filed out and followed Copper's instructions with perfect execution. The three in front of me reached the bottom of the stairs and began sweeping the room. My feet hit the floor, and my eyes immediately went to the figure in the corner of the room. I pointed my gun at the figure and quickly hit my tactical light.

"Phoenix!" I yelled, already running toward him. He wasn't moving. "Phoenix!" I yelled again, louder and more panicked this time. Nothing. Not a twitch or a flinch. Just...nothing.

Oh, fuck no. I slid on my knees the rest of the way to him. "Phoenix man. Can you hear me?" I gently shook him and still got no response. My trembling hand went to his neck, but I couldn't tell if he had a pulse or if what I was feeling was my own hand shaking.

Judge came up beside me. "Let me, brother," he said in a tone gentler than I have ever heard from the big man. He brushed my hand aside and placed his huge fingers against Phoenix's neck. He turned his eyes back to me, "He's got a pulse. It's weak but it's there." There were a few quick cheers but they quickly died down. We didn't want to be discovered, well, not yet anyway. Judge looked to Copper, "We need to get him to the hospital, now. He won't make it much longer if we don't."

Copper didn't hesitate, "Go." I got to my feet, unsure of what to do. I wanted to stay, to fight with my brothers, but one of the Croftridge members needed to go with Phoenix. Copper made the decision for me. “Dash, help Judge get him to the car. Both of you go to the hospital with him. Take Byte and Coal with you. We’ll finish up here and meet you at the hospital.”

In the blink of an eye, we were flying down the road toward the hospital, with a barely breathing Phoenix in tow.

CHAPTER TWENTY-EIGHT

Ember

"Ember, sit down. I swear, you're wearing a path in the floor with all of the pacing you are doing," Jamie said, for probably the tenth time since we had been locked in the panic room.

I knew it wasn't going to be quick, but I didn't think it would take this long for Dash to get back. With each minute that passed, my fear grew. What if he hadn't come back because he couldn't? Because he's in the hospital, or he's lying somewhere hurt, or he's dead? No! I couldn't think like that. I wouldn't.

He's fine. They were all fine. It was taking so long because they were being careful. Making sure they'd covered everything, so they could get in and get out without running into any problems. Yes, that was why it was taking so long.

My attempts to soothe myself were not working in the slightest. I needed a distraction, or at least an outlet for all of this pent-up emotion circulating through my body. I turned to Jamie, "Get up."

He looked shocked. "What? Why?"

"I need a distraction, and I need to get rid of this nervous energy. We're going to fight. Get up."

"Have you lost your damn mind Ember? I'm not fighting you. Dash would kick my ass."

"Not if I kick it first. Come on, hotshot, get up," I taunted. I was baiting him, and he knew it. I didn't care, I just needed him to take it.

"Is there a camera in here? A recording device of some kind? Something I can use to prove that I was clearly against this?" he asked, glancing around the room.

"Here. Jot down your ass-covering statement on this piece of paper, and then get your ass over here," I demanded.

Jamie's eyes widened, and then a smile slowly spread across his face. "Did little miss Ember just say ass?" He covered his mouth with his hands, like he was trying to hold his laughter in.

I rolled my eyes, "Oh, fuck off, pretty boy."

He bent at the waist, pointed at me, and shook with silent laughter as he struggled to breathe. Finally, he managed to get out each word between laughs, "You. Said. Fuck." More guffawing.

This went on for several minutes. I was starting to really lose my patience. "Are you done?"

He straightened and wiped his eyes, blowing out a long breath. "I think so." He laughed some more. "Damn, I have never heard anybody say fuck as dainty and lady like as you did. Promise me something?" he chuckled.

"What?" I stupidly asked.

"Promise me you'll say it again, just like that! Please!" He fell over on the couch in a fit of laughter again. Oh, I was so going to whoop his ass and not feel bad about it at all.

***

"I think the bleeding has finally stopped. I'm going to grab some fresh ice for you." I quickly grabbed some ice from our tiny freezer, placed it in a plastic bag, and wrapped it in a towel for Jamie's nose.

"Do you at least feel better now? I mean, am I in all this pain for no reason?" he griped.

"This definitely has provided me with a distraction," I hedged.

"Not what I asked," he said flatly.

"I'm still worried, like seriously worried, but I don't feel like my insides are trying to crawl through my skin anymore."

"I'll take that as a yes then."

"I'm really sorry Jamie. I didn't mean to break your nose. I've grappled and sparred with Dash tons of times and nothing like this has ever happened," I explained, truly upset that I hurt him. To really hurt him was never my intention.

He scoffed, "I have a hard time believing that Dash would go bare-knuckle with you."

Well, didn't that make me feel like an idiot. "Oh, I guess you're right. I didn't think about that."

Ring! Ring! Ring!

I leaped from the couch to grab the phone, “Dash?”

A deep voice filled my ear, “Sorry, sweetie, it’s Bronze. Copper sent word for me to get you and Jamie to the hospital.”

“Why?” I shrieked. “Who’s hurt?”

“Besides that boy down there with a broken nose, I don’t know. He didn’t have time for details. Just said to get you there. Oh, and he told me to say, ‘Release the Flame.’”

“How did you know about that?” I asked.

“I just told you, Copper said to say that, said it was the passphrase.”

“Not that. About Jamie’s nose?” I huffed.

“I’ve been sitting outside this damn door the whole time watching you two on the monitors. There are four cameras in there. You didn’t know?”

“No, I did not. Wait! You’ve been outside the door the whole time? If you’ve been here, why were we locked in this shoebox?!” I yelled into the phone. I was furious. We’d been in there for hours, wondering if and when anyone would come back for us.

“I was just following orders. Seriously though, open the door, we need to get going,” Bronze ordered.

I slammed the phone down and turned to Jamie. "We're being taken to the hospital. You should get that looked at while we are there."

***

Bronze led Jamie and I to a waiting room somewhere deep in the hospital. When my eyes fell on Dash, I took off running. I launched myself into his arms and thankfully, he caught me. "It's not you!" I said into his neck.

He pulled back from me, "You don't know?"

"No one told me anything, just that we needed to come here," I said, irritated.

He pulled my hand and led me to a chair to sit. "I can't say much, given where we are and all, but we found Phoenix."

My eyes started to fill with tears, "Is he okay?"

"We don't know anything yet. He was in a bad way when we found him. We brought him here right away, and we haven't heard anything yet."

"What was wrong with him?"

"All I can tell you is that he was unconscious, and he was barely breathing when we got there." He held me close to his chest and I let the tears fall before I pulled myself together and waited to hear from a doctor. I was determined to be strong for my dad.

I looked up and glanced around the room to see who was in here with us. I noticed Byte and a few of the members from the Devil Springs chapter spread out around the room. My eyes landed on a guy that looked oddly familiar, but I couldn't place him. I leaned into Dash and asked, "Who's that?"

"You don't recognize him?"

"He looks familiar, but I can't place him."

Dash whispered in my ear, "He's from the farm." I immediately stiffened. Why was he here? "It's okay. He's the one who helped us find Phoenix. I'll explain more later." He helped them? And he was from the farm? Nothing was making any sense.

I leaned forward, "Hi, my name's Ember. Thank you for helping them find my dad." I held my hand out to him.

He reluctantly took my hand and gently shook it. "I'm glad I was able to help. I'm Coal by the way. My parents work at the dairy farm. Or they did..."

Dash cleared his throat, effectively interrupting him, "We can talk about all that later, when we have more privacy."

Coal looked sheepish, "Yeah, sorry, man. This is all new to me."

"It's all good."

It was two more hours before a doctor finally came to speak to us. "Family of Phoenix Black?"

I leaped to my feet. "Yes! That's me! I'm his daughter. Please, how is he?"

"He's stable at the moment." He looked around the room and eyed the bikers warily. He lowered his voice, "I am quite concerned as to how he acquired his injuries."

Dash stepped up beside me. "So are we. We found him like that and got him here as soon as we could. If you haven't already notified the authorities, I will. We were just waiting to hear how he was doing first."

The doctor's whole attitude changed after Dash spoke. "Yes, we have informed the police. It's hospital policy to report things of this nature. Mr. Black was unresponsive due to a significant amount of drugs in his system. We were able to counteract some of them with medications, but we still need to monitor him closely until all of the lab work has come back and we're sure everything has been flushed out of his system. It appears he was beaten, rather severely, with a blunt object of some kind. He has significant bruising over the majority of his body. He has blood in his urine due to a contusion on one of his kidneys. Currently, there is no active internal bleeding that we could find, but again, we will continue to monitor him closely. He has five fractured ribs, his left tibia is broken, and his right shoulder was dislocated. We have stabilized his ribs, set his tibia and casted his lower left leg, and reduced his shoulder. He is not awake, but he is breathing on his own. He's going to be moved to the ICU shortly."

"Can I see him? Please?" I begged.

"As soon as he gets to the ICU, you can see him. Any other questions?"

Tears fell freely down my face. "I don't think so. Thank you for saving my dad."

He looked at me with gentle eyes, "He's not out of the woods yet, but he's doing a lot better than he was when he got here. He's in the best place he could be to beat this. I'll go let the nurses know they can move him to his room now. You can go on up to the waiting room and they'll come get you when you can visit."

Dash held out his hand, "Thank you, doctor." They shook hands, and the doctor disappeared down the hallway.

I grabbed my things, and our little group

made our way a few floors up to the ICU waiting room. I was shocked to find Copper and Badger sitting there.

Copper stood when he saw me. “Hey there, little cousin. How’s your pop?”

“They say he’s stable right now. I haven’t seen him yet, but they should be bringing him up soon,” I sniffled. “He’s hurt pretty bad. Um, bruises, broken ribs, broken leg, dislocated shoulder, and something about blood in his kidneys. Oh, and he had been pumped full of drugs.” Saying it out loud like that made me feel dizzy. The room started to spin, and I felt myself sway to one side.

Dash wrapped his arm around my waist to steady me. “Sit down, baby. You feeling okay?”

I slowly nodded. “Yeah, I just got a little light-headed for a moment. I’m good.”

He looked at me skeptically. “When was the last time you ate anything?”

“I’m not sure.” I couldn’t remember when or what I ate last.

“If you don’t remember, it’s time to eat. It’s been quite a day, and I think everything is starting to catch up with you.”

A few minutes later, Badger returned with a sandwich, chips, a banana, and a bottle of apple juice. “I don’t know where you found this, but bless you, Badger. I didn’t realize how hungry I was until food was placed in front of me.”

He winked, “I have my ways.”

I swallowed the last bite of the best bag lunch I had ever tasted just as a nurse came out and told me I could go visit Phoenix.

I stood and Dash did as well. “I’m sorry, sir. Only one visitor at a time.”

“She got dizzy and almost fainted just minutes ago. Unless you can promise to stay by her side the whole time she’s back there, I’m going with her,” he said in a tone that brokered no argument from the nurse.

“Right this way.” She led us to a room full of medical machinery the likes of which I had never seen before. There, in the middle of tubes and wires, lay my father, barely recognizable to my own eyes.

I placed my hand on his, afraid to touch him anywhere else, and just cried. “Oh, Daddy, please be okay. You have to be okay. I love you so much. I just found you. I can’t lose you now. I won’t lose you. You fight to get back to me. Please.” I was ugly crying. Tears, snot, and maybe even saliva dripped all over me, him, the bed, and Dash. I didn’t care one bit as I sobbed and wailed at my father's bedside.

Dash scooted a chair up behind me and instructed me to sit. That's where I stayed until the nurse told me visiting hours were over for the night. I didn't want to leave him, but I didn't have a choice. I placed a gentle kiss on his cheek and whispered, "I love you, Dad. I'll be back first thing in the morning."

I walked into the waiting room and was immediately tackled by Reese.

"Ember!" she screamed at the same time I yelled, "Reese!"

"What in the hell is going on?" she demanded.

I sighed, "It's a long story and honestly, I don't even know all of it."

"Give me the short version, a couple highlights, anything."

"I can't right here. Let's wait until we get back to the clubhouse or at least in the car."

"Fine. Car it is. I'm riding with you," she stated matter-of-factly and walked out the door. It seemed I would be dealing with sassy Reese.

I filled Reese in on everything that had happened that I knew of.

"Let me see if I have this right. Pete attacked Jamie and Dash, and then you killed him. Copper and his crew came to the cabin to take down Octavius and his men who showed up to take you back. Back at the clubhouse, Dash found everyone except Phoenix in the panic room. While you and Jamie were in the panic room, Coal helped the guys find Phoenix. They brought Phoenix to the hospital, let you out, and here we are."

"That sounds about right."

She was silent for a beat, eyebrows furrowed. "Hold up. Things are missing. Like, what happened to Octavius? Who is Coal and how did he know where to find Phoenix? Where was Phoenix? And most importantly, why did Octavius take Phoenix anyway?" She held up a finger for each question she ticked off.

"Coal's parents work at the dairy farm. They live on the property, so he grew up there. Other than that, I don't have the answers to anything you asked me." She remained silent, clearly thinking over everything we discussed. I didn't want to talk about it anymore at that moment, so I changed the subject.

"How's Duke?" I should have asked about him way before now. I felt awful about that. I'd been so wrapped up in my own drama that I'd forgotten about my best friend, my only friend.

She shrugged, "The same. Awake, but barely

speaking. When he does talk, it's usually so he can say something mean to me."

"And you? How are you?" I asked.

She looked away from me, "I'm fine. I don't let what he says get to me."

She could say that until she was blue in the face, but that wouldn't make it true. She wasn't fine, and what he was saying did hurt her. I couldn't put my finger on it, but I had a strong suspicion something else was going on with her as well. Hopefully, most of my dust would settle soon so I could pay more attention to her.

"Why do you keep going up there if he is being so unpleasant?"

"I stopped going after the first time he was so ugly to me. I didn't want to be there today, but Duke needed some of his things, and no one else had time to bring it to him. I was just going to drop it off and leave, but Carbon texted me and told me to stay in his room until he said otherwise. Let me tell you how high that ranked on the suckage meter."

"I bet it was up there with my day," I giggled and then yawned. And yawned again. I must have fallen asleep because the next thing I vaguely recalled was the feeling of being carried and the scent of Dash surrounding me.

CHAPTER TWENTY-NINE

Dash

Ember fell asleep on the way back to the clubhouse. I was surprised she didn't crash sooner, but my girl hung in there like a champ. I carried her to my room and tucked her into bed. Reese asked if she could stay in there with her, and I let her because I had no idea when I would make it back to my room. "Just make sure you keep the door locked. I'll use my key if I need to get in, but no one else needs to come in here, unless your brother comes by to check on you."

"Got it. Thanks, Dash. Night."

Once the girls were tucked in for the night, I made my way down to Church, called by Copper and Badger. I stopped by the kitchen to grab a bite to eat and some coffee. I was fucking exhausted, but this had to be done, and it was likely going to take a while.

I was the last one to enter. The moment my ass dropped into my chair, Badger banged the gavel and began. "We need to go over everything that has happened today. Not a one of us has been present for every single event that has taken place, and we haven't had the time to discuss much in between the fires we've been putting out. Copper and I have crudely put together a timeline of the series of events and will take turns sharing details as it pertains to us. Please hold any and all questions and comments until we have reached the end unless you are specifically called upon by one of us. Understood?"

Sounds of affirmation went up around the room. "Okay, let's get to it."

I knew most of what had happened up until the part where I had to leave for the hospital with Phoenix. Copper was sharing that portion of the story, "...so we told them to get him to the hospital and we would handle things there. I used Octavius's phone to text his council members instructing them to meet him in their main office in 15 minutes. They made it easy for us, too. Not a door in sight was locked. We walked right into that office, positioned ourselves accordingly, and waited to capture our prey. There were 10 of them and 14 of us, so we took them down with ease. Much as I wanted to put a bullet between their eyes and make the world a better place, Badger and I thought it might be best to keep them breathing in case we need to extract more information from them. We borrowed some more of those fancy SUV's Octavius has stockpiled at his place, loaded up the fuckwads, and tossed them downstairs in the cells. Ultimately, we have to decide if we want to handle them in house or if we want to turn them over to the police, when we're done with them of course, but we'll come back to that."

The two of them continued on until everyone was brought up to speed. The next words out of Badger's mouth were music to my ears, "I say we table everything for tonight. It's late, and it has been one hell of a day. Everybody can get some sleep, and we'll come back to the table with a clear head. Any objections?" Not a one. "All right.

Night, brothers." Badger banged the gavel, and Church was dismissed.

I fell face down on my bed, fully dressed, and passed the fuck out with Ember beside me and Reese on the other side of Ember.

***

I forgot to turn my fucking alarm off, and I couldn't find the right button to hit to make the shit stop squawking at me. Pissed as hell, I finally sat up only to realize it wasn't my alarm clock, it was my phone ringing. Who would have the balls to call me at six o'fucking clock in the morning?

"This better be good," I answered gruffly.

Goosebumps spread across my skin when he spoke, "I want to see my daughter."

"Phoenix?"

"Who the fuck else would it be? Get your ass out of bed and get my daughter up here." I heard the click of the call disconnecting. Oh hell, Phoenix was awake, and he sounded pissed.

"Ember, baby, wake up." She rolled away from me and pulled the blanket tighter around her. I gently shook her. "Ember. I need you to wake up. Your dad is awake and he's asking for you."

She shot straight up. "What?"

"You heard me. Get dressed so we can go."

Thirty minutes later, we walked into Phoenix's hospital room. "Dad," she rasped. "How are you feeling?"

He gingerly held his hand out to her, "Been better, baby doll. Come here and give your old man a hug. I've been so worried about you."

She went right to him and carefully wrapped her arms around him. "I'm fine. I've been worried about you. What happened?"

Phoenix patted her back and sighed, "You both should probably grab a chair and sit down. I have a lot to share. Has anyone called my grandparents?"

I shook my head. "Not that I'm aware of. You want me to call them?"

"No, not yet. I'll call them myself. They won't believe I'm okay unless they hear it from me, and I don't want them hopping on the first flight to Croftridge just yet."

"Gotcha. I'll let Copper and Badger know as well."

Phoenix's brows furrowed in confusion, "Copper?"

I chuckled, "Guess we have a lot to fill you

in on as well."

"You go first. I have a feeling my part will tie up any loose ends of your story."

I told Phoenix everything that happened in the last 24 hours. He remained silent throughout the entire explanation, patting Ember's hand at various parts of the story. All in all, he took things better than I thought he would.

He cleared his throat and adjusted himself to a more comfortable position in the bed. "I'm going to fill you in on what I know, but I want you to keep it to yourselves until I've had the chance to tell the club myself."

Ember and I readily agreed to not say a word.

"Night before last, I was at a loss as to what to do with Octavius. Our leads were hitting dead ends, and I was quickly running out of options. I decided to call my Pop and ask him if he knew anything about the farm, not the rumors that everyone in town has heard, but anything concrete or factual. Turns out, he did know some things about the farm, a lot of things actually. My mother, Julia, was married before she married my father. She married a man named Zayne." Ember gasped and covered her mouth with her hand, but didn't say anything. Phoenix turned to me, "Zayne was Octavius's father. According to Pop, as soon as they were married, things started to change. They moved into a house on the farm property, and Zayne became increasingly controlling. She stayed with him for a little over a year before she told Pop she wanted out. Pop didn't go into a lot of detail, but he said she felt like she was a part of a cult and that she thought his family might be involved in illegal activities." He cast his eyes toward the window, away from us, and took several deep breaths.

He remained silent for several minutes before he continued. When he did, his voice was thick, and I knew he was trying to get his emotions under control. "This next part was hard to hear, and it is even harder to say." When he turned back to face both of us, his eyes were haunted, and he looked lost. "She was desperate for Pop to help her get out of the marriage and get away from Zayne because she was pregnant, with me."

Ember reached out and grabbed his hand in an attempt to give him some comfort. I sat there stunned with absolutely no idea what to say. All that came to mind was, "What the fuck?" I remained silent and patiently waited to see what other bombshells he might have to share.

"Pop didn't say what it was, but she knew

something they wouldn't want getting out. Pop used that as leverage to get the marriage annulled. He threatened to expose them if any of them ever tried to contact her again. Then, he shipped her off to California to start a new life. She married Phillip when I was an infant, and I was raised to believe that he was my father." He paused and then continued with more vehemence, "He wasn't my biological father, but he was my *Dad*."

I leaned forward in my chair, my elbows resting on my knees, "So, this makes you and Octavius half-brothers, right?" He nodded. "I'm just not following, Prez. This is shocking news, but how does it relate to Ember's situation?"

"I had the same exact question after I talked to Pop, but I still couldn't piece it together. Since Octavius was the only one around who could fill in the blanks, the boys and I decided to ride out and pay him a visit. We were gathered in the common room, seconds from walking out the door, when him and his men rolled up and started tossing concussion grenades left and right. Next thing I knew, I was coming to at the bottom of a damn staircase, my hands bound behind my back, with none other than Octavius standing over me. He drug me over to a corner of the room and explained everything to me as he beat the hell out of me."

Tears were running steadily down Ember's face. She choked on a sob after his last sentence. He squeezed her hand, "Hey, hey, none of that. I'm okay, baby girl. It's over, I'm okay, and he can't hurt me, you, or anybody else. I'll make sure he never hurts anyone again." She sniffled and nodded. "You need to hear the rest of it, but it's not a nice story. You think you can handle it right now?"

She wiped the tears from her face and straightened her spine, "I'd rather hear it now. I'll drive myself crazy thinking of all kinds of horrible things if I wait."

Phoenix patted her hand and continued, "As you know, when I was 15, I moved back to Croftridge to live with my grandparents after my parents died in a car accident. My first day at Croftridge High ended with me getting into a fist fight with Octavius. I saw him grab a girl's arm and shove her down to the ground. I intervened, and the little punk swung at me." Phoenix shrugged, "So, I swung back and handed his ass to him. He got up spouting some crap about being Octavius Jones and he would make me pay. Unbeknownst to me, this was the catalyst that unveiled 15 years' worth of secrets and set the stage for the next 20 years."

"Octavius wanted to make me pay for humiliating him in front of the whole school, so he started digging, trying to find out anything and everything he could about me. It didn't take him long to find out who I was and why I had moved to Croftridge. When he didn't find much on me, he started researching my parents. That's when he found the newspaper article announcing the marriage of my mother and his father. It didn't take a genius to put the dates together and figure out that I'm Zayne's child. What did he do with this information? He confronted his father, which was a big mistake on his part. Zayne had no idea of my existence. Once my mother was gone, he moved on to the next woman almost immediately because he needed a male heir in order to take over the farm from his father. Enter Octavius. What Octavius didn't stop to consider was the fact that I am actually the first male heir, not him. Had he kept his mouth shut, no one would have ever known otherwise. Once Zayne knew about me, he completely disregarded Octavius and began focusing on how to become a part of my life so he could bring me into the fold. Pop found out what he was doing and put a stop to it, using the same threats he used to get Mom's marriage annulled. Zayne backed off at the time, but Pop didn't know that Zayne planned to try again once I turned 18. For the next three years, Zayne either ignored Octavius or treated him like shit. It didn't help matters that Octavius and I had become rivals at school, completely unintentional from my side. Whatever I did, he tried to do and was never able to best me. Football, wrestling, grades, friends, girls, you name it, I was better. Zayne also threw this in his face often. It didn't surprise me when Octavius told me he killed Zayne just before I turned 18 to prevent my true paternity from being revealed to me and my existence revealed to their people."

Phoenix repositioned himself, took a few sips of water, and went on, "The summer before my senior year of high school, I met Annabelle, your mother. I fell for her hard and fast. We all know how it ended, but I now know that Octavius is responsible for Annabelle's disappearance. He wanted her, but she wanted me. I had no idea he had even approached her. After she rejected him, he stepped back and began plotting. He did his research and found out that Annabelle's parents were worthless trash who spent any money they had on cigarettes, alcohol, and gambling. Octavius had the brilliant idea to loan them money, a large sum of money they would never be able to pay back. The day after I deployed, Octavius rolled up to their house and informed them that they would be repaying their debt to him by working on the farm, effective immediately, and Annabelle was coming along, too. Octavius planned to shower her with acts of kindness and lavish her with gifts to win her over, but she wasn't interested. He changed tactics and said he would reduce the amount of debt her parents owed him if she would give him a chance. She hated her parents so that didn't work for him either. He continued his efforts until she finally told him she was in love with me and pregnant with my child. Octavius was furious with her, but having learned from his previous mistakes, his words, not mine, he thought about things before he acted."

Phoenix squeezed Ember's hand again and softly said, "Baby girl, this is the hard part. You still want me to keep going?" She nodded quickly. Phoenix took in a deep breath and looked down at their joined hands, "He went back to Annabelle and told her that he would allow her to keep the baby, even provide her with medical care, if she agreed to marry him after the baby was born, and then bear him a son. At this point, he didn't really want her; he just wanted to ruin her in my eyes, again his words, not mine. He promised that he would let her leave free and clear after she gave him a son, but the son would remain with him. She refused at first, but he told her he would have her baby aborted, lock her away, and continue to impregnate her until she gave him a son. Then, he would kill her. Obviously, she chose the first option."

Ember's eyes widened and filled with tears, "Then how did I end up at the orphanage? They told me my mother died during childbirth, which we know isn't true since Annabelle was still there for a while as Annelle." She clutched her chest as if she were in physical pain. Horror washed over her face as realization dawned, "Oh, no. Does this mean Nivan is my brother?"

Phoenix appeared to be in pain as well. His brows were furrowed, jaw clenched, lips in a thin, hard line. "From what I gathered, you ended up in the orphanage as leverage to make sure Annabelle stuck to her end of their agreement. He was clever in his wording, leading her to believe she would keep and raise the baby, when he really meant he would allow the baby to live. As far as Nivan being your brother, I don't know the answer to that. I was damn near unconscious again from all the blows I had taken by the time he finished talking. I do remember demanding to know what happened to Annabelle." Phoenix looked down and shook his head. "That fucker grinned at me and said, 'I'm the only one that knows, and I'll never tell you a damn thing about her.' Then, I saw his boot flying toward my face. The next time I opened my eyes, I was in this room, and here we are."

"Damn, Prez. That's one fucked up story. You believe everything he told you?" I asked, genuinely curious. I wasn't sure how I would react if I was ever in his position. Hell, I didn't even know how to react as a bystander, but I did know that we shouldn't blindly believe everything Octavius told him.

"Yeah, I think so, most of it anyway. He was blurting it all out in a fit of rage. Plus, he had no reason to lie at that point. He thought he had won. He had me with no one to come save me, or so he thought, and he was going to have Ember back in his grasp within a few hours." Phoenix grinned. "He didn't count on me having a contingency plan in the form of another chapter, led by my family."

Phoenix clapped his hands together and

looked directly at me. "Now, boy, have you got something you need to say to me?"

Oh shit. Straightening myself, I met his gaze, "Yes, Prez. I'm in love with your daughter and would like to make her my Old Lady." I held his gaze for what felt like an eternity, but it couldn't have been more than 30 seconds.

"You touched her?" he asked sternly.

"Dad!" Ember yelled, her cheeks turning a telling shade of red.

"We have rules, baby girl. I cannot allow those rules to be broken. If I allow one to get away with it, others will think they can, too, and then everything goes to shit. Honor, respect, and loyalty are the foundation of this club. Without those principles, we are nothing," he explained.

"I understand that, Dad, but we had a good reason for waiting to tell you and that reason is based solely on respect, so you can't hold it against him for upholding a founding principle," Ember pleaded.

Phoenix quirked an eyebrow, curious as to what she was going on about. He turned his attention to me, "Explain."

"I didn't want to tell you over the phone. I thought anything less than a face to face conversation would be disrespectful. I was planning to come talk to you the night Ember got shot. After that, I didn't get a chance to talk to you before we left for the cabin," I explained, meaning every word I said.

"And I asked him not to say anything to you until this was over because I wanted you to be focused on what was happening down there and not worried about what was happening between me and Dash at the cabin," Ember blurted out.

"She did do that, but that's not why I waited. Like I said, I felt like it was a conversation to be had in person. I know I should have waited to move things along with us until I had spoken with you, but I didn't, and I'm not sorry about that. She has made me the happiest I have ever been in my entire life. I didn't know how everything would turn out, so I wanted to have every second I could with her in case our time was limited."

"I can understand that, more than I care to," Phoenix said quietly. Then, he perked up, "I get it, and you two have my blessing, but I still have to black your eye or something visible, so the boys don't think I'm getting soft."

I was about to say I understood when I was hit in the face with Phoenix's sledgehammer of a fist. "Fuck!" I grunted and fell back into my chair.

"Daddy! Are you okay?! Should I get the nurse?" Ember's frantic voice had me lifting my head to look at them.

Phoenix had his good arm wrapped tightly around his ribs and was pressing some kind of handheld button for dear life. He said through gritted teeth, "No. I'm fine. Just. Need. The drugs. To kick in."

I shook my head and laughed to myself, "You fucking Blacks and your iron fists. I'm okay, by the way. In case my Old Lady was curious."

Ember's eyes shot to me. She winked, "I wasn't worried, baby. I know you can take a punch." I fell a little bit more in love with her in that moment.

Phoenix started swatting her hands away, "Stop fussing over me. I'm fine now. Besides, I need to have a chat with Dash, alone. Can you step out for a few minutes?"

I stood, "Not until I make sure someone is out there. Can't be too careful." Phoenix gave me a chin lift, his eyes full of respect.

I returned to Phoenix's room and sent Ember out to sit with Badger. "What's up, Prez?"

"Have we identified the men we have in the cells yet?"

"Not sure. Last I heard, Byte was working on that with Coal's help."

"We need them identified, and then we need to figure out what in the hell we are going to do with them. It's going to have to be quick, too, otherwise both sides of that farm are going to start wondering what happened to the ever present assclowns."

"I'll track down Byte as soon as I get back. What are you thinking we should do with them?"

"I think we should hand them over to the authorities. This is too big for us to handle in house without drawing attention. We've always gotten along with the local cops, and I don't want that to change. Also, a few guys I served with are now with the FBI or work closely with them, so we've got options. Only problem is, Octavius is mine. I'm not turning him in."

"How are you going to do that?" I asked.

"Still thinking on that. For now, I want him kept separate from the others. I don't care if they can hear him, but I don't want them to be able to see him. Can you make sure that happens for me? Starting today?"

"Sure thing, Prez. Anything else?"

"Actually, yes. I want you to marry my daughter," he stated bluntly.

I choked on my own spit when he said that. I coughed so hard I thought my eyeballs were going to shoot out of my head. When it subsided, I looked up to find Phoenix watching me closely. "What? You're dating her, making her your Old Lady. You can't put a ring on her finger, too?"

I blinked stupidly at him. "Uh, I, yeah, I can. I just thought it was maybe too soon for that, you know? Girls look at that stuff differently."

He scoffed, "Marriage is the same as becoming an Old Lady in our world."

"I know that and you know that, but she doesn't."

"So, explain it to her and then marry her. I don't want her becoming a mother before she is married," he put his hand up and quickly added, "and I don't want to know anything about her chances of becoming a mother or lack thereof. That's my baby girl, and I'm not used to my role as a father yet. I know she's grown, but I still don't want to know anything about you two being together like that."

I chuckled, "Got it, Prez. I'll talk to her."

"See that you do. And one more thing," he paused and narrowed his eyes, "If you hurt her, Carbon's techniques will look like child's play when I'm through with you."

"I wouldn't expect anything less, Prez." We shook hands and did the best we could for a half hug/back slap given his current state before I left to get Ember and follow through on Phoenix's requests.

CHAPTER THIRTY

Ember

We arrived back at the clubhouse and things seemed almost normal, which was weird. Things shouldn't be normal at all. I wasn't sure how things should be, but normal wasn't it. I looked around the common room and noticed most, if not all, eyes were on Dash and I as we entered the room. I leaned in close to him and whispered, "Why are they all staring at us?"

He grinned and whisper-yelled, "Because I'm holding your hand and they want to know why." He raised our joined hands in the air and announced, "She's mine! With Phoenix's blessing." The roar of cheers and applause that immediately followed was almost deafening. I was hugged, squeezed, patted, and had my hand shook more in the 30 minutes that followed than my whole life put together.

Everyone seemed genuinely happy for us, except for one person. The one person I thought for sure would be happy for me. Reese.

"Congratulations," she said in her monotone robot voice. "I'm so happy for you two."

There were a couple of ways I could have handled her response. I could have gotten mad and yelled at her. I could have cried and said she hurt my feelings. I could have ignored it and accepted her fake congratulations. I chose none of those. I placed my hands on her shoulders and looked directly into her eyes, "What. Is. Wrong. With. You?" I punctuated each word with a gentle shake of her shoulders.

She jerked back from me and ran from the room. I went after her, but a large arm wrapped around my waist and stopped me from going any farther. "Let her be," Carbon quietly rumbled near my ear.

"Get your fucking hands off my Old Lady!"

Dash roared from the other side of the room. The crowd parted, creating a clear path for the raging bull, otherwise known as Dash, to come charging toward Carbon.

Carbon immediately released me and put his hands up. “No disrespect, brother. I was only looking out for my sister. She’s having a tough time right now, and I was telling Ember to let her be.”

“Still doesn’t explain why you had your hands on her. You can talk to her without touching her,” Dash spat.

“Reese can lash out, verbally and physically, when she feels cornered or threatened. Didn’t want her doing that to Ember. That’s the only reason I used my hands to stop her,” Carbon explained, his eyes full of honesty and a deep sadness I guessed was put there by his sister.

“Fine. Just keep your hands off next time. Feel me?” Dash grumbled.

“No problem, brother. Again, didn’t mean any disrespect.”

“Come on, Ember, I need a shower, and then I have a few things your father asked me to take care of today.” Upset at Reese’s reaction and slightly embarrassed at the show of machismo, I followed Dash to our room without question.

As soon as we crossed the threshold, I started, “Something is going on with Reese. Something major and I am seriously worried about her. Carbon says to let her be, but that is not helping her.”

Dash stalked toward me and captured my lips with his. He mumbled against my mouth, “Don’t want to talk about that right now.”

I pushed back from him, “Dash, I’m worried about my friend and you’re what? Trying to have sex with me right now? Really?”

He sat down on the end of the bed and pulled me to stand between his legs. “I’m sorry, baby. I know you’re worried about your friend. It’s just, well, a lot has happened and it’s been stressful. Sometimes a man needs to relieve that stress, and there’s only one way I want to do that right now.” He rubbed his hands up and down my sides in a gentle caress. He lowered his voice, “Do you think you could help me out with that?” He pulled me closer and nipped at my lower lip. “Give your friend some time to get herself together.” He continued to place little nips from my neck to my ear and back. He squeezed my butt with both hands and growled, “You gonna let me fuck you, baby?”

I could only reply with a soft moan. I really

should have been angry with him, but there was no use in fighting it. He had me where he wanted me and he knew it. "It's going to be hard and fast. If you can't handle that, say it now," he warned.

What would happen if I couldn't handle it? Would he go find what he needed somewhere else? He must have seen something on my face, worry or fear, or complete devastation. "If you don't think you can, I'll just go to the gym or get one of the guys to get in the ring with me. After I fuck you," he winked. "I don't want you to do anything you don't want to do."

"It's okay. I want to. I mean, I want to see if I want to. Ugh, why is this so hard?" I swallowed and took a quick second to organize my thoughts. "I'll never know if I like it that way or not if I never try it. So, consider this me volunteering to try it."

I thought I would get a laugh out of him with my ramblings of inexperience, but I was very much mistaken. He squeezed my butt even harder before pushing me away from him. "Strip!" he barked.

I jumped from how loud and stern his voice was. He had never spoken to me like that. It was kind of scary, but a little exciting, too. I jumped again when he roared, "Now!"

Not wasting another second, I moved quickly

to do as he bid.

He pointed to the floor in front of him, "Knees."

I sank to my knees in front of him. I was trying to trust him, to not question him. He knew I had limited experience. Surely, he would guide me through the next steps.

He stepped closer to me. Cupping my cheek with one hand and giving me a gentle caress, he unfastened his jeans with his other hand. He shoved his pants and boxers down just far enough to free himself. He stopped caressing my cheek and moved his hand to the back of my head. "Open," he commanded.

I opened my mouth without hesitation. He took another step closer and slid his cock into my mouth. I instinctively closed my lips around him, but I was unsure of what to do. The next second, I learned that I didn't have to do anything. He held my head in place and slid himself in and almost all the way out of my mouth over and over. "Ember, baby, that fucking mouth," he groaned.

His thrusts began to go deeper and deeper until he was hitting the back of my throat. I felt the urge to gag, but he would pull back each time before anything actually happened. I was beginning to wonder how much longer I could keep my mouth open that wide when he pulled me off of him and lifted me to my feet with the hand he had fisted in my hair. "On the bed. Hands and knees," he barked, turning me and punctuating his demand with a sharp slap to my butt.

I crawled onto the bed and remained on my hands and knees, not sure of what to expect from him. He grasped my cheeks with both hands and pulled them apart. I squeaked in protest, knowing he could see all of my most private places. He completely ignored me and shoved two fingers inside me. I moaned like a shameless hussy and started pushing my hips back into his hand.

"You like that, baby? You want me to fuck you with my fingers?" I moaned and vigorously nodded my head. He slapped my butt hard, "That's not going to work. Beg me. Tell me what you want and beg me to do it."

"Please, Dash. Please fuck me with your fingers. I need it. Please," I begged.

He slapped my butt again, "You should have been more specific." I could hear the sarcasm in his voice, but I didn't understand until I felt something I had never, ever felt before. His fingers were still inside me, but something, I'm guessing his thumb, had entered me elsewhere. I squealed and started to rise up, trying to turn around and tell him no. I lifted my hands off the bed, but he slapped my butt so hard I stilled from the shock of it. "Hands on the bed, eyes to the wall. You want my thumb out of your ass, you ask me to take it out. But you don't want that, do you, baby? If you did, you wouldn't be pushing that ass back into my hand, would you?"

He was right. My traitorous body was doing exactly what he said. I pushed back and he pushed forward, thumb and fingers. "That's right, baby, fuck your pussy and your ass on my fingers." He pumped his fingers forcefully in and out of my holes several times. I groaned loudly and arched my back. I was close to climaxing, just a few more thrusts. "Don't you dare come, Ember!" He smacked my butt, alternating cheeks, several times.

"Dash, I'm going to come! You have to stop!"

He removed his fingers from me and fire blazed across my butt from the rapid-fire swats he delivered. "You don't give me orders. Now, roll the fuck over and spread those legs wide."

I rolled over and gasped when my butt

touched the sheets. I spread my legs and tried to raise my butt off the bed to keep the blazing skin from coming in contact with anything. He smirked, "Put that ass on the bed or I'll redden it some more." I reluctantly let it fall back to the bed. "Now, play with your tits for me while I fuck your sweet pussy."

I looked at him with wide eyes. I had never done anything like that. I knew people did touch themselves, but I was always too afraid someone at the farm was watching or would walk in on me. He smacked my thigh, not nearly as hard as he had smacked my butt, but it still caused me to suck in air. "Pinch. Your. Nipples." He punctuated the first two words with a light swat to each thigh, and the last one with a swat to my sex.

I brought my hands to my chest and began playing my nipples for him. I briefly wondered if I should be angry with him for the way he was talking to me, but I was enjoying myself far too much to worry about how I "should" be reacting.

All coherent thoughts ceased when he grabbed my thighs and slammed into me. He was relentless with his thrusts. He grunted, cursed, and said all kinds of filthy things to me. "You better fucking come, Ember. I'm about to fucking blow and I'm not stopping for you." He lightly tapped my clit and that was all it took. I fell headfirst into the most intense pleasure.

When my sense of reality returned, Dash was hovering over me, sweaty and panting, with his hand over my mouth. "They're going to think I was killing you with the way you were screaming," he laughed. "Twenty bucks says someone is knocking on that door within two minutes."

I blushed from my head to my toes, "You're not serious, are you?"

He grinned, "Yeah, babe, I am. They're used to hearing that shit come from Carbon's room, not mine."

I frantically tried to push him off of me. "Let me up! I've got to get some clothes on!"

"Wait! Let me clean you up first," he said as he started to move himself off of me.

"I can do it in the bathroom," I argued. I just wanted to get some clothes on before anyone came knocking.

"That's not what I meant," he cast his eyes away from me. "I'm sorry, baby, I forgot the condom." I gasped. "I pulled out. I know it's not fail-safe, but I didn't realize until the last second." He glanced at my stomach, "Anyway, let me get something for that."

He returned quickly with a damp cloth and cleaned his mess off of me. He pulled me into his arms and kissed my temple, "Are you okay?"

"I'm fine, are you okay?"

He chuckled, "Hell yeah, I'm okay. That was the best sex of my life."

I beamed at his words, "Really?"

"Yes, really. I got a little carried away. Are you sure I didn't go too far?"

"I'm sure. I, um," I looked down at my lap, fighting the urge to rub my palms together. I lowered my voice and said, "I liked it. A lot."

He kissed my temple again, "I did, too. I'm sorry about the other part. I'm clean, so you don't have to worry about that. We can get you one of those Plan B pills if you're worried about pregnancy."

I don't know what came over me, but I said exactly what I was thinking without even considering how he would react, "I don't want that. If I get pregnant, I get pregnant. If I don't, I'll make an appointment and get put on birth control."

"If you get pregnant, we're getting married right away. Your dad specifically told me not to make you a mother before you were married," he said, completely serious.

“What?” I shrieked and then stopped myself. “Wait. Let’s worry about this when and if the time comes, okay?”

“Sounds good to me, baby.”

We cleaned up and got dressed. “Oh, by the way, you owe me $20,” I reminded him.

He scoffed, but handed me $20. “I’ve got to go, baby. Your dad asked me to get some things done for him as soon as possible.”

Dash left to go do whatever Dad had asked him to do. I laid back on the bed and pondered over what to do about Reese. The more I thought about it, the more I thought Carbon was wrong about letting her be. That’s not what she needed. She needed to talk about whatever was bothering her. She needed to get it out in the open and let people help her. She didn’t have an abundance of friends like most people our age. I was pretty much it for her, just as she was for me, but she also had a club full of bikers who considered her a part of their family. Then it dawned on me! Duke. He could help.

I quickly changed into something more presentable and went in search of Dash. Twenty minutes later, he was nowhere to be found. Frustrated, I went to the common room and planted my butt on one of the couches. I planned to stay in the exact same spot until I found someone who knew where he was. Surely, someone who did would come through there sooner or later.

It was Copper who finally gave me a straight answer, "He's busy taking care of something for Phoenix. It's best if he's not interrupted unless it's an emergency." He raised an eyebrow as if to say, "Well, is it?"

"It's not an emergency," I said, deflated. "I just wanted to see if it would be okay for someone to take me to see my dad. That's all."

Copper smiled. "I'll go run it by him. If he's okay with it, I'll take you up there myself. I planned on going up later this afternoon, but now works just as good."

With Dash's approval, Copper took me to the hospital to see my dad. I just had to figure out how to ditch him, get to Duke's room, and back to my dad's room without anyone noticing. That might not be as easy as I originally thought.

After spending some time with Dad, who was looking remarkably better, I excused myself to use the facilities and stop by the cafeteria to grab something to eat. I hurried to the nurse's station and asked for Duke's room number. She clicked around on the computer screen until she found it. She told me his room number without any fuss. I rushed to the elevators, rode up two floors, and walked straight into Duke's room.

His eyes widened when he saw me walk through the door, but he didn't make a sound. I pulled a chair up next to his bed. "How are you doing, Duke?"

Nothing.

"Are they going to let you go home soon?'

Nothing.

"Did you know my dad is here in ICU?"

That got a response, possibly a flicker of surprise, but it quickly disappeared. Still no words. Did I miss something? Did something happen to his vocal cords or his tongue? Was he physically not able to speak or make a noise? I had a strong feeling he could talk, he just wasn't.

Feeling a bit bold, I reached out and pinched the fire out of him. He jerked his arm away and yelled, "Ow! What the fuck, Ember?"

I jumped to my feet and pointed my finger at him, "Ha! You can talk! What the fuck indeed?" Yes, I actually said fuck. Like I said, I was feeling bold.

Duke clamped his mouth shut and glared at me. He was going to test every bit of patience I had left, which wasn't much. Why was everyone playing the silent game? I flopped back into my chair and sighed loudly. "Nothing is ever solved by not talking. Do you think any part of my issues would have been resolved if I had refused to talk?" Not waiting for him to answer, I went on, "No, they wouldn't have. In fact, silence on anyone's part could have caused things to turn out worse than they did. More people could have been hurt, more people could have lost their lives. More good people, that is."

He just sat there. He wasn't looking at me, and I honestly couldn't tell if he was even listening to me. This was turning out to be a total waste of time. "It was stupid of me to come here. I thought you would be able to help her! She won't let me in! She won't talk! You won't talk! I know something is wrong. You just sit there in your self-centered silence and do nothing. I will figure out another way to handle it."

I stormed out of his room and let my rage keep my tears at bay. I paced around his floor several times like a crazy woman. When the nurses started to eyeball me like they were considering trying to catch me with a butterfly net and haul me to the mental health floor, I decided it was probably a good time to head back to my dad's room.

I arrived to find my dad and Copper deep in conversation. Neither had noticed how long I was gone and neither questioned it when I returned. "You guys look like you're in the middle of something. Do you want me to wait outside?"

"No, of course not, baby girl. Come on in." Dad looked me over from head to toe. "Something wrong?"

I sat down on the edge of his bed and let my shoulders sag forward like I had the weight of the world on my back. "Yes. I'm worried about Reese. Something is up with her but I don't know what. Carbon tells me to let her be when she gets in one of her moods, but that's obviously not solving anything. It just gives her time to push her issues to the back of her mind until they surface again. Rinse and repeat. On top of that, Duke has apparently taken a vow of silence and refuses to speak. I just don't know what to do."

My dad took my hand in his much larger, severely bruised and battered one, "Baby girl, sometimes there is nothing you can do, no matter how much you want to. I know you want to help Reese, especially because she has done so much for you, but this time, I don't think there is anything for you to do except let her know that you love her and you'll be there for her when and if she needs you."

My head popped up, "You know what's going on with her?"

He shook his head. "No, I don't, but I do know her brother and a good bit about what their family has been through. No one goes through all that and comes out unscathed, but that's not my story to tell."

I sighed again, "I don't like it, but it sounds like there really isn't anything I can do, other than be there for her." I leaned over and kissed him on the cheek. "Thanks, Dad."

CHAPTER THIRTY-ONE

Dash

Three days after we found him locked in Octavius's basement, Phoenix came walking through the clubhouse doors and shocked the shit out of everyone. He was limping and struggling, apparently, he refused to use crutches, but he was there.

Shouts of "Phoenix" or "Prez" and some form of "Welcome home" greeted him.

"Why didn't you tell us you were getting out? We would have had someone pick you up," Badger asked, sounding a bit offended.

Copper appeared from behind Phoenix. "I was there visiting when the doc sprung him, so I brought him."

"He rode bitch on the back of your bike?" Badger asked, clearly not believing them.

"I ought to knock you on your ass for that," Phoenix grunted.

Copper just laughed. "I had to pick up a few things, so I took a cage when I left this morning. Worked out well." I couldn't put my finger on it, but something did seem off about their explanation, not that I would ever accuse either one of them of bullshitting us.

Phoenix growled, "I'm here and that's that. Where are they?"

"In the cells," Badger answered. "Dash busted his ass putting up a new cell with solid walls, just for Octavius. Did a damn fine job, too."

"I appreciate that, Dash. I'm going to visit our guests. Officers can come down. No one else." With that, he hobbled toward the stairs that led to the basement. He looked like he was going to fall over at any second. I just knew he was going to go tumbling ass over elbow down the stairs, but I didn't offer to help him because I didn't have a death wish. Surprisingly, he made it down the stairs and to the cells without incident.

"Have we got them all identified?" Phoenix asked no one in particular.

Byte stepped forward with a piece of paper in his hands. "Yes, we do. Everyone we have is listed on this paper with a basic description of who they are and what they did for Octavius."

Phoenix took the paper and looked over it. He folded it and shoved it in his pocket without saying a word. He then walked into the walled off cell containing Octavius and closed the door. We all looked at each other worriedly.

"Should one of us go in there with him?" Carbon asked. Before any of us could answer, we heard a sharp cry of pain, and then Phoenix hobbled out the door. "Church!" he bellowed.

He was in a mood, a foul mood, which was a rarity for Phoenix. He was a force to be reckoned with and not a man I would ever want to cross, but he was rarely this cold and calculating. He slammed the gavel down on the table and started without preamble. "We're going to get some of the drugs similar to what Octavius injected me with and pump him full, to the point he's near death. We are going to carefully string him up and stage it to look like he hung himself. The drugs should slow his breathing and heart rate enough to make it look like he is dead. We'll even put some makeup or some shit on him and really make him look dead. We have a contact at the funeral home that can help us with any documentation we need to prove that he hung himself, they picked him up, and cremated him. Backing up a bit, after he is discovered in his cell, we'll let a few of his people see him hanging there. After the funeral home comes to pick him up, we will call in the local authorities and fill them in on what we know about the farm. Since we also have contacts in the department and are handing over a huge case to them, they will overlook the little lapse in time between our discovery and our call to them. Once the cops have taken them all away and finished getting our statements, Octavius will be brought back here for me to deal with in any way I choose for as long as I see fit. Any objections?"

All hands went up in the air except for mine. Badger was the first to speak. "Are we missing something here? Why do you want to keep Octavius here as your personal torture toy?"

Phoenix fell back into his chair. "Fuck! Sorry, boys, the pain meds are fucking with my head. I was so damn focused on making sure I didn't fuck up my plan of action, I forgot that I hadn't told any of you, with the exception of Dash, the reasons behind all this."

All heads turned to me. "He told me to keep it to myself until he had a chance to tell all of you himself, so that's what I did. The only reason I heard it before you all is because I was at the hospital with Ember and she was going to need someone to lean on after he told her."

Phoenix cleared his throat to get the room's attention. "That was my decision and I stand by it. While this is club business, this is also my family business. More so than any of us originally thought. Ember had the right to know first and as my future son-in-law, so did Dash. Now, quit your bitching and listen up 'cause I ain't going to tell it a second time."

Phoenix spent the next hour retelling the story of his past and how Octavius was involved. It took quite a bit longer than when he told Ember and I due to frequent angry outbursts from the men Phoenix had appointed as officers of his club, who were also his closest friends, his brothers.

When all was said and done, Phoenix called for a vote on his plan for Octavius and his men. It was approved unanimously.

I felt sure we would be dismissed after the vote, but that wasn't the case. Phoenix pulled a piece of paper from his pocket. He smoothed it out and started reading off the names and descriptions. It was the list Byte had given him earlier.

When he finished, he looked pointedly at each one of us. "Tell me, brothers, if this is a complete list of our captives, where the fuck is his son?"

Men cursed, fists banged the table, someone jumped to their feet so quickly it caused their chair to crash to the floor. How in the hell did we miss that? I knew Coal was posing as his son, but I assumed his real son had been one of the ones captured the night we found Phoenix. Fuck. Fuck. Fuck.

"Quiet!" Phoenix bellowed, louder than he should be able to given the state of his ribs. "Obviously, he's still out there. My best guess is that he's been running the farm since we nabbed all of their top dogs. That would explain why things appear to be running smoothly out there instead of the complete chaos I expected once the slaves figured out all of the 'executives' were MIA."

"You want us to go get him?" Carbon asked

excitedly.

"No. We'll let the cops get him when they raid the farm. If we show up out there in those SUV's again, he'll know it's us and he'll run. He may try to run when the cops swarm the place, but he won't be able to get very far, not after Ember fills them in on every secret passage, trap door, hidden room, and underground tunnel that exists out there. Only way in or out is with the chip in their cars. A strip or two of tire spikes will stop anyone trying to escape with one of the vehicles." Phoenix shrugged. "It's a huge property with a large number of places to hide. It may take more than a day or two, but they'll find him."

The room fell silent for a few beats, which I took to think over this last chunk of information Phoenix just delivered. "Let that be a lesson to you boys. When you think you've tied up every loose end, crossed all your t's, and dotted all your i's, go back and look over everything at least two more times. Lucky for us all, this time everything came out just fine. It could have just as easily royally fucked us all. That's all I'm going to say about it, because I am damn proud of how everyone pulled together and how quickly you boys got shit turned around when it went sideways. Damn proud! Now, let's get this shit done so we can celebrate!" He slammed the gavel down, effectively dismissing us.

***

The next morning, I got out of bed when it was still dark outside, careful not to disturb Ember. I met Carbon at the basement door. He stood there with his creepy, evil grin and a large syringe twirling back and forth between his fingers. "Ready?" he asked, far too chipper for the time and the task at hand.

"Yep." I followed him quietly down the stairs and into the cell containing Octavius. We silently slipped inside. I quickly placed my hand over Octavius's mouth and nose, preventing any air from entering or escaping, thus silencing any protests he would have made. Carbon quickly jammed the needle in his neck and pressed down on the plunger. Not even a full minute passed before Octavius went limp. "He's out," I whispered.

Carbon nodded. He wordlessly picked up a sheet and began tying it into a makeshift noose. Somewhere in the back of my mind it registered that I should be alarmed at how fast and accurate

Carbon was at creating nooses out of sheets. When he was finished, we hoisted Octavius up, careful to not actually cut off his air supply. We slipped out of his cell and back upstairs without being noticed.

We didn't wait long to come down the stairs with breakfast for our prisoners. Usually, we fed them much later in the morning, but they had no idea what time it was, which worked to our advantage. I was the one to go in and "find" Octavius. I yelled for help, telling the other brothers to get Patch. I left the door wide open so the other prisoners could see me trying to hold Octavius's body up. Carbon rushed in to help me while we waited for Patch. He flew down the stairs with his medical bag, acted like he was checking Octavius over, then shook his head and told us he was gone. We cut him down and placed him back on his bed. Hector and the other men were screaming and yelling, some angry, some sad, some silent with shock. Whatever, as long as they bought it.

We made a big show of "calling the authorities" to report the death. Two guys that Phoenix got from who knows where came in dressed in cheap suits, asked some questions, jotted a few notes in little notebooks, told us to call the funeral home, and left.

Phoenix's contact at the funeral home came over to pick up Octavius's body. He loaded his limp, seemingly lifeless body onto the stretcher and wheeled him away. Instead of putting his body in the hearse and taking him to the funeral home, he pushed the stretcher into an empty room near the back of the clubhouse. Carbon and I followed him into the room to handcuff Octavius's arms and legs to the stretcher, as well as place a gag in his mouth in case he woke up. Patch stayed there to monitor him and make sure he stayed alive.

Once everyone had finished their assigned tasks for the morning, we all gathered in the common room. Phoenix clapped his hands to get everyone's attention. "I'm going to place a call to my buddy down at the police department so we can get those fuckwads out of my clubhouse and finally put an end to that damn farm. We've been over this several times, what to say and what not to say. If any one of you feels like you can't handle this, speak up now." He paused and made a point to meet each and every brother's eyes, even the prospects'. "Good. Let's get to it."

***

There were freaking pigs everywhere, crawling all over the clubhouse, trying to get statements from everyone, including our captives. Phoenix suggested they move the party down to the police station, but they were having none of that.

Slipping quietly from the room, I grabbed Carbon and hoped our exit went unnoticed. I grabbed a large laundry bin that we used for the general clubhouse laundry, like towels, dishcloths, and shit. I pushed it as quickly and quietly as I could to the room we had Octavius in. Patch jumped to stand in front of him when I opened the door. “It’s just me and Carbon. We’ve got to get him out of here before they find him. They are coming up with every excuse in the book to enter the bedrooms.”

“His vitals are coming back up, so I don’t necessarily need to watch over him anymore. He’s not in danger of dying from an overdose, but he shouldn’t be waking up anytime soon either,” Patch informed us.

“Good. Let’s dump his ass in here and move him to the shed furthest out. Maybe even the one by the lake if we can make it that far without being discovered,” I suggested.

"Sounds good to me," Carbon agreed. The big bastard removed the cuffs from Octavius and tossed him into the bin as if he weighed nothing. He didn't even break a sweat. Carbon grinned at me, flexed his arm muscles, and said, "I drank my milk and ate my vegetables."

"Shut the fuck up, man. We don't have time for this right now." We covered the top of the bin with a fitted sheet and discretely wheeled it out the back door. We did have an industrial sized washer and dryer in one of the sheds out back, so I headed in that direction in case we were spotted.

We made it to the laundry shed without incident. "You think we should put him in here or you want to try to make it out to the lake?" I asked. I would rather have him farther away, but we would have to risk being seen to do it.

"I think we can get him to the shed by the lake. Move out of the way and let me push that thing. Try and keep up, junior."

He wasn't kidding. The big beast of a man should not be able to move that fast. I had to jog, at a fast pace, to keep up with him. When we reached the shed, Carbon repositioned Octavius, cuffed his arms and legs to the bin, pushed it inside, locked the door, and dusted his hands off. "That's how it's done." The cocky son of a bitch.

We returned to the clubhouse to find that even more officers had arrived. I made my way over to Phoenix, "Got started on some of the laundry that was piling up since it looks like we won't be going anywhere anytime soon. It was starting to stink and I figured you didn't want the whole clubhouse smelling like it. What did I miss?"

Phoenix didn't miss a beat. "Good thinking, brother. I like my clubhouse fresh and clean. You didn't miss much. As I expected, this is too big for the local boys to handle. The ones that have just gotten here are federal agents from one or more of the three-letter agencies."

"Shouldn't they be heading out to the farm instead of hanging around here?"

Phoenix sighed, "They want to get all the info from us and the local officers and formulate a plan before they go out there. That one right there," he pointed to a well-dressed man in his early forties, "is the one in charge. That's Luke Johnson, served in the Marines with him. He asked if they could set up a makeshift command center here in the common room. I'm not happy about it, but I couldn't exactly say no either. You,

Carbon, and Byte go make sure shit is locked up tight and do it without drawing attention to yourselves."

"Got it. You need anything else?"

"Yeah. When you're finished with that, wake my daughter up and let her know what's going on. They'll want to talk to her at some point. I'm surprised they haven't asked for her already."

***

Finally, the clubhouse was free of anyone related to law enforcement. They stayed all day. I think they would have stayed longer, but Phoenix plainly stated that his daughter's safety was his number one concern; therefore, the gates would be locked at 10:00 pm and would not open again until the morning. If they didn't want to be locked in for the night, they needed to pack up and leave. They gathered their belongings and scurried off to the only motel in Croftridge.

I sat back on one of the sofas and put my arm around Ember's shoulders. "How you doing, sweetheart?"

"Okay, I guess. None of this stuff bothered me, but I'm still worried about Reese and I'm also worried about my dad. He's doing too much.

He just got out of the hospital yesterday."

I kissed her temple and pulled her closer to me. "He's a grown man, darlin'. He can handle himself."

She rolled her eyes, "That may be true, but he's still my dad, and I'm allowed to worry about him."

Phoenix hobbled toward one of the couches, looking very unstable. Ember jumped up and grabbed his hand. "Daddy, let me help you. You need to sit down. Please!" she begged. Phoenix looked down at Ember and reluctantly allowed her to help him to a seat. He pulled her in for a hug and whispered something in her ear. She nodded and quietly left the room.

As soon as she was out of earshot, Phoenix ordered, "Somebody go get that cockwad and put him back in the cell. We'll figure out what to do with him in the morning if they come back."

A loud commotion at the back door drew everyone's attention. Carbon entered the room like only a muscled ball of fury could. "He's fucking gone!" he roared.

Everyone in the room jumped to their feet, loudly voicing their disbelief. Every single person, except Byte. He remained relaxed on the sofa, legs stretched out in front of him, crossed at the ankles. He waited until it quieted down enough for him to be heard. He rubbed his fingernails on his shirt over his chest as if he were buffing them without a care in the world, "Relax, would ya? I've got this under control."

Phoenix took several threatening steps closer to Byte. "The fuck you talking about?"

Byte grinned from ear to ear. "Well, see, after your speech about checking things twice and yada yada, I got to thinking about how to prevent further mishaps in situations similar to our current predicament."

Phoenix growled, "Cut the shit and spit it out."

Byte sighed, deflated, "After Octavius was doped up and moved to the back bedroom, me and Patch put a tracker in him. His own tracker, ironically. I was able to reprogram it and secure the feed so that only I can see it, or those who have clearance." He shrugged. "So, relax, I've known the fucker's location the whole time."

Phoenix's face reddened to a very unhealthy shade, but it was Badger's fist that collided with Byte's face.

"Ow! What the fuck, Veep?" Byte shouted.

"You're fucking smart. I'll give you that, but you're a cocky, sarcastic little shithead. You should have told us you did that! And you should have told Phoenix the minute, no the fucking second, you knew he was on the move!" Badger slapped Byte in the back of the head. "What in the hell is wrong with you?" Byte reached up to rub the back of his head with the hand that wasn't cradling his cheek. "Never mind. Don't answer that. Just go get him. Now!" Badger bellowed.

Byte scurried out the door, Patch not far behind him. It didn't even take 10 minutes for them to drag Octavius through the front doors. They unceremoniously tossed him on the floor at Phoenix's feet. Byte kept his eyes on the floor and muttered, "Sorry, Prez. Won't happen again."

"See that it doesn't. It was good work, good thinking, all except not telling me or Badger about it."

"Got it."

Phoenix looked down to the lump on the floor. Octavius lay curled on his side, handcuffs still attached to his bloody wrists and ankles. There was blood coming from somewhere on his torso, but it wasn't obvious as to where exactly or what caused it.

"Where'd you find him?" Badger asked.

"About 50 yards from the shed by the lake. He wasn't going to make it much farther with his ankles in the state they're in, not to mention the metal rod that was sticking out of his back," Byte explained.

"How'd that happen?" Phoenix asked.

Byte shrugged, "I'm guessing he was rocking back and forth, doing whatever he could to get that laundry bin to fall apart. When it did, he must have fallen on one of the rods that framed the bin. We found him crawling on hands and knees with a two-foot rod sticking out of his back. Patch yanked it out, and we carried him back here."

Phoenix looked to Patch, "You need to do anything else to him?"

Confusion washed over Patch's face, "You want me to fix him? Isn't that counterproductive?"

Phoenix laughed, an evil, cold laugh, "Not at all. I plan to keep him alive for the time being. I have a feeling he's going to become your number one patient."

Octavius grunted and tried to raise his head, "You can't do this to me! You're not going to get away with this."

Phoenix gave him a hard kick to his ribs. "That's where you're wrong, *little brother*, I can do this, and I've already gotten away with it. Everyone thinks you're dead. Your boys saw your body hanging by a sheet from the ceiling of your cell this morning, saw the police come and take statements, saw the funeral home wheel your body away." Phoenix leaned down closer to Octavius's face, "I'm feeling generous, so I'll give you a choice. You tell me what happened to Annabelle and I'll show you some mercy. You don't, I'll keep you alive and torture you for years to come. I'll make sure every one of your executive council has the 'full prison experience', especially your son." Phoenix kicked him again and hobbled away, clutching his ribs. "Get him out of my sight."

Patch and Byte carted Octavius to the basement, Badger followed Phoenix to his office, and I went to see my girl. Nothing sounded better than crawling in bed beside her and sinking into her warm, wet body.

EPILOGUE

Ember

One month had passed since Octavius was found dead. Federal agents raided the farm the very next day. What they uncovered was unheard of in a little town like Croftridge. Octavius was forcing people to illegally ship drugs and guns for him. He even took their children from them to keep them compliant and working. That's how the "orphanage" came to be. All of the kids knew what it was and why they were there, all of them except for me.

After the raid, the people forced to work

for Octavius were allowed to leave the property and their children were returned to them. Since those people ended up being forced into the drug and gun trade because they had been illegally gambling, they couldn't get off without some form of punishment. It was eventually decided that each person, children excluded, would be put on probation for two years.

Several families were in a very bad situation. They were suddenly homeless, jobless, and carless with a new criminal record and children to provide for. I couldn't help myself. I wanted to help them, especially the kids. They were innocent in all of this, just like I was. If I could prevent even one kid from having a crappy childhood, I was going to do it.

As luck would have it, Phoenix, being Zayne's firstborn son, became the rightful owner of the dairy farm. Well, owner isn't the right word, more like a CEO. He could do anything and everything with the farm, except sell it, destroy it, or intentionally ruin the business. The man who started the dairy farm—it actually was just a farm in the beginning—some ancestor of mine, had a legal document drawn up giving control of the farm to the firstborn son of each generation when their respective father died or retired. If said son did not want to run the farm—which had yet to happen—they were to hire a third party to manage the farm until the next male heir came of age. The document was quite impressive. It outlined who the farm was passed on to in every circumstance imaginable from no heirs to only female offspring. The man really covered all of his bases.

Once all of the contraband was removed from the property, the criminals were arrested, and the families were set free, there was a lot of available room on the property. It seemed wasteful to let so many buildings sit empty, particularly when Croftridge had a sudden influx of homeless families. The ideas started flooding my mind, faster than I could write them down. Once I finally had my thoughts organized, I set off to find my dad.

I knocked excitedly on his office door. "Come in!"

"Hey, Dad. Do you have a minute?" I asked, barely able to contain my excitement. I think I actually bounced the whole way to his office door.

He looked at me curiously. "I don't know. I'm not sure if I'm going to like whatever you are obviously about to spring on me."

I laughed, "You'll like it, Dad. I promise."

He closed his laptop and leaned back in his chair. "You have the floor."

I rubbed my hands together and began pacing back and forth. "I was thinking that it's a shame to let all those buildings on the farm property sit empty, especially when they can be used to do good things for the people of Croftridge. For example, there's an entire barn and dairy farm set up just sitting there, not being used. Coincidentally, there are a bunch of people that are looking for work, but have a very new criminal record. A lot of those people have kids, who now don't have food, water, or shelter."

My dad was smiling at me. Not his fake smile. No, this was a real one, reaching his eyes and lighting up his face. "You want me to take the fake farm and make it a real farm, hire the forced workers as legit employees, and provide them with living quarters. Correct?"

"That's the gist of it, though I don't think it should be another dairy farm. I don't think that would be profitable since we currently have a good balance of supply and demand. I was thinking maybe horses and organics."

"Horses and organics? I'm not sure I'm following you, baby girl."

I shrugged, “I like horses. I thought maybe we could breed them or train them, maybe have riding lessons for kids or a camp or something.”

“And the organics?” he asked, his head was cocked to the side with the strangest look on his face. I wasn’t sure if I should continue or not, but he gestured for me to go on.

“Uh, like organic fruits and vegetables. People are all over organic food and clean eating. If it turns out to be a flop, it wouldn’t be a huge monetary loss. If it turns out to be a big hit, then we could possibly invest in the equipment needed to yield larger crops.”

He was still smiling with that same look on his face. “Sounds good. You’ll need this and this. Oh, and these.” He slid a stack of papers over to me, his credit card on top of the pile. Wait. What just happened?

“What’s that?” I pointed to the pile.

“New hire paperwork for the employees, a list of all buildings on the property, a log of who is currently living in what building and where, and my credit card. Hire the people, assign them rooms, start ordering the shit you need for your horses and your yuppie food.” I stood there completely dumbfounded. He said yes? “Well, take this stuff and get a move on it. Businesses don't start themselves."

I squealed and ran around the desk. He stood in time to catch me. I hugged him as tight as I could. "Thanks, Dad. I love you!"

He grunted and set my feet back on the floor, "Careful, kid. I'm not completely healed yet."

I gasped, "Oh, crap. I forgot. Did I hurt you?"

He laughed, "Tiny little thing like you? No way."

I pointed my finger at him and narrowed my eyes, "Hey, now, we both know I could if I wanted to."

He scoffed, "You might be able to take Dash down, but there's no way you can take me."

"Want to bet?"

"Hell, no. I will not get in the ring and fight my daughter. Now get out of here and go make dreams come true."

"Nice try. I'm on to your distraction techniques. We'll revisit this when you're completely healed." I grabbed the stack of papers and his credit card from his desk. "Thanks, Dad! See you later!" I said as I hurriedly left his office.

I was almost to the common room when I heard Dad call my name. "Yeah?" I answered.

"Don't forget about the party tonight," he reminded me.

"Thanks! I had forgotten. I'll be back in time.

Do you need me to make anything?"

"Nope. We're doing the cookout thing tonight."

"Okay, see you then. Love you."

"Love you, too, baby girl."

Dash

I dropped into my designated seat and waited for Phoenix to begin Church. This was an impromptu meeting, which had me a little on edge since I had no idea what Phoenix may hit us with.

The gavel banged on the table and Phoenix started speaking. "Sorry for the short notice, brothers, but I needed to have a quick sit down before the party gets started tonight. As you all know, Octavius is still locked up in the basement. Since we've reinforced the locks and added soundproofing panels to his cell, I feel confident we will have no more near discoveries." About two weeks ago, Ember insisted she heard pained groans coming from below the common room. Ultimately, I convinced her what she heard was one of the club whores getting Carbon's special brand of fucking. She plugged her ears and left the room with a scrunched-up face. Mission accomplished.

"Octavius still refuses to give up any details on Annabelle, nothing new there, but I do have some news. I went to visit Hector today. I figured it wouldn't hurt to ask him a few questions, see if he would willingly answer or if I could trip him up enough for him to let something slip. Turns out, he is pretty pissed at Octavius and was more than willing to share what he knew out of pure spite. We may need to visit with him more in the future, but today I went specifically to ask about Nivan since there has been absolutely no trace of the boy since this all started."

Phoenix took a sip of water and leaned back in his chair. "I didn't think there could be much more to this fucked up story, but apparently I was wrong." He dropped his head, shook it from side to side, and then raised it to continue. "Nivan's dead, has been for years. According to Hector, Nivan died when he was five years old. Somehow, Octavius managed to keep that fact hidden from everyone else. Now, I know what you all are thinking. I thought the same thing, too. He's lying to protect him. Hector told me where a hidden safe was located on the farm.

He said the proof I needed would be in that safe. Gave me the combination and everything. Being that I don't know what else is in that safe, I think it would be wise to wait until tomorrow to ride out there and find out. We are way overdue for a celebration and I don't want anything that might be in there to put a damper on the party. Any objections to that?"

Heads shook. He was right. We needed tonight. Even though things came to a head a month ago, it was still one thing after another. Things were just really starting to settle. At least they were until we were gifted this newest tidbit of info.

"Good. Badger and I will go tomorrow. Since Hector was speaking so freely, I asked him about Annabelle." Phoenix paused for a moment, "He said he truly doesn't know what happened to her. One day she was there, the next day she was gone, and Octavius forbid anyone from saying her name again. He couldn't confirm if Annabelle was Nivan's mother or not. That's all I have in regards to Octavius."

I hated watching what this was doing to Phoenix. He'd already been through this exact same thing. Lost her, searched for her, grieved for her. Now that he thought there was a chance that she was alive, he would search for her and when he didn't find her, he would have to grieve for her again. I couldn't imagine losing Ember once, let alone twice.

Badger's deep voice brought me back to the present. "We have a couple of different reasons for the party tonight. One, it's our way of giving thanks to Copper and his crew for saving our asses when they needed saving. They should be arriving in the next hour or so. Two, as per the vote last week, Prospect Jamie will be patched in as Edge tonight. Three, Coal will receive his Prospect patch. If those weren't enough reasons to party, we will likely have one more reason to celebrate before the night is over..." he trailed off and cast his eyes to me.

I cleared my throat and stood, "With Phoenix's blessing, I'm going to ask Ember to marry me tonight." The brothers at the table slapped me on the back and gave me their congratulations.

Duke grumbled, "Don't congratulate him yet, you stupid fucks. He hasn't asked yet, and there's no guarantee she'll say yes."

I grinned, "She'll say yes. She's already my Old Lady. You fuckers just try to hold off throwing back your liquor until I've asked her. I don't want anyone ruining this for her." They all nodded their agreement. In the short time she had been around, they had all come to love Ember. She was the little sister, favorite cousin, and/or best friend to most of my brothers. To me, she was the world.

Also by Teagan Brooks